The House at Bridal Veil

By Anita Birt

Binford & Mort Publishing
Portland, Oregon

This book is dedicated to the people who built the house and all those who came after. The story of their lives echoes in the lives of us all.

For the Franciscan Sisters of the Eucharist who rescued the house from a slow death and brought it back to life, they have my love and appreciation. And so too, do all their special friends who have given untold hours of labor helping to restore the site.

Acknowledgements

My thanks to all those who let me enter their lives and share their memories of The House at Bridal Veil. They made the story come alive.

For help with the Jacobson story. Mrs. Elizabeth Leitzel Dowling and Mrs. Irene Jenny Pringle.

For the Lawrence family. Dr. Donald B. Lawrence and Mrs. Elizabeth Lawrence, Mrs. William Lawrence II, William Lawrence III and Mrs. Jean Lawrence Thorpe.

For the Kathryn Reynolds' story. Mrs. June Reynolds Cusack, Mrs. Linda Reynolds Johnson and Michael Collier, Frank Fabian, Gordon Fabian, Mrs. Janice Fabian Thomas and Mrs. Nellie Harwood.

For the Columbia Gorge Nursing Home. Mrs. Madge Nepper, Mrs. Annette Gilbert and Ms. Phyliss Clarke.

For the Redemptorists. Brother Oliver, C.S.S.R.

For the Fathers of the Divine Word. Father Ed Borkowski and Brother Nick Carlin.

Special thanks to the Franciscan Sisters of the Eucharist at Bridal Veil and their many friends who encouraged me to write the story of *The House at Bridal Veil*.

Special thanks to Dr. Donald B. Lawrence, Professor Emeritus, Department of Plant Biology, University of Minnesota, Saint Paul, Minnesota.

Anita Birt, Victoria, B.C., Canada

Contents

Acknowledgements iv

The Arrival 1

The Columbia River Gorge 17

The Jacobson Mansion 27

The Second Arrival and Moving In 49

The Lawrence Villa .75

Kathryn Reynolds and the Reynolds' Health Studio . . .101

The Columbia Gorge Nursing Home 125

The Redemptorists .135

The S.V.D. Fathers .143

Making Progress — 1975 151

A School Is Born 167

The Community Develops 183

Challenges and Responses 221

The Way Ahead 251

Epilogue 273

Sources 275

Index 277

The Arrival

December 31, 1974 and a steady rain is blanketing the area in and around Portland, Oregon. It's a day of damp, bone-chilling cold. The weather is blowing in from the east, a typical easterly that in winter can rage through the Columbia River Gorge bringing down trees and uprooting shrubs. At times, heavy snow or freezing rain will close the roads. Yet spring, summer and early fall are times of sunshine, warmth and abundant growth, creating a perfect environment for the plant life that abounds in the gorge.

For the three Roman Catholic Sisters watching the rain from the front window of their small rented house, this will prove to be an eventful day. They are waiting to be picked up by their new friend and real estate agent, Frank Joseph. He is to drive them into the countryside east of Portland to look at a house. One that is empty and for sale.

Mother Mary Michael, Mother Francine and Sister Paula Jean are members of the Franciscan Sisters of the Eucharist and are associated with the Franciscan Life Center Network. The women have relocated in Portland after working in a parish and Diocesan setting in Vancouver, British Columbia. They are educators in the full sense of the word. Between them they have graduate degrees in psychology, education, educational administration, English, drama and French. Mother Francine is a Clinical Member of the American Association for Marriage and Family Therapy.

She is now employed as Director of Catholic Education Programs and Sister Paula Jean as Director of Religious Education for the Portland Archdiocese. Mother Michael, the senior of the group, is creating programs for senior citizens in two parishes.

They have a vision beyond their present work. They want to create a small community of nine or ten Sisters whose focus will be on life education. This is no small vision. Life means just that—the reality of people's life experiences from birth to death. Weekend after weekend they have been searching the area in and around Portland looking for a big house with some land on which to create their center. Nothing suitable has come their way. The fact that they have no money other than their salaries does not discourage them. They figure that if they find the right place at a fairly reasonable price, they will work something out. Theirs is a faith that in a pinch can move a mountain or two.

Their dream is beginning to unravel a little as the weeks slip by and no house appears on the horizon. Then on Christmas Day, just a week ago, a small miracle began to unfold. The seed for the miracle was planted back in early spring when Mother Francine and Sister Paula Jean travelled to Portland to be interviewed for the positions they now hold. Mother Michael came along for the ride and decided to wait for them in a cafe across the street from the Chancery office.

"I drank some coffee, read the local paper and decided I was bored just sitting there." Wondering how to make the time interesting, she remembered her teenage years back in Lewiston, Idaho, when she babysat for the Rudfelt family. One of their boys, Dick, was a special favorite.

She hadn't seen him for thirty-odd years but somewhere along the way had heard that he, his wife and family had moved to Portland.

"I think I'll see if he's in the phone book." There was a pay phone near the door with a chained, dog-eared and much-thumbed phone book dangling underneath. She found his name and dialed.

A woman answered. Mother Michael in her usual cheerful, confident voice asked, "Is this the home of Dick Rudfelt who used to live in Lewiston?"

Katie Rudfelt wasn't at all sure about this caller. "Who's calling please?"

"Well, you don't know me but I used to babysit Dick back in Lewiston. I'm Mother Mary Michael Costello," then she laughed. "If he's there, just tell him it's Mary Costello."

"What a wonderful surprise! Dick has often talked about you. Just a sec and I'll call him."

"Mary," Dick's voice echoed his pleasure at hearing from his old friend. "Where on earth are you?"

"I'm right here in Portland waiting for two of the Sisters who are being interviewed for jobs. We'll be moving to the city by the end of June or early July. Now tell me, how are you and the family?"

They exchanged family news and caught up on what they'd been doing for the past many years. Then Dick asked, "But where are you right now?"

She looked out the cafe window and told him the name of the street. He was taken aback. "Mary, that's a terrible part of town. You stay right there, I'm coming to get you."

"Oh, Dick, I'm just fine. The others will be here any minute now. Don't you worry, I've been in lots worse places than this."

He was still not convinced that he shouldn't come and get her but finally agreed that if the other two Sisters didn't come within the hour, she was to phone. Mother Michael promised to get in touch once they were settled in Portland. And so she did. Dick and Katie became close and loving friends.

When Christmas came, the Rudfelts asked the Sisters to celebrate the day with them and to share their Christmas dinner. It was Katie's brother, Frank Joseph, dropping by to wish them all a Happy Christmas who helped the Sisters' dream become a reality. Interested in them and the work in which they were involved, he heard about their fruitless search for a house.

"What kind of a place are you looking for?"

"It has to be big enough to house nine or ten of us and we'd really need some land, not a lot but some. You see, life education to us means to be connected with the spiritual, psychological and intellectual values of each person with whom we are involved. We also follow the teachings of St. Francis who urged his followers to have close contact with the earth and growing things." As Mother Francine was speaking, Frank remembered something.

"Before I was in real estate, I sold stereos. Years ago I delivered some equipment to priests who were living in a big old house out near Bridal Veil. Do you know that area? It's on the old Crown Point Highway. I've heard the place is empty and it just might suit you. Let me check it out and I'll get back to you."

He was as good as his word and drove up to their house right on time. They ran through the pouring rain to the car. As they settled themselves, Mother Michael wiped the rain from her face. "My father used to say when it rained like this 'just look at that, it's raining pitch forks and hammer handles' and when I was little, I wondered why I only saw rain."

On the forty minute drive to Bridal Veil, Frank filled them in on some details about the house. "It's owned by the Fathers of the Divine Word and has been empty for six or seven years. What I remember is it's some kind of mansion with a gatehouse near the entrance. I wasn't able to find out the asking price but one of the Fathers is to meet us and he'll know."

Bridal Veil is no longer a town. It had been a thriving lumber and mill town early in the century, now it's a collection of a few small and large houses stretching along the highway. There's an old cemetery and some derelict buildings. The town was named for the beautiful falls pouring down the gorge cliffs behind it. The story of its naming is part of the local lore. A woman passenger on a steamer travelling down the river saw the falls and was heard to remark, "they look just like a bride's veil." The falls can no longer be seen from the river or road. Trees have grown up and obscured the view.

Frank turned into the drive but had to stop the car. A huge tree had fallen across the entrance, victim of some wintry storm. Despite the pouring rain, there was nothing for it but to climb over the tree. Mother Michael, being older and wiser, decided there had to be a better way. The three-foot girth of the tree didn't appeal to her as a fun thing to circumnavigate. They looked around and finally were able to climb through the dirt piled up by the tree roots. Then slipping on wet leaves and picked at by blackberry thorns, they struggled to the main driveway.

Stopping to catch their breaths, they looked up at the house glimmering whitely through the dripping trees.

Mother Michael remembers: "It looked so beautiful in the rain even though it seemed so neglected and run down and overgrown and everything. Then right away I thought, we can make a go of this."

For Mother Francine, the harder it was to walk up the drive, stumbling over fallen branches and climbing over yet another fallen tree, the more she felt "this was the place where we should be. It had an aura about it. I had such a strong sense that this was the place for us to establish our foundation."

Sister Paula Jean as she stared up at the house had a feeling of awe. "I knew this was a special place yet I couldn't find words to describe that feeling."

They were quiet as they walked slowly up towards the house. A feeling of mystery surrounded them. When they talked about it later, they found it hard to describe what it was about the place that so quickly drew them to it. Was it a plea from a derelict house and its desolate grounds that touched the women at a deeply spiritual level?

Arriving at the front of the house, they were faced with what must have been a fishpond. It was beautifully shaped with cement curbing but now was filled with leaves and debris from the surrounding trees. They stepped up to the door and rang the bell.

Father Borkowski greeted them and invited them in. They entered a small reception area, then followed him up a short stairway and through French doors into the huge living room.

"Why this is like a ballroom," Sister Paula Jean whispered to the others.

Water was running in a steady stream over the stone fireplace at the far end of the room and Brother Nick Carlin was busy mopping up the water that was fast accumulating on the floor. The women looked around. It says much for their courage that they didn't turn and walk away. The oak floor had heaved up three feet in some places and was like a wavy wooden sea. Huge sheets of black plastic covered the enormous windows and French doors that led to the terrace. Light from some oddly shaped chandeliers only served to shed some dim light on the wreck of the room.

Father Borkowski took them on a tour of the house. There were two French doors on either side of the huge, wet, stone fireplace. They led to a curious room. The

Sisters were told that it was the community chapel and had once been the library. There were no bookshelves, just plain, dull wood walls. The three tall windows gave little light since a small forest of trees was pressing up against the outside walls.

Going into the dining room, they were met with sodden walls, a sagging ceiling and a floor covered in linoleum, cracked and dirty. French doors led off to one side into a solarium. It had a floor of white and black marble. At one end there was a small and exquisite white marble fountain with catchment basin set in the floor. The fountain had the face of what looked to be an ancient Greek god.

Entering the kitchen through the back hallway brought them to the only really dry room on the main floor. It was dirty. Cobwebs and dust clung to the greasy film on the walls. Two pantry areas led off either side. One appeared to be a food storage area. The other must have been a china pantry but the small panes of glass in the cupboard doors were covered in paint. Pink paint.

Returning to the front of the house, they were shown a small room that connected to the living room through yet another glass door. Going up the front stairway, the Sisters looked back and saw the elegant vaulted ceilings of the small reception area and the hallway that separated the living and dining room areas. On the second floor there were two separate wings. The women were astonished at the number of rooms. They were very small. A previous owner had put up plywood partitions in the large bedrooms to create small sleeping areas. Some had no windows.

A back staircase led down to the rear of the house. By the dim light of a dusty bulb, they went down to explore the basement. Father Borkowski returned to the watery main room to help with the mopping up.

"It's a whole other world down here." Sister Paula Jean felt like an explorer. They stood in awe as they stared at the enormous furnace.

"This looks big enough to heat the Empire State Building." Mother Michael was not mechanically oriented and to her inexperienced eyes, it looked terrifyingly complicated.

As they walked slowly through the vastness of the basement, peering into large and small rooms, a mouse suddenly ran in front of them. Mother Francine saw it first and jumped back, nearly knocking Sister Paula Jean down.

"There's a mouse!" she yelled. Brave as she was about most things, she had a real fear of mice and rats. Her fear would be put to the test in the months ahead but now in the company of others, she put aside her fright and they finished their tour.

A short flight of stone steps led from the basement to the outside, exiting to the west of the terrace. Some small grass snakes had slithered down into the lower level so as well as mice, there were snakes in the basement. Yet to be discovered by the Sisters were rats sheltering in a crawl space.

When the women emerged the rain had let up and was now a misty drizzle. Father Borkowski joined them. Walking around by the terrace they could see the magnificence of the house that faced them. The terrace of red brick, totally moss covered, stretched almost the full length of the house. The beautiful French doors and the tall windows with fanlights were elegant. The harmony of the overall design was breathtaking.

They walked as well as they could through the tangled weeds of what had once been a lawn. Thick and thorny blackberry branches lying close to the ground were a hazard to avoid. A bordering wall separated the "lawn" from the next level. The opening in the center of the wall was graced with a large round, bowl fountain with a ceramic centerpiece in the shape of a pineapple. Steps on either side led down to a large piece of weed-strewn ground. Looking back was to see yet another fountain. This one with the face of the Greek god Poseidon as its focal point.

Slipping on muddy stone steps, brought them to a large depression in the earth. Here and there bits of rock wall showed through. Father Borkowski said it used to be a trout pond. It was filled with years of fallen leaves in various stages of decay. The place was a mess.

Following him back up and around the house, he led them up a slippery rocky path that edged alongside the gorge wall. Rounding a mossy outcropping, they stopped and stared. They were facing a roaring, tumbling waterfall. This was Coopey Falls, 171 feet high and named for the man who once owned the property at the top of the gorge through which the stream flowed that fed the falls.

Use of the water came with the property. Under the falls was a large, stone-walled reservoir. It was filled with rocks that had fallen from the cliff face. A stream flowed haphazardly east of the house.

Walking back and away from the house, they passed a derelict swimming pool. It was a chain-link fenced, moss-encrusted, blackberry-filled disaster. A sorry sight like the rest of the property. There was a small barn, old but might be made useable.

"I'll bet we could soon fix that up and keep some chickens." Mother Michael was already populating the place with laying hens, a perfect natural environment for them.

As they approached the gatehouse, an overpowering smell greeted them. Local people had forced open the garage doors and were using it as a handy dump. It was packed five feet high with trash, much of it with so-called "disposable diapers," all in a state of stinking decay.

Around the house were five wrecked cars, two refrigerators, numerous mattresses with bedsprings, car tires, every kind of junk imaginable. The smell was sickening. The women hurried inside the house to inspect the apartment but had to beat a hasty retreat. The stench from the garbage had infiltrated every nook and cranny.

Staggering outside and hurrying to where the air was more breathable, Mother Michael called Frank aside. "What do you think they want for this place?" He'd been thinking about this as the Sisters were viewing the property.

"I think if it was fixed up and the grounds were in decent shape, oh, maybe $250,000.00."

"You mean a quarter of a million dollars! Why this place is a wreck." She took a deep breath and gathered her wits together, "Well I'm going to ask Father anyway. It won't hurt to ask," and off she went, catching up with him by the front door.

"Father what are you asking for this place?" They stepped inside the house.

"I talked to my superior yesterday and told him I was going to show you the property. He really wants it to go to another religious community and he's a bit short of money. He's asking $70,000.00 cash. He wants to get it off our hands."

As they joined the others she wanted to jump up and down and shout for joy. She kept her cool. "We'll talk it over with each other and with our major superior and get back to you."

They said good-bye and walked down the obstacle course that was the driveway, concentrating on their footing. Wet, leaves, branches and fallen trees needed their full attention and it wasn't until they were in the car and driving away that Mother Michael told them the asking price.

This set off a burst of talking. Yes, they wanted the property. Yes, they would make a go of it. Yes, it was perfect for them. Yes, they were sure they would be able to come up with $70,000.00.

"Frank, what do we do now?" Mother Michael asked. He wasn't convinced that buying the Bridal Veil house was such a good idea.

"Are you sure you want to do this? That place is more dead than alive and will cost a fortune to fix up."

Nothing now would deter them. "Okay, here's what you do. You make a formal offer, I'll look after that and send them a check for maybe $500.00 or so as earnest money and wait to see if they'll accept." He went on. "It's usual to offer less than the asking price and then negotiate. Why not offer them $60,000.00 and see what happens."

"We'll have to call Mother Rosemae in Connecticut to get her okay for this. I'm sure she'll say to go ahead and will lend us the $500.00. What did you call it? Earnest money?"

The Sisters had been having lengthy discussions by phone and in person with their major superior and she was as interested as they were in the possibility of establishing a life education center near Portland. Calling as soon as they were back home, they had her okay to go ahead. The earnest money was wired and sent with the formal offer.

January 1st was a holiday. It was the second day of 1975 when Frank brought the offer around for their signatures. The reply came within a week:

"We accept your offer of $60,000.00 and are returning your $500.00 check. It is not required."

The house at Bridal Veil was theirs and the great adventure was about to begin. The Provincial of the S.V.D. Fathers was concerned that the Sisters might have second thoughts about the purchase when they had more time to spend at the house. He said they could have forty-five days before making their final commitment. They were given the keys. He encouraged them to spend all the time they wanted at Bridal Veil. The women were quite sure their decision to buy was the right one and were appreciative of his thoughtfulness.

Also, before the final decision was made, the major superior of their Franciscan community was to see the property. Fortunately, her representative, Mother Suzanne was visiting San Francisco with two other Sisters and before returning to Meriden, Connecticut, stopped off in Portland. She was as enthused about the find as the Sisters and encouraged them to go ahead. The larger community could not finance the Bridal Veil Sisters. It was up to them to find their own money, however they managed it.

Friends from Vancouver came to Portland for a visit. The Macdonalds looked around the house and grounds. Angus Macdonald said without hesitation, "Don't buy it. This place will kill you."

Mother Francine's mother, Mary Barrett, came down from Seattle, looked around and said, "Buy it!"

And who are the Franciscan Sisters of the Eucharist? A relatively new religious order, they had originally been members of the Franciscan Sisters of Perpetual Adoration. Vatican II had shed new light on the study of theology and had called upon all Catholics to undertake a renewal of their faith from within. This call was heard by some of the Franciscan nuns who were involved in the formation of the younger Sisters, as well as the Novice Mistress of their mother house. These women undertook a serious study of theological changes emerging from Vatican II. They began to make changes in their work of formation with an emphasis on the type of community life that would result from this theological renewal.

When the young Sisters, prepared for a new kind of community life as taught and modelled by the formation team, were sent out to the various Franciscan centers, they met a lifestyle that did not match their expectations. So many of the young Sisters left after Vatican II that the formation team petitioned the mother community for permission to form four houses. Young Sisters would come and live there with professed sisters who were willing to accept the challenge to renew their religious lives. They would nurture the commitment of the young Sisters and continue their own personal spiritual growth.

These experimental houses worked very well. Mother Michael was involved. As Provincial of the Western Province, she agreed to have her Province participate. Mother Francine was superior of one of the houses.

Distinctive patterns were established within the four houses scattered across the country and they developed close bonds with one another. They then asked the mother community if they could establish their own province since they were discovering that in issues of authority and religious formation, they were becoming more and more differentiated from the mother community. When they attended the general chapter meeting of the whole community, they found themselves using a different vocabulary from the others and had difficulty relating their experiences of community life to those not involved in the experiment.

Permission was granted for the formation of a new province. They were still under the authority of the mother community. After two or three years as a separate province, this new grouping had become stronger and stronger. They then began to be perceived as a threat to the rest of the community. The younger Sisters wanted to participate in the renewal activities and some of the major leaders of the mother community also wished to begin sharing in this new experience.

At the chapter in 1973, those involved in the renewal communities were given an ultimatum. They were told to return to their original provinces, dissolve the experiment or leave religious life. This was a very difficult and stressful time. None of the Sisters wanted to leave their mother community, they did not want to form their own community and had no desire to leave religious life. They wanted to renew and energize. Loving and respecting their Sisters, it was not their intention to change them nor their way of serving God and their church. They had created another way of serving and wanted to live that choice.

"It was a pretty terrible and difficult chapter," recalls Mother Francine. "At the end, fifty-two of us decided that although we didn't want to leave the community nor religious life, we could no longer integrate ourselves back into our former provinces. We felt we had gone far beyond what was going on there. As a body, we left the mother community and petitioned Rome to hold our vows while we established a new religious community." Their appeal to Rome was duly taken under consideration and their vows were held for them. With much prayer and reflection, they were able in due time to present their constitution to the authorities in Rome.

The Decree from Rome reads:

"A group of Religious of the Franciscan Sisters of Perpetual Adoration, because of special circumstances, have several times respectfully petitioned the Holy See to be allowed to separate themselves from their Congregation in order to establish a new religious institute, called The Franciscan Sisters of the Eucharist.

The Sacred Congregation for Religious and for Secular Institutes, having carefully examined the matter and gathered information from the local Ordinaries concerned, decided to accede to the petition and by virtue of the faculties granted by the Holy Father, Pope Paul VI, with this present decree establishes and erects the new Institute, The Franciscan Sisters of the Eucharist, all other conditions of law being observed.

Rome, December 2, 1973."

The Sisters breathed a collective sigh of relief upon receiving this official document. They could now use their energies in serving the people of the regions where they are located. Each of the communities will be completely self-supporting through professional services rendered by the Sisters. In order to do this, each Sister must, within her spiritual development, acquire specific professional competence to meet particular cultural needs on both a professional and spiritual level.

The Sisters are completely on their own financially. They ask nothing in the way of money from their church. It is their spiritual home and they revere the teachings of their founder, St. Francis.

Out in the world, they have to earn their living like everyone else.

The Columbia River Gorge

When the three Franciscan Sisters were taken out to Bridal Veil on that cold, wet December 31, 1974 and shown the house that was destined to become the center of their foundation, it was the second time they had visited the area.

On Mother Michael's birthday, August 7, they decided to drive out into the country. She had been taking driving lessons and her instructor, hearing about their quest for property, advised her to look east. "It's too built up north, south and west of Portland and you'd spend hours driving back and forth to where you're working."

So east they headed on the Interstate. They were feeling a bit frazzled and needed a break. Without knowing much about neighborhoods when they moved to the city, they had rented a small furnished house in a less than salubrious area. Drunks staggered on to their back steps to fall down, sometimes to sleep, sometimes to be sick. Noisy, all night drinking parties in surrounding houses kept them uneasy at night.

"We've got to get out of here!" Mother Francine was feeling stressed and mentioned their dilemma to a friend. Word made the rounds that the Sisters needed a better place to live. The grapevine paid off. A bungalow belonging to someone's aged parents was available for several months. The Sisters would be able to move in September.

"Well, let's celebrate your birthday Mother. Who knows we may be lucky and find a place to buy!" Sister Paula Jean, like the others was ever hopeful.

They turned off the highway at the Bridal Veil exit and taking a right, headed westward up the Crown Point Highway as it wound its way to Crown Point and the magnificent view of the Columbia River and the western portal of the Gorge. Had they taken a left instead of a right turn after leaving the freeway, they would have driven by their future home.

The countryside through which they were now driving was so appealing that Mother Michael remarked wistfully, "I sure wish we could live out here. It's so beautiful."

The Columbia River rising in the the Columbia Ice Fields in the Rocky Mountains of Canada and fed by hundreds of tributary rivers and streams is one of the great rivers of the world.

The Gorge with Bridal Veil nestling near its west portal is a deep east-west canyon through the Cascade Range, carved nearly to sea level by the Columbia River. It has no counterpart in the Americas nor elsewhere in the world. Its location midway between the Equator and the North Pole results in large differences in strength of the sun's rays on opposing slopes. With much greater intensity on the north (Washington) side than on the south (Oregon) side, there is marked variation in local climate and kinds of plants and animals on the opposing slopes. For this reason, in winter when the sun is low in the southern sky, even at noon, Bridal Veil gets little direct sunlight.

The magnificent river was discovered in 1792 by Captain Gray in command of the ship, *Columbia Rediviva*. Although Indian tribes had known of the river for centuries before the arrival of Captain Gray, he was the first white explorer to discover and name it. He called it, Columbia, after his ship and claimed it for the United States.

In 1805 Lewis and Clark, travelling down the Snake River reached the Columbia. The splendor of this great waterway and the surrounding country was spellbinding. Passing down stream they came upon an unusual sight. Dead tree trunks of varying height and width stood in the water, and down river from this drowned forest were several miles of rapids.

Lewis made note of this phenomenon as did many explorers and settlers after him. He thought that the river had been dammed at the Cascade Rapids drowning the trees up stream. This explanation proved to be correct although his timing was out. The trees had drowned some six hundred years earlier when a great landslide brought them down from the sides of Table Mountain. Lewis thought they had been in the water for about twenty years.

"The Drowned Forest of the Columbia River," the whys and wherefores of its origins, provided both professional and amateur scientists with a fascinating puzzle. The solution to the puzzle gradually became clear as geologists and botanists began a close study of the drowned trees, the surrounding gorge wall, its rock formations and tree life. Dr. Donald B. Lawrence and Elizabeth Lawrence had a part in unravelling this mystery.

It was about A.D. 1250 when the slide occurred at Table Mountain sending tons of rock and soil deep into the gorge and up the south wall. This natural dam effectively blocked the river creating a huge lake that stretched eastward for many miles. Giant Douglas firs and other trees came crashing down with the slide, many of them remaining upright.

As the lake formed behind the dam, the trees left standing, slowly died. The pent up water created tremendous pressure on the rock and earth dam and eventually broke through into the river bed creating miles of rapids. The bare trunks of the trees now stood like sentinels in the river channel.

An ancient Indian legend tells of a natural bridge across the Columbia. Although there is no word in their language for bridge, the legend has it that their ancestors crossed the river without wetting their feet and their fathers could voyage in their canoes to The Dalles without meeting any obstruction. It is possible that the Bridge of the Gods legend is a piece of oral history passed down over the centuries by the Indians and refers to the time when the great wall of earth and rocks dammed the river. The people could then walk across with dry feet.

With the building of the Bonneville Dam several miles east of Bridal Veil, the submerged forest disappeared forever beneath the lake formed behind the dam. A modern two lane steel bridge now spans the river and taking its name from the Indian legend is called "The Bridge of the Gods." This feature is memorialized in the famous romantic novel with that title by Frederick Homer Balch.

Settlers began trickling into the region during the early years of the nineteenth century, some coming overland from the east and others by boat from the west. Down river from the Cascade Rapids, ocean tides were noted in autumn when the river was low. At Cape Horn just across the Columbia from Bridal Veil, they found harbor seals sunning themselves on a little rocky island. It is named Phoca Rock for the scientific name of these marine animals.

John Jacob Astor was one of the first businessmen to realize the potential of the fur trade in the northwest. He had information that the powerful British Northwest

Company was expanding into the west. With little delay, a ship was outfitted to take men and supplies to the mouth of the Columbia. It arrived in April 1811. Fort Astoria was built sending a signal to the British that the fur trade in the area was in American hands.

Numerous small Indian tribes lived along the river and farther inland. With the coming of the white settlers, their traditional hunting and fishing territories were invaded. Some Indians made an uneasy peace with the newcomers although some stole what they could, given the opportunity. Other tribes were openly hostile. Raids on farm homes and the stampeding of horses were commonplace. Companies of volunteer soldiers kept order as best they could but when the Yakimas attacked settlements at the Cascades in 1855, federal troops had to be called in to drive them off and secure the area. The troops were led by Lieutenant Philip Henry Sheridan who distinguished himself there and later in the Civil War. He was made a lieutenant general in 1869.

The land along the river was heavily timbered with areas of rich soil along many of the tributary streams. There was land here to be farmed, trees to be cut and a river on which produce, logs and furs could be moved to market. Towns and villages were established. Bridal Veil was one of them. A planing mill built in the town provided work for some men while others felled trees in the forest. Teams of oxen with their skilled drovers hauled the logs out on skid-roads. The town of Palmer, two miles uphill from Bridal Veil was built at the same time. Both were lumber and mill towns.

With women and children now established in simple but adequate houses, a store and a school had to be provided. A company store was built and stocked, a school erected and two teachers hired.

Railway lines were laid on both south and north banks of the river. The small communities were no longer as isolated. The children had woods to play in, the river to fish in and chores to do around the house. For young Alva Horton who arrived with his widowed father and brother in 1889, there was much of interest. He said he and his friends "made rafts by placing three railroad ties close together in the water, nailing a couple of cross strips to hold them. I fixed some oars." The boys were rafting in the millpond which was just as well. Alva, a non-swimmer, fell backwards from the raft when his paddle slipped from the oar lock.

"I went right down out of sight. As I came up I was right by the raft and got my arm over it and paddled to the shore."

The school he attended had thirty to thirty-five boys and girls and all grades were taught, "only they weren't called grades then. It was first, second, third, fourth and fifth readers. Arithmetic, writing, spelling, grammar and geography were also taught."

The mill manager, J.S. Bradley and his wife, were well liked in the town. According to Alva Horton, Mr. Bradley, "always had a kind word and gave good advice to us. Mrs. Bradley was more influential than any other person. She was never cross or scolded us and in the Sunday School class she was always so kind and soft to us boys who were inclined to be a little loud. But every day, Sunday or not, if we were thinking about something mean, if we thought Mrs. Bradley would not like it, we did not do it."

Since there were no movies or theatres in Bridal Veil, nor in any other small town at that time, "Mrs. Bradley proposed an evening of reading. We had no library available so she invited everyone to her home, two evenings a month, for a reading circle. Each person would take a turn at reading. The first book was *Corporal Cy Cleg*. This was a Civil War story. The next book was *Aunt Samantha at the World's Fair*. There would be an attendance of fifteen or twenty people and the program would last about two hours. It was a democratic situation where the owner of a big business opened his house to his most humble employees."

When they weren't in school, the children liked to go up to Palmer and watch the teams of oxen hauling logs. Heaving and straining, the patient animals dragged the logs to the mill. However, the mill soon needed logs faster than the ox teams could bring them out and more modern equipment was brought in. The Smith and Watson donkey engine became the pride and joy of the loggers.

Flumes to send the timber down to the millpond were part of the logging operation and to this day, remnants of the flumes can be seen in and around Bridal Veil Falls.

A memorable flood hit the town in 1894. The railroad was under several feet of water. Some of the children rowed themselves to school, others thought it great fun to paddle their makeshift rafts over the top of the railway bridge and peer down at the tracks below.

That same year, 1894, long before vaccinations and inoculations were available to prevent life threatening childhood diseases, diphtheria, a deadly illness, crept into Bridal Veil like a thief in the night leaving a trail of grieving parents in its wake. One family lost four children and their father, stricken himself, barely pulled through.

With the passing of the epidemic, life slowly returned to normal. Lumber from the Bridal Veil and Palmer area was highly prized and the mill was kept busy filling orders. The company store in Bridal Veil supplied the people of Palmer as well. "Every day a wagon hauled by two teams of horses brought freight and groceries up to the Palmer Mill."

The summer of 1902 was hot and very dry. By September the forest was like tinder and sparks from a passing train set the surrounding brush ablaze which quickly roared up the hill east of Bridal Veil. With the fire head-

ing straight for Palmer, word was telephoned to the town
warning residents to flee. Some managed to outrun the
flames, others jumped into the millpond protecting themselves as well as they could while their town burned to
the ground.

With everything lost, the people of Palmer were
without the barest necessities of life. When the Meier and
Frank Company of Portland heard of their plight, they
had freight cars loaded with food, clothing and bedding
and dispatched them immediately to the stricken people.
"No one living in Palmer at that time ever forgot the
generosity of Meier and Frank who were first to respond
to the disaster."

Within two years Palmer was rebuilt on a site two
miles from the original town. The lumbering business
slowly declined over time as the surrounding land was
depleted of usable trees. With the shortage of timber to
harvest and mill, Palmer became a complete ghost town.

The entwined histories of Bridal Veil and Palmer echo
those of many towns dependent on a single industry and
one with a finite resource. The hills and valleys were
stripped of their trees. Nature was left to renew the
forest.

Bridal Veil is no longer a town as such, it is more a
postal address boasting the second smallest free-standing
post office in the United States.

By 1915 a highway had been built from Portland past
Crown Point. This road linking western and eastern
Oregon enabled travelers to visit parts of the state not
previously accessible. Not completely paved for another
decade or so meant a bumpy ride at times. The Gorge
area became an early tourist attraction. Its many waterfalls, varied plant life ranging from giant trees to rare
wild flowers were then and still are a source of interest to
those who take the time to observe and protect them.

It was over this road as it was being built that Donald Lawrence, younger son of Louise and Will Lawrence, second owners of the property, traveled often as a boy with his family on their way between Portland and their apple orchard at Hood River. He was intrigued by his observation that the Douglas fir trees pointed their branches westward down-river from Crown Point and Bridal Veil but pointed their branches eastward as he approached Hood River.

A local explanation had arisen to account for the differences in the fir crowns of the west and east parts of the gorge. The winds of the gorge were thought to arise in the valley of the Wind River halfway through the gorge, swirl around Wind Mountain and so become separated into two winds going in opposite directions. They would then pass forth from that region simultaneously eastward and westward so that the prevailing winds would blow outward from the center of the gorge.

Young Donald thought this couldn't be the correct explanation. These deformed trees interested him so much that he later devoted several years of study to determine the correct causes. He found that wind blows through the whole gorge mainly from the west in summer and from the east in mid-winter, gradually gaining strength as it passes through the gorge. It never blows in opposite directions from the center at the same time as past local lore would have it.

In the western part, especially near Crown Point and Bridal Veil, violent winter winds, sometimes accompanied by freezing rain storms break off eastern branches. Or on clear days, dries them out enough to kill the needles. In the eastern part of the gorge winds from the east are never strong and winter precipitation occurs as snow that gently sifts to the ground without sticking to needles and branches.

The summer story is a different one. The westerly wind gradually increases in velocity so that from Cascade Locks eastward, the branches bend around the trunk as they grow, making graceful streamlined crowns all pointing eastward. But at Bridal Veil and Crown Point, the summer wind is too weak to bend the branches.

For Donald Lawrence his study of the deformed fir crowns became part of his doctoral thesis at the John Hopkins University. Now Professor Emeritus, Department of Plant Biology, University of Minnesota, Saint Paul, he has done much ecological research in the Pacific Northwest including Mount St. Helens, Mount Hood and southeastern Alaska as well as the Columbia River Gorge.

Writing with passion about the importance of preserving the Gorge area, he sees it as a "unique resource worthy of national care." He would like to see the whole of the Bonneville Landslide area extending southeastward from Table Mountain, Red Bluffs and Greenleaf Park to the Columbia River and beyond to include the toe, now named "Ruckel Slide" on the Oregon side, be preserved undisturbed insofar as possible at this late date in the conservation effort.

A heavily traveled freeway, Interstate 84, now borders the south bank of the Columbia, beside it the busy railway brings long lines of freight cars thundering past.

It is sometimes difficult to imagine Bridal Veil being the center of bustling commercial activity, to remember that not far to the east at The Dalles, as recently as 1855-56, Indians were attacking settlers. And in 1910, one housewife in Bridal Veil lost a quarter of beef to a hungry cougar down from the hills looking for an easy meal.

The Jacobson Mansion

August 8, 1916. With the signing of the required legal documents, Dorothy H. Jacobson was now the owner of 15½ acres of land in the Columbia River Gorge area. She had purchased the land from Minnie Franklin, a widow, living in Vancouver, Washington. Ten acres lay on the river side of the newly built Crown Point Highway. The balance of the property on the south side of the road sloped up towards the towering rock wall of the gorge.

Dorothy and Clarence Jacobson had been searching for the perfect location on which to have a summer residence built. They wanted to be close enough to Portland for easy access. Clarence was the part owner of a thriving clothing business in the city. He would have to make frequent trips into town. But they also wanted their summer home to be far enough from the city so that friends coming to visit would have a feeling of reaching a destination, of arriving at a special place.

The location of the property a mile or so east of the town of Bridal Veil was ideal. The Crown Point Highway came twisting and turning down from the top of the gorge to Bridal Veil, where it then proceeded in a more sedate fashion as it followed the river upstream. The drive from Portland to the Jacobson property would take from one to one and a half hours.

The Jacobsons were very wealthy. Dorothy was a millionaire in her own right. Her father, reputed to be the tobacco king of the United States, presented each of his three adult children with one million dollars. Clarence was Dorothy's second husband. She had always lived luxuriously and travelled extensively. Clarence enjoyed seeing the world with her.

Although the United States in 1916 was not yet involved in the mass slaughter in Europe, known as World War I, travel to that continent was out of the question as was travel to the Near and Far East. Dorothy Jacobson liked to be "on the go." Moving around the world by train and luxury liner being impossible, she needed something to occupy her time. Having a summer residence built and friends coming to stay when it was finished seemed to be the perfect solution. Both Dorothy and Clarence had warm, outgoing personalities that drew people to them.

Clarence loved fine automobiles and owned three, a Locomobile, a 12-cylinder Packard and a yellow sports Oldsmobile. He and Dorothy spent many pleasant hours driving on the new highway as they searched the area for a piece of land suitable for their house project. They would take along a picnic basket filled with treats from the kitchen of the Benson Hotel where they kept a suite of rooms.

The land they purchased was totally wild and would need careful development to turn it into the work of art that Dorothy had in mind. One of the beautiful features of the property was the 171-foot Coopey Falls that tumbled over the gorge creating a rushing stream on the east boundary.

As part of the purchase, Dorothy had an agreement to have the use of 50% of the Coopey Falls water. Besides household needs, it would be used to generate electricity.

On one of Dorothy's trips to Italy she had visited friends who owned an elegant villa on the Mediterranean coast. The Italianate style of white stucco walls, tall arched windows and red tile roof appealed to her. It was usual for villas of this type to have formal gardens falling in terrace fashion towards the sea. The gardens would be graced with sculptures, fishponds and numerous fountains. It was such a house and such gardens that Dorothy envisioned on the Bridal Veil site.

Having found the land, the next problem she had to deal with was finding an architect in Portland who could bring her dream house to life. Portland in 1916 was not the sophisticated city it is today and its architects might have neither the travel experience nor expertise to design and build the Jacobson house. As luck would have it, they found exactly the right person. A chance meeting at a party given by friends acquainted them with Morris H. Whitehouse. He was well known in Portland for his excellent work on many public buildings and some private homes. Upon being introduced to him as one of the leading architects in Portland, Dorothy mentioned that she was looking for an architect to design a summer residence in the gorge area near Bridal Veil.

When she described the kind of house she had in mind, Whitehouse wanted to hear more. With her usual enthusiasm, she went into detail about the house and gardens she had imagined.. Whitehouse then told her about his own love for the Italianate style.

Although born of Portland pioneering stock, he came across as a second century Roman patrician. In a 1935 interview he said "to interpret the present, it is necessary that the principles of the past or classical period be understood. After these have been mastered, the architect can create modern architecture but unless he is familiar with the principles of proportion, ornamentation and proper treatment of mass, he will never create real art."

Speaking with Whitehouse was to be caught up in his artistic vision of how a building should fit into its surroundings. For him "Architecture is the art that harmonizes beauty and utility. It is the most useful of the fine arts and the noblest of the useful arts. It is considerably more than merely drawing pretty pictures." This was a man with strongly held beliefs. "One is never through learning," he said. He had a list of skills that architects should have. "They must know general engineering, especially structural, heating, sanitary, electrical and other types of engineering, that enter into the construction of buildings. He must be a trained research worker for architecture is the projection of all our experiences of the past into the present and future."

Whitehouse thought it vitally important that an architect know how to get along with the contractors and workmen since he must act as disbursing agent and provide the owner with proper certificates of payment.

He had the feelings of a true artist. "There is a satisfaction and thrill to a finished building that you have guided from inception to occupancy that cannot be described. It is the thrill of seeing a bit of creative art reach the point of achievement, and is augmented by knowledge that it is one of the most durable and useful arts. Architecture is an art that affects every human being in some manner constantly during his or her life."

When he graduated from M.I.T. in 1906, he received the first travelling fellowship ever granted by the school. It gave him more than a year abroad, during which time he studied the fine architecture of the old countries. He also spent several months at the American Academy in Rome. He visited the Mediterranean coast and discovered the singular beauty of the Italian seaside villa. The same villas that so enchanted Dorothy Jacobson. The graceful lines of the houses and their formal gardens were much to his liking. He never expected to be designing one of these villas in the Columbia River Gorge area, yet that is what Dorothy Jacobson was proposing.

"Would you consider designing and overseeing the building of our summer home?" she asked. Whitehouse was pleased to accept. He had already been approached by Simon Benson, promoter of the Crown Point Highway and former chairman of the Oregon State Highway Commission, to build a hotel in the gorge area. Whitehouse presented Benson with a plan to build the hotel along the same lines as the Jacobson house. So it was agreed.

With the contracts signed between Whitehouse and themselves, Dorothy and Clarence picked him up on a bright and sunny day for the drive out to the Bridal Veil site. They chose the big Packard for the trip. Parking on the roadside, they looked over the land.

"Your house should be built on this side of the road," Whitehouse opened his arms wide as he took in the slope of the land, the gorge cliffs and some magnificent trees. They picked their way through the blackberry bushes, scrubby shrubs and weeds of every description until they reached the high point of the property and could see the full watery, rocky beauty of Coopey Falls. The Jacobsons had already ascertained that electricity could be generated from the falls.

"I think the first work to be done will be to build a holding reservoir here below the falls and run piping down to a power house which will be best located at the lowest point down slope." Whitehouse walked down from the falls to the road and looking back up decided where the powerhouse would be placed. Although he would be using an electrical engineer and contractor to build the reservoir and powerhouse, he, true to his calling, knew exactly where and how the electricity could be produced.

With the eye of the true artist, Whitehouse thought the house should be placed on the high point of the site, close to the stream that rushed down the east boundary and with a view of the falls if possible. He was picturing windows or French doors looking towards the falls with a view of the rocky gorge over which it fell and the hanging vegetation that thrived in the mist.

He shared his thoughts with the Jacobsons who had waited quietly as he walked with them over the land.

"The house should be about here," and he paced off its location, "the formal gardens can be in terraces looking towards the river. We can put a fishpond at the lower level and perhaps one near the front entrance."

Dorothy broke in, "We also wanted a swimming pool. Where would be the best place for that?"

"And," here Clarence interrupted, "I've hired a chauffeur and told him he could decide the kind of house he wanted to have for himself and his family when they move out here."

Whitehouse laughed "Good! I think I have enough information to go on. I'll come out with one of my construction foremen to make accurate measurements and then make my sketches," he paused to look around, "you have chosen well. Although the acreage is small for the kind of estate you want, I think we'll come up with something that will be pleasing to you."

His sketches were works of art in themselves. The Jacobsons knew they had found the right person to build their home. Whitehouse also consulted with John Leitzel who had been hired as the Jacobson chauffeur. He and Clarence had met in Portland when John was driving a sightseeing chain drive bus around the hills of Portland. Their mutual interests in automobiles resulted in a relationship more like friends than employee and employer. Clarence wanted a chauffeur to drive him back and forth to Portland and John Leitzel was not only an excellent driver but a skilled mechanic to boot.

Whitehouse decided to build the Leitzel house near the entrance to the property. John said it must have a three-car garage so the cars could be parked easily. The house was built around and over the garage. On one side was a toolroom with an exit to the outside. On the same side was a wood lift that could be filled with mill ends from the Bridal Veil lumber company. It then was cranked up to the kitchen on the second floor where Mrs. Leitzel used it in her wood stove. On the opposite wall, a door opened into a stairway that led to the living area above. It was a spacious apartment consisting of three bedrooms, a living room, a large kitchen, a dining area and a bathroom.

With his designs approved, Whitehouse set about engaging the contractors, engineering expertise and skilled workmen to bring his design to fruition. Italian craftsmen who had worked on building the fine stonework that bordered parts of the Crown Point Highway were hired. To enhance the grounds, Whitehouse had them line the stream edges with stone. Then had them create beautiful small arched bridges over it. A large trout pond with an encircling wall of cut stone blocks was evidence of the fine work of the Italian stonemasons. A stone pedestal was placed in the pond at Dorothy's request. It was her intention to have a statue of a Greek or Roman goddess placed on it sometime in the future. She was thinking ahead to the end of the war and a return to Italy and Greece to find the perfect goddess for her garden.

The finished house was a work of art. It had white stucco walls, a red tile roof and tall arched windows, both inside and out. It has been described architecturally as "a modified rectangle with wings, staggered hipped roof with overhanging eaves and modillions, one interior and one exterior chimney; Ionic pilasters flank the front door with semi-circular arch lunette and support the pediment with dentil molding, a cartouche protrudes from the center of the pediment. The second floor has 6/6 double hung windows; recessed mid-block has 6/6 double hung windows on the second floor and casement windows in recessed arches on the first floor; one story wing protrudes at the south end with modillions beneath metal copings; north facade has recessed French doors with semi-circular arched fanlights, two doors lead to the porch (terrace with red brick floor) down to a fountain in an enclosed garden."

The preceding is a cool, clinical rendering of the exterior of the house. It's a bit like describing a human being as skin, this much; hair, that much; fingers, this many; and so on. As with a live human being, so with the Jacobson mansion, it had to been seen in its totality to be appreciated. The house was a thing of beauty both inside and out. The elegance of its design, the brilliant use of materials, the wonderful arched windows, the red tile roof, all contributed to an overall feeling of seeing something quite special and something quite unusual in the Columbia River Gorge.

Whitehouse had spent many hours discussing the project with the Jacobsons. They wanted their guests to not only enjoy staying at the house but to enjoy their arrival. A rock wall now bordered the property by the road and the wide entrance had wrought iron gates that opened to the driveway. To the right, the Leitzel carriage or gatehouse echoed the design of the big house. White stucco walls with red tile roof and small arched windows on the stairwell pleased the eye.

The architect decided to create a winding driveway that would curve in two graceful loops around the trees and shrubs that were to be planted. Although the distance from the road to the front door of the house is only three hundred feet, the driveway is well over one thousand feet. The artist in the architect wanted there to be an unfolding of the scene as the visitors drove slowly up to the house heightening the sense of arrival at a special place. Creating a "sense of place" was Whitehouse's plan. There had to be a harmonious blending of all the elements to enhance this feeling.

The swimming pool, placed about twenty-five feet to the right of the last curve of the driveway, was made of poured concrete, painted a delicate turquoise color. White marble benches were set in the landscaped lawn around the pool. A steam pipe running underground from the house furnace was used to heat the water. Pathways from the pool led to the lower rock garden.

A long terrace of red brick was an inviting feature of the north side of the house. Tall French doors led from the main room to the terrace. Standing in this central doorway, the eye was drawn outward and downward past the wide expanse of lawn, through an opening in the lawn-bordering white stucco wall, to the formal rose garden and thence to the trout pond with the stone pedestal awaiting its goddess. Beyond lay the mighty Columbia and the hills of Washington. The view was one to give delight and an appreciation of the formal and informal ambience of the scene.

Three formal fountains graced the gardens. One on the wall below the terrace, one in the shape of a pineapple set in the wall above the rose garden and another below that facing the garden. This latter fountain had the face of the Greek god of the sea, Poseidon.

Water was much in evidence around the grounds. The driveway at the front of the house encircled a large goldfish pond. In it stood three crane sculptures. There were pink water lilies, multi-colored fish and on the stone edging, a small bronze frog from whose mouth water spouted.

Stepping into the house was to enter a dwelling of surpassing beauty and overall perfection of design. Beautiful polished wood railings and balustrades of the front hall staircase met the eye. A few steps up and the hallway branched to the right and left. French doors led from the left into the magnificently proportioned main living area. It was a full forty-two feet long, some twenty-five feet wide and soared two stories high. A huge fireplace of carved stone dominated the east end of the room, with French doors on either side leading to the library.

But one of the most interesting features of the room was the second floor balconies. At both east and west ends, the balconies stretched the width of the room. The one to the east had as part of its back wall, the great stone chimney of the fireplace. The balconies had slender railings and were supported by finely carved wood beams. Bedrooms gave on to these balconies. To give the connecting upper hallway a view of the room below, unusual windows had been placed along the wall. With their protective lower railings, they were a reminder of the Italian architecture which so appealed to Morris Whitehouse.

The library fireplace although not as large as the one behind it, was created with as much care. And as Whitehouse had envisioned, wide French doors offered a view of the craggy gorge wall and its multitude of hanging plants. The sound of the stream pouring down from the falls added to the loveliness of the scene. Polished wood shelves stretched from floor to ceiling and the walls between were hung with imported silk coverings. Tall windows on the east and north sides allowed daylight to flood the room.

Fine oak floors were a feature of the house except for the dining room, solarium and kitchen area. Centered in the dining room was oak flooring surrounded by black and white marble squares. This room also had a white marble fireplace. French doors led from the dining room to the solarium which was also floored in black and white marble and more glass panelled doors led to the outdoors. The light fixture in the solarium was quite beautiful. It was of alabaster in a bowl shape with three small bronze mermaids seated on the rim. A delicately crafted white

The living room/ballroom as it appeared when the Jacobsons lived at Bridal Veil. Much of the furniture was covered in red plush. The tiger and leopard skins were brought back from one of Dorothy Jacobson's travels.
Note the balcony over the fireplace and the windows that opened the upstairs hallway for viewing the room below.

marble fountain with catchment bowl in the south wall added to the charm of this room.

The vaulted ceilings of the first floor hallways gave a sense of spaciousness. Dorothy Jacobson had asked Whitehouse to create a special room for her collection of Chinese artifacts. This was in the northwest corner of the house and could be reached from the living room or the front hall. In it she placed her tables inlaid with mother-of-pearl in oriental designs, a three-panel screen with colorful pictures embroidered on silk, a four-poster Chinese bed and a glass-fronted cabinet holding small items, including several fans inlaid with mother-of-pearl.

There were five guest bedrooms on the second floor each decorated in a unique style. The master bedroom was large with a pink marble fireplace, a walk-in closet lined with imported cedar and a bathroom *en suite*. There were two other bathrooms for guests. Staff quarters were at the back of the house, with a bathroom attached.

The basement stretched far and wide beneath the house. Thirty double batteries in the laundry area stored the electricity generated in the power house. The great furnace burned wood and coal and that in turn heated the water for the radiators. All the radiators in the main rooms of the house were covered with decorative screening.

The kitchen was very large and a wood range was used for cooking. A dumbwaiter built into the wall gave the kitchen staff access to the basement area for moving laundry up and down and items in and out of storage.

The china pantry lay between kitchen and dining room. It was lined with glass-fronted cupboards. Dorothy was fond of brightly colored china and had several sets, all in bright primary colors. A very large safe was located here, in size, almost like a small bank vault. On the opposite side of the kitchen, a door led to a pantry. Outside the kitchen, the hallway connected the back entrance, a second staircase, a small washroom, and into the solarium.

Incorporated into the house was a telephone system. Every room was wired. A line was also strung to the Leitzel house by the main gate. John Leitzel was called out of bed at three o'clock one morning by Clarence Jacobson.

"John can you get up here right away. I think someone is trying to break in. We can hear all kinds of funny noises at the back of the house."

John pulled on his pants over his pajamas, stuck his feet in his shoes and ran up the path. Clarence met him at the front door and they both stepped quietly through the solarium, into the back hall and to the basement door.

"Listen to that. What do you think it is?" John put his ear against the door. The thumping continued.

"Well the only way to find out is to open the door." With that John pulled it open, switched on the light and found himself facing a large pack rat trying to drag an old work boot belonging to the gardener down the stairs. Startled by the light and the unexpected appearance of two human beings, the rat dropped the boot and scurried away into the basement. It was out of sight by the time the men reached the bottom of the stairs.

"Well, Clarence, it looks as though you're going to have to call in someone to get rid of that thing. There's bound to be more and I tell you, they'll take all kinds of stuff."

How they had come in and where they were nesting had to be left for an expert. The last thing the Jacobsons wanted in their beautiful new home was a family of pack rats.

Calling for outside help meant driving into town. There was no telephone service into the Bridal Veil area, nor would there be for many more years.

The Jacobsons had a fairly large staff to maintain the house and grounds. Dorothy had her own maid, Margaret. She also assisted Mdme. Carteau in the kitchen when needed. Mdme. Carteau was French and specialized in her country's cuisine. She was disappointed not to be able to buy carp in Oregon.

"A wonderful fish," she told Margaret, "and the way to get the muddy taste from its flesh, is to pour vinegar down its throat." When she was on vacation, the Jacobsons were able to engage the remarkably talented Henri Thiele as their chef. He had opened a restaurant in Portland which became a great success and the Jacobsons had met him while enjoying his fine food. Using their considerable charm, Dorothy and Clarence persuaded Henri to spend a week or two at Bridal Veil cooking for themselves and their friends. Always generous to those who worked for them, Henri was paid well for his culinary skills.

Three gardeners were engaged full time. Mr. Hefty was head gardener and he had two helpers. Trees and shrubs were imported from abroad. Beautiful roses were planted in the rose garden and two rock gardens were created, one behind the house and one below the swimming pool. The one behind the house and close to the stream was raised above ground level with a stone retaining wall. Winding steps led up to the garden. It was in this garden that Dorothy had Mr. Hefty place a bronze sculpture of the Buddha that she had brought back from the Orient.

Furnishing the house gave Dorothy much satisfaction. Her taste was excellent. All the dining room furniture was custom designed and hand crafted. The great living room had large sofas and chairs with many pieces upholstered in red velvet. On a trip to Africa she had brought back a tiger skin and a leopard skin. These were on the floor.

Dorothy and Clarence were fond of music and she played the piano well. She had purchased a Chickering piano for the house. Chickering pianos were noted for their fine tone. Made in Boston, they ranked with Steinway in the piano world. Pianists with a fine ear could discriminate between a Chickering and a Steinway. The Chickering had an English tone, the Steinway, a German tone.

The Jacobson house became known locally as the "Jacobson Mansion." As soon as they were settled, Dorothy and Clarence invited friends for weekend parties, some came for longer visits. Dorothy was a beautiful woman with a mass of auburn hair. Perfectly self-assured, she defied the conventions of the day and smoked. Her long cigarette holder kept the smoke from

Dorothy Jacobson

irritating her eyes. When her friends were not visiting, she wrote them long letters. Her hand writing was elegant. She always used maroon ink and a pen with a maroon feather attached to it.

The swimming pool was often the center of attraction for guests on hot summer days. After a swim and a change of clothes, they would have luncheon on the terrace. On clear nights, the terrace was a wonderful place to sit, watch fireflies and gaze at the stars.

The Jacobsons had no children and Dorothy was especially fond of little Elizabeth Leitzel who was three when her parents moved to Bridal Veil. She liked to bring Elizabeth presents from time to time and one day came in with a pretty romper suit she had bought in Portland. Elizabeth didn't like the look of this at all.

"I don't like it!" She stamped her foot.

"Come now Elizabeth, just try it on." Her mother seldom raised her voice and now was gentle with her child.

Dorothy joined in, "I want to see how you look in it and then come up by the house so I can take your picture."

Elizabeth liked having her picture taken and consented to put on the romper outfit. She wasn't pleased though and after she and Dorothy had gone up to the house and the picture taken, she let her displeasure be known.

"I don't want you to come down to my house ever again," she pouted and ran off down the path. But Dorothy loved the child too much to take this to heart and very soon they were quite the best of friends.

One of the delights of little Elizabeth's life was to go hand in hand with her father, across the road to where the chickens were kept. The Jacobsons owned ten acres of land on the north side of the highway, sloping towards the river. On it they had a chicken coop built and kept a sizeable flock of birds to supply them with eggs and

Irene Jenny, Elizabeth Leitzel and baby Clarence Leitzel behind the gatehouse.

poultry for roasting and frying. John Leitzel adored his daughter. Walking over to collect eggs, he told her stories about how he left home when he was thirteen.

"But Daddy, why did you?" Elizabeth couldn't imagine anyone wanting to leave home. Hers was such a happy, loving place, she thought all children had parents like hers.

She heard the whole sad story when she was older and able to understand, how his mother had died when he was eight, his father remarried a widow with two boys and she treated John so badly, he walked away when he was thirteen and never returned.

Clarence Jacobson and his dog Duke.

Caroline Schmidt, with whom he fell in love and married in 1913, was a woman of gentle ways, quiet of voice and manner. Theirs was a great love.

And these were pleasant times for the Jacobsons. They enjoyed themselves to the fullest. Clarence wanted to take a yachting trip up the West Coast and north to Vancouver, British Columbia. He had John Leitzel make all the arrangements and then insisted that he accompany them. They stopped off in Vancouver and boarded the train to take them on a visit to Banff and Lake Louise. While they were gone, Caroline Leitzel, Elizabeth and their new baby, Clarence, stayed in the big house. The Leitzels were so fond of the Jacobsons that they named their son after Clarence.

The pleasure the Jacobsons had in their lovely Bridal Veil home was short-lived. Clarence died very suddenly of a heart attack in the late fall of 1919. Dorothy was devastated and felt unable to stay in the house. She and Clarence had planned it together, delighted in entertaining their friends and now their shared joy had turned to ashes.

John Leitzel was stunned by his employer's death. He felt as though he had lost a close friend. Dorothy closed up the house, the furniture was covered in dust sheets, valuables were locked away in the safe and the Chickering piano, which could not be left in an empty house, was given to the Leitzels. Elizabeth was to take piano lessons.

Although Dorothy pleaded with John to stay on and act as caretaker, he and Caroline decided to leave. Without Clarence, the three cars to drive and maintain, John knew he would be like a fish out of water. This was not the life he wanted. With Dorothy's permission, he offered the caretaking job to his cousin, Chris Jenny. The Jenny family moved into the gatehouse. John bought a garage in Sutherlin, Oregon and he and his family moved there. Dorothy headed for New York.

Not quite ready to sell the house, she left it in the care of Chris Jenny. The ten acres to the north of the Crown Point Highway were sold. Dorothy remarried within two years. Her husband was Roy Carruthers, associated with the Waldorf Astoria Hotel in New York. In the March

House and Garden, March 1926

Italy in Oregon

1926 issue of *House and Garden* magazine the house at Bridal Veil is featured.

The caption reads: "ITALY IN OREGON. You might encounter this house somewhere on the road between Florence and Perugia, but you actually find it on the Columbia River Highway at Bridal Veil, Oregon. Its

Dorothy Jacobson Carruthers Cole on tour.

owner is Roy Carruthers and its architect, M. H. Whitehouse."

Dorothy was to marry again. Her fourth husband, a Mr. Cole, Vice-President with Standard Oil. The last mention we have of her is when the house is sold in September 1926 to Louise B. Lawrence. Her signature on the documents is, "Dorothy H. Cole."

She left the house wrapped up and closed in. It was empty for six years. During that time Chris Jenny kept the house in good shape although there was a continuing problem with pack rats climbing the wisteria vine at the back of the house and burrowing under the tiles. Water seeping into a corner of the library damaged the silk wall coverings.

The lawns and gardens could not be maintained as they had been previously when three men worked on them full time. Chris struggled to keep them trim and neat but was no match for the creeping weeds in the flower beds.

One of the Jenny daughters, Irene, was married at Bridal Veil. Her father promised that if the day was rainy, he'd remove the dust covers in the living room and hold the reception there. However, the June day dawned bright and sunny. The wedding feast was spread on tables down by the gatehouse.

Dorothy had no children and now disappears from our story. She corresponded for many years with the Leitzels then suddenly her letters stopped and they were never able to learn what happened to her.

It is sad to lose sight of Dorothy Jacobson. Through her wealth and excellent taste combined with the genius of Morris H. Whitehouse, the house at Bridal Veil came to life. Its haunting and timeless beauty still echoes with her spirit.

As for Morris Whitehouse, his love of classical form and the overall design of the house and grounds remain a living monument to his name.

The Second Arrival and Moving In

February 17, 1975 and it's raining. Mothers Michael and Francine are on their way to the airport to pick up Sister Margaret who is joining their small community.

"Let's take her straight out to the house!" Mother Francine is so enthused about their find at Bridal Veil that she wants to show it to the newcomer that afternoon. "Do you think she'll be too tired?"

"I doubt it. You know how she is, she's so at peace within herself and so centered, she'll probably come off that plane looking better than we do." Mother Michael laughed, "At least she won't be bedraggled from the rain. Anyway she'll want to see the house so we'll go right out there."

They were both anxious to see how Sister Margaret would react when she saw the house. There was a mind-boggling amount of work to be done before the place was remotely liveable and she, with the other three, had to set about and do it.

She already had a full-time job waiting for her. Her training in the food sciences and years of managing food services in institutional settings were in great demand. Her ability to work harmoniously with people while directing their activities makes her the perfect person for the hospital setting where she will be employed. Her reputation as an outstanding cook and her skills at food preparation make her doubly welcome everywhere she lives. Sister Margaret's gentle, loving presence attracts children, adults, dogs, cats, animals and birds. Gifted with almost a sixth sense, she seems able to communicate with birds as difficult as peacocks. More of that later.

"Thank goodness the flight's on time." Mother Michael is thinking about how quickly the afternoon light will fade and it's a half hour drive to Bridal Veil.

"Well, hello." Sister Margaret's smile lit up her face. She had been flying cross country for hours, changing planes once but looked fresh and relaxed. "It's so good to see you both." They were old friends and hadn't seen each other for months so lots of warm hugs had to be exchanged before collecting her luggage.

She wanted to know all about the house and whether they had made a final decision about purchasing it.

"We're waiting for you to see it." Mother Michael paused, "It's a real mess but I think we can fix it up. The place hasn't had a thing done to it for six or seven years but the house seems solidly built. We're going to have a structural engineer come have a look to make sure we know what we're getting into." She turned to smile at Sister Margaret, "There's a little, old barn on the property so you'll be able to have some chickens."

As they headed out on the Interstate, they described in detail the house and grounds. "And guess what!" Mother Francine is bubbling with excitement. "There's a gorgeous waterfall on the property. We couldn't believe it when we saw it. Can you imagine having our own waterfall?" She is sure Sister Margaret will like the place but wants to give her a real feel for some of its special charm.

She is so busy listening to them talk that Sister Margaret hasn't realized they are on the Interstate and not on their way to Portland. When Mother Francine took the Bridal Veil exit, she realized where they were going.

Parking at the front gate, Sister Margaret jumped out of the car first and then saw the tree blocking the entrance.

"Wait a minute, you don't have to climb over it." Mother Francine is laughing. Sister Margaret, in a hurry to see everything, has already got one leg up and over the huge trunk and is preparing to scramble over it.

"We've found a way around by the roots but watch your stockings, there are hundreds of blackberry bushes everywhere and they are covered with awful thorns."

Easing their way around the tree, through the mud, the slippery leaves, the blackberry bushes and broken pieces of stone, they stop and are quiet. All they can hear is the rain. Sister Margaret looks around and then up at the house. She is quite still. For her it is an emotional moment.

"This is it." She wonders if she should say this out loud. "Maybe they'll think I'm crazy if I do."

Mother Francine is unable to stand the silence any longer. "What do you think?"

"You'll think I'm out of my tree but this is it." She has a strong feeling that the place is holy. For her, it has a spiritual quality. "I don't know what it is, but there's something here that feels right."

As they walk over the land, she senses it is good and picking up some earth, lets it filter through her fingers.

"This is good earth. We'll be able to grow things here." She was born and raised on a farm and her prediction about the quality of the earth was born out in the years that followed.

Going up to the falls, she noticed bits of a well-laid brick path under the creeping moss. The more she saw of the grounds, she realized that under the mess of weeds, broken trees and garbage was an underlying unity of design. "We can bring this place back to life."

They entered the house. Like the land around it, the house had a special quality that came through despite years of neglect and structural changes that might have destroyed a less beautifully designed building.

"All this place needs is to be cleaned up and given lots of loving care." Months later when some of the cleaning up and clearing out had been done, Sister Margaret remarked, "The way this house responds to care is just wonderful. As soon as the floor in the living room dried out, the wood went right down. Why even the little wooden pegs were there and we were able to tap them gently back in place. There isn't a nail in that floor, and you know, as we were working away tapping at the pegs, we kept saying to each other, 'Just look at that. Isn't that something.'"

When they returned to town, Sister Paula Jean was home from work. They began making their plans. They had been out at the house often enough to realize they were going to need some help. With full time jobs, they could only get out after work and on weekends. Someone had to be there to help with major tasks and keep an eye on the place. The leak in the roof had to be repaired and none of the Sisters was inclined to tackle that job. The original red tiles had long gone from the house and a previous owner had the roof shingled. The whole roof had to be redone.

When the Sisters were working in Vancouver, they had met Brother Jerome, O.M.I. (Oblates of Mary Immaculate). He had been employed as a carpenter and general maintenance man at a school on a nearby Indian reservation. It had been taken over by the government and he was between assignments. Mother Michael approached his superior to ask if he could help them out for a couple of months. Permission was given and Brother Jerome proved to be a willing and hard worker.

The sale of the Bridal Veil house to the Sisters spread around the local community. On one of the first Saturdays they were working at the house, Don Gibbon, a rancher living a couple of miles away, dropped by. He looked at the fallen trees and decided that the neighborly thing to do was to bring some equipment and one of his hands over to cut the trees apart and stack them for firewood. Although not a Catholic, he liked the Sisters and admired them for taking on the restoration of the house and grounds.

"I think you're crazy you know, taking on this place but maybe you're crazy enough to make it work!" Being a man used to hard physical work, Don wondered to himself how a small group of women, none of whom looked particularly robust, could tackle the sheer physical labor facing them.

Before Sister Margaret's arrival, the others had been coming out to assess what needed to be done. One evening Mother Francine and Sister Paula Jean decided to make a sketch of the whole interior of the house. Neither had any drafting skills but that didn't bother them. They figured they could measure walls, doors and windows and draw lines between them. The fading light of a wintry January evening gave them enough light to see what they were doing on the first and second floors. Although the power was on, many light bulbs were missing and they hadn't thought to bring a flashlight.

Sister Paula Jean's dog, Shabar, was with them. He had been named for a character in the book of Joshua. This was a difficult naming considering the numbers of people and places found in that Old Testament book. The Sisters named their dogs by opening the Bible at random and picking a name on whatever page appeared. Mother Francine's beloved dog, Jessica, an animal of unusual mien and testy of temper, was named for a biblical character.

Shabar having run through the house, headed down the basement stairs ahead of them. It was pitch dark.

"Feel for the light switch," whispered Mother Francine.

"I did and it's not working," Sister Paula Jean whispered back.

"Well, let's feel our way down, there must be a switch somewhere." Mother Francine began running her hand along the wall as she stepped carefully down the stairs. Her companion was right behind.

They reached the basement floor and began moving slowly keeping close against the wall. Suddenly there was a loud crash. They stumbled back to the stairs and ran up with Shabar scrambling behind them.

Catching their breath at the top, they began to laugh and the dog began to bark. "Do you want to go down again?" Mother Francine was laughing so hard, she had to sit down on the top step. "I really don't think there's anything down there and if there is, it'll be long gone."

So down they went. They listened for any strange noises as they felt along the wall for a longed for light switch.

"There!" Sister Paula Jean found one and it worked. The single bulb shining through its coating of dust revealed the cause of the crash. Shabar running on ahead had stepped on a piece of sheet metal covering a drainage line. It had tipped over, rattling and banging to good effect.

"Do you think there are any mice?" Now that she could see, Mother Francine thought she'd better keep an eye out just in case. Her brain told her that only a stone deaf mouse would be silly enough to come out with a dog prowling the basement, but the part of her that feared mice and rats kept running interference. She stamped her feet and talked loudly to warn lurking pests that she was there.

Finding light bulbs working in a couple of rooms, they removed one, took it to an empty light socket and gave themselves enough light to make their measurements. Relieved to be finished, they hurried upstairs, locked up and ran to the car.

"One of the first things we have to do is buy a whole bunch of light bulbs. It's kind of creepy when you can't see." Sister Paula Jean made a note, buy light bulbs and underlined it.

With the arrival of Sister Margaret, the women began to deal with the trash both inside and outside the two houses. With the driveway now clear, dumpsters were brought in and filled with the filthy garbage in the gatehouse garage and the junk lying around, the dead cars, refrigerators, dirty mattresses, bedsprings, tires and one rusty old stove. They hired a man with a front end loader to pick up the rubbish and drop it into the waiting dumpsters. The revolting mess left by some of the neighbors was soon cleared away but the smell lingered on.

One of the old cars had been a nesting place for a fox. Frightened when the Sisters began their clean up, she ran off.

With Brother Jerome due to arrive, the apartment in the gatehouse had to be made habitable. The women swept, scrubbed, disinfected and scrubbed some more and still the smell persisted.

"It didn't smell so great when he arrived," said Mother Michael, "I don't know how he stood it but bless his heart, he did."

The Sisters divided their energies between the gatehouse and main house. With the gatehouse cleaned out, they concentrated on their own kitchen, the only really dry room in the house. Having no appliances, they brought out sandwiches and thermos jugs of coffee after work, ate a quick supper and set to their assigned tasks. They kept at it until midnight or later, drove back to

Portland and to bed, hoping to catch enough sleep to function at a reasonable level the next day.

The kitchen was filthy. Ceiling, walls, floor and cupboards washed down three and sometimes four times gave up years of grease, spider webs, mouse droppings and soil. The kitchen at Bridal Veil eventually becomes the domain of Sister Margaret. As a specialist in food preparation and with an artistic flair for doing magical things with whatever she touches, the Sisters can count on nourishing, simple meals, beautifully presented. Leftovers turn up in a variety of disguises.

Weekly work lists kept them on some kind of schedule but diversions happened often enough to throw their best laid plans awry. Sister Paula Jean's discovery brought them running.

On her knees scrubbing the foyer floor by the front door, she sat back to rest and looking up decided there was something wierd about the paneling edging the hallway. The few steps leading to the hall from the front of the house had finely turned, beautiful wood bannisters.

"That plywood doesn't look right," she thought, "it doesn't match those bannisters." Putting down her scrubbing brush, she picked up the scraper she'd been using to get rid of ground-in dirt from the tiles, "I'll just see if I can pry off some of that stuff."

It took awhile but eventually she managed to press the double plywood wall apart with enough space for her to peer inside. "Well, I'll be darned."

Excited at her find, she called the others, "Hey, where are you? Come here, I want to show you something." The others working at the back of the house didn't hear her. She ran to get them.

Persuaded by her excitement, they dropped their tools and followed her.

"Just look at this!" And like a magician showing off a special trick, she let them peek one at a time inside the crack in the plywood wall. It reached from floor to ceiling and covered wood railings that duplicated the staircase bannisters.

"Do you know what this place is like?" Sister Paula Jean posed the question and didn't wait for an answer, "It's like an archeological dig. Who knows what we'll turn up next."

Her remark was a portent of the future as little by little the house gave up its secrets.

Having glimpsed the hidden railings, the Sisters threw aside their work schedule, called Brother Jerome to bring some crowbars and with his help, they took the wall down.

From the foyer, the delicate railings followed the line of the curving bannisters, and the French doors to the living room brought light into what had been a dark and gloomy passageway.

"Now why did someone do that?" Mother Francine wondered aloud as they stood and admired the original design. They left the question unanswered since it seemed impossible to imagine why a previous owner had made something so graceful and beautiful into something ugly. Many times in the future as they worked through the house, the same question puzzled them. "Why did someone do that?"

Brother Jerome changed all the locks, repaired a broken window beside the front door and helped with much of the heavy work. The Sisters found used hypodermic needles in some corners of the main floor rooms and shreds of marijuana. A tavern across the road closed down shortly after the Sisters bought the house, the tavern owner being charged with criminal activities. Strangely enough, the house was not vandalized while standing empty for seven years. Although the garbage and trash in and around the gatehouse was smelly and unsightly, the vandals broke only the garage doors and nothing else.

The Sisters' friends, the Rudfelts, sent up a full cord of firewood. With fires lit in the living and dining room fireplaces, the walls, ceilings and floors began to dry out. Brother Jerome, up on the roof to assess what had to be done, repaired the leak.

The furnace presented a problem as the Sisters hesitated to touch the controls. Totally inexperienced in dealing with such an enormous heating unit, they decided to call in some help. Converted to oil sometime in the past, there wouldn't be coal to shovel. Their friend, Terry Falls, came out. He checked the burner, the controls, the oil in the tank and turned it on. Without so much as a groan or glitch, it flared into life. The radiators throughout the house warmed away the damp.

The Sisters learned all too soon that heating a house of some five thousand square feet was beyond their meager finances. To conserve oil, the thermostat was set low. They heated the living room with log fires, the fireplace being almost big enough to roast an ox. The kitchen was fairly snug when meals were prepared. All the other rooms and hallways remained cool during the winter months. A friend of one of the Sisters who made the mistake of visiting during a cold January, vowed not to return until the sun shone and the world heated up. The Sisters' defense against the cold? Thick sweaters and warm socks.

On one of their working weekends, Sister Margaret discovered a rat in the basement. With that, they decided that getting rid of both mice and rats took priority over everything else. They called in an exterminator.

He lived in a nearby town and was both pleasant and helpful. Going over the house carefully, he gave them his estimate. His price seemed reasonable enough. Their problem, they couldn't afford it. He did, however, offer them advice on the proper poisons to use and where and how to spread them around. He pointed at a crawl space in the basement. "There are rats in there. The poison has to be laid down right in that space."

The Sisters bought the deadly ingredients and spread them around in the designated places. Some of it had to go into the crawl space. One of them had to go in there. Of the four Sisters, Mother Francine was the smallest and the only one of the four with a phobia about mice and especially rats.

Years later, she shudders at the memory. "It was awful! I was absolutely terrified, my heart pounding and me shivering with fear. I thought, 'I'm going to die in here with the rats.' Mother Michael shone a flashlight in for me to see."

"I crawled in on my stomach and the rats' eyes were shining and they were squeaking and I had to go right around the space putting the poison down. The rats scurried out of my way." Putting her hand to her throat she relived the horror. "Can you imagine what it was like? I knew that if one of them jumped on me, I'd start to scream and die of fright!"

Holding on to her sanity, she backed slowly out and helped down by Mother Michael, stood shaking on the basement floor.

"Thank goodness she was there to hold me up. I couldn't stop shaking and she just put her arms around me and kept saying, 'It's all over, it's all over, just take it easy, you'll be okay,' and when she figured my legs could move and I seemed reasonably normal, she led me back up to the kitchen and sat me down."

" 'Let's have some coffee.' And she called the other two to join us. They'd been scrubbing the tile floor in the solarium. I gave them a blow by blow description of the rats. Maybe, I thought, the memory will fade if I talk it out." Mother Francine is laughing at herself now, "I can still bring it back it in full and living color. I told them then that whatever else needed doing at the house, I was bowing out as the exterminator. That experience just about did me in."

And a seemingly endless amount of work waited to be done. Fortunately what remained of the winter was mild and spring brought fine weather with little rain. The house warmed up. With spring sunshine flooding in, the extent of the damage done to the house became more and more apparent. They had taken down the sheets of black plastic covering the beautiful windows and French doors facing the terrace. The question of who had covered the windows remained in limbo.

Thinking back on the day they first saw the house, Mother Michael shakes her head. "Why it was just like Niagara Falls in there, all that water coming down over the fireplace. What a mess! But even under water this place spoke to us. Funny how a piece of land and a house can speak if we care to listen."

The Sisters never lost that first profound feeling of being in the presence of something holy. They tackled the repairs to the house always with a sense that they were creating something. What that something was eluded them at times. Education for life was the path. How it would be played out in the future was not always clear. As faithful followers of St. Francis, they were comfortable within themselves and the work they were doing both professionally and at Bridal Veil. Building their foundation slowly, the future would reveal itself.

In the meantime, in the basement of the house they found hundreds of strips of movie film hanging in one of the rooms. "Someone must have been a movie buff." Sister Paula Jean gathered up bundles of tangled film to take outside and burn. "I wonder why they left this?"

"Well it makes a great fire with all the other junk lying around down there." Confined in a burning barrel, the film blazed into ash.

On the second floor, they began taking down the plywood partitions. The box-like cells disappeared leaving the beautifully proportioned bedrooms. Only a dusty and mouldy smell remained. But a room at the back of the house had a terrible smell. The Sisters scrubbed it up and down, even taking up the old linoleum covering the oak floor. The smell persisted.

"We'll have to leave this for now." Ever practical Mother Michael, "We've got to fix up our own rooms if we expect to move in by Easter." Shutting the door, they left it.

When the Sisters first looked at the house on that rainy, gloomy, grey New Year's Eve morning, they fell under its spell so completely that they failed to notice something curious about the large living room. Perhaps with the rain pouring down the fireplace, the oak floor like a wavy wooden sea and the sheets of black plastic over the windows, they failed to take a good look at the ceiling.

Now with bright daylight and sun shining through the windows, they saw that something was quite wrong with the overall symmetry of the room. Two steel beams, like pillars, supported the ceiling. A couple of exotic looking chandeliers, Venetian in their appearance, seemed out of place amidst the general wreckage. At both ends of the room, a line of carved wooden shapes lined the ceiling edge.

Exploring more thoroughly, they discovered the damage done to the room. A previous owner lowered the ceiling, braced it with the steel beams and created small bedrooms on the second floor above the living room. Months later the Sisters were given a picture of the room as Morris Whitehouse designed it. The beautiful balconies with their elegant wooden supports disappeared leaving only bare vestigial remains. The graceful viewing windows of the upstairs hallway that added such an unusual touch to the soaring height of the living room vanished without a trace.

"I guess whoever did it must have had a good reason." Mother Francine looked around. "I wish I'd seen it before it was like this." Something else bothered her. Someone had painted the carved stone fireplace and its sweeping stone chimney pink. Upstairs where it continued through one of the created bedrooms, the stone was painted blue.

Moving In

Working slowly and methodically, the Sisters with the help of Brother Jerome made the kitchen fit to cook and eat in. Friends in Portland having their own kitchen remodelled gave them their old stove and refrigerator. Another friend provided a table and chairs. Their bedrooms were cleaned thoroughly and given a quick coat of paint.

With Holy Week approaching, the Sisters decided to spend their first night at the house on Holy Thursday. They asked a priest friend to celebrate Mass with them that evening and bless the house. Mother Shaun, Mother Rosemae and Sisters from their Astoria community came along for this special occasion.

With no beds as yet, the Bridal Veil Sisters brought along their sleeping bags. They packed up food for the evening meal and something for breakfast. A piece of plywood set on two sawhorses and covered with a white cloth served as the altar in the dining room, with candles, bread and wine ready for the celebration of the Eucharist.

Before Mass, Father walked with them through the house, blessing it and the foundation being established there. It was a beautiful and moving ceremony. Tears filled the eyes of the four women who had worked so hard to bring them this far along.

Mass began. In the middle of the liturgy the doorbell rang. Startled by this sudden intrusion, they looked at each other. It was pitch dark outside. No one was expected. The bell rang again. Mother Francine went to see who was there as Mass continued. A man stood on the front step.

"I am Mr. Moffatt," he announced in a loud voice, "and I want to know what you're doing here. This is my house. I have first option to buy it." He took a step toward the door. Mother Francine stood in his way.

Staring him down and holding the door close to her side, she gave each word a solid emphasis, "That is very strange. We purchased it several months ago. You are quite mistaken! This is our home!" And she started to shut the door.

"That's not possible." His voice became louder. "I have first option to buy this place and you have no business here." He made another move toward the door. "I want to come in and see what's going on."

"No! You are not coming in!" Determined to slam the door in his face if need be, she raised her voice a notch or two. "You can call us in town tomorrow," and pulling a pad of paper and pencil from her pocket jotted down their phone number. Then with a parting shot, "And don't try to use any key you have because all the locks are changed." With that, she slammed and locked the door before he had a chance to push past her.

"Oh, my God." She leaned her head against the door, close to tears. "How can I hold myself together until Mass is over." Feeling sick inside, she returned to the dining room. With Mass ended, she told them what had happened. She choked back her tears. "After all our hard work and the house being blessed and all our plans for our foundation, why this? Why now? What are we going to do?"

"Now just a minute." Mother Michael, confident as usual leaned over and gave her shaken colleague a quick hug, "This man is mistaken. We've been through all the legal business and title search. What we'll do tomorrow is get in touch with the S.V.D. Fathers and clear this all up."

Then making the best of a worst case scenario, she added, "If God means us to have this place, then we'll have it, if not, it may be because there is something better in store for us." This bit of cheerful wisdom failed to lighten their mood. To start somewhere else? Too terrible to think about just then.

Sister Margaret wondered aloud, "Why has this man suddenly appeared? There's something strange about this. What's he been doing since January when we bought the place?" She smiled a wickedly gentle smile, "I think he's trying to scare us off but we don't scare that easily."

Sister Paula Jean like the others was shaken and asking herself why God was letting the devil play with them like this. It all seemed so cruel.

The priest and the Astoria Sisters left, promising to pray for a happy outcome. Knowing the work the others had done at the house, they were devastated at this turn of events.

Mother Francine, recovering from the shock of dealing with Mr. Moffatt, realized how angry she felt that this special Mass and blessing of their house had been violated by this man.

"I wish I'd just shut the door in his face and not given him our phone number. He must be crazy to think he can barge right in here." She looked over at Sister Margaret. "I think you're right. There's something very strange about that character."

"Okay, there's nothing we can do about it tonight so let's pray and go to bed. We'll cope with this better in the morning." Mother Michael wanted her little community calmed by prayer and their minds at rest for the night.

Gathering up their sleeping bags and followed by their two dogs, they went upstairs to sleep. Their symbolic moving in did not turn out as planned yet with the morning, their spirits brightened. Back in town, they put in a long distance call to Father Shigo, Provincial of the S.V.D. Fathers.

He wasn't in his office. Away visiting he couldn't be reached until the following day. The Sisters waited. The hours dragged on. Another night to pass.

Father Shigo was surprised at their news. "I'll tell you what I'll do. Our lawyer will go through the papers and I'll get back to you."

It was Easter weekend. No one was working. By Monday, the Sisters were on tenterhooks. Doing their best to concentrate on the Easter mysteries and the joyful celebration of the resurrection, they found a prayerful resting place.

Father Shigo phoned on Monday afternoon. He'd found a letter in their files from a man named Moffatt. Part of it read "...I can't come up with the $134,000.00 right now but I hope to do so in the future."

"He doesn't say anything about an option to buy so he has no legal claim to the property. But our lawyer wants some time to do a thorough search. I'm not sure how long that will take."

It took three weeks. Then Father Shigo phoned. "The property is yours. Everything is fine. I'm sorry this took so long but for your sake and ours, we had to be absolutely sure that this Moffatt character had no legal claim that might backfire."

During the difficult three week waiting, the Sisters stuck to their schedule of work at Bridal Veil. Their strong faith and their prayers sustained them. As the days passed and spring warmth brought the land back to life, their sense of being in the right place strengthened.

Now that Mr. Moffatt and his threats were out of the way, the purchase price of the property became the next hurdle to pass. Sixty thousand dollars, cash, to be exact. With no credit rating to fall back on and no assets other than their salaries, no bank would finance them. They turned to friends and relatives. Within days they managed to borrow the cash. It says much for these Franciscan Sisters that they repaid all of it within two years.

Still more money was needed, another five thousand dollars to replace the roof. Not only had it leaked over the fireplace but shingles had blown off in many places. Seepage stained some of the ceilings on the second floor.

Sister Paula Jean turned to her uncle to lend them the money. As he wrote the check, he teased her. "I'll bet I won't see this again." He admired the courageous attitude of his niece and her colleagues. Whether he ever saw his money again didn't trouble him. He thought it was a good investment in the small community. Repayment of the debt made him smile. The Sisters proved to be a good bet.

With the coming of May, they moved their odds and ends of furniture from the rented house in Portland. Slowly they acquired a secondhand sofa, some comfortable chairs and a used television set. The small room off the living room, once Dorothy Jacobson's Chinese room, became the chapel. The house felt like home when they moved in.

Snakes–A Discovery–A Repentant Thief– Assisi–The FBI

Living in the house gave them more time to spend both cleaning it and clearing some of the wild growth close by. Weedy trees unchecked for years crept in from the forest to a stopping place against the east wall of the house blocking the windows. Blackberries, wonderful fruit for pies, jams and jellies, but left to run wild, become an impenetrable thicket with thorns to rip and tear skin and clothes. The Bridal Veil climate suited them well. They thrived.

Sister Margaret wanted a small vegetable garden close to the west wall of the house. Fresh herbs, lettuce, radishes and green onions for a start. First, the jungle outside demanded attention.

"I can smell snakes out there," she told the others, "and I don't want to get into that tangle by myself. Who'll help?" Sister Paula Jean volunteered. She felt like working outside for a change of scene.

"Just look at the size of those blackberry branches, they're as thick as my wrist." Garden clippers were useless. They used a saw to cut through the branches.

"Ouch!" Sister Paula Jean ripped the skin of her hand on a thorn. Both women wore thick gloves. Now they wrapped two layers of green garbage bags over them to protect their hands and arms.

The snakes proved to be harmless grass snakes. Hundreds of them lived undisturbed for years in their cosy habitat now falling to the strong, saw-wielding arms of the nuns. They beat a hasty retreat.

The weedy trees, a kind of alder, to the east of the house, gave them some trouble and Brother Jerome helped clear them away. To take down an invasion of trees is no small task. Sawing, chopping and dragging away is not work for the faint of heart. With them out of the way, light streamed through the glass. The windows, with some oiling of hinges and locks, creaked open.

The room now freed of its window-blocking trees, still seemed dark and featureless. Father Borkowski referred to it as the original library of the house. When a previous owner converted it to a chapel, the architect's design underwent a complete change.

On a bright sunny Saturday, the Sisters decided to have a good look at this room. Plywood panels covered all the walls so taking claw hammers and a crowbar, they set to work removing them. Sets of bookshelves appeared between the graceful windows. The once beautiful wood was marred by nails. Filling the holes right then was not a priority item.

The south wall, facing the falls, was solid brick under the plywood. The most startling discovery was yet to be found. As they removed the last of the panels on the wall between the two French doors to the living room, a great gaping hole met their startled gaze. Stone edged the opening. On the floor inside lay chunks of the same stone. It matched the fireplace in the living room.

Kneeling down and peering inside, Mother Francine could hardly believe her eyes. "Why this must have been a fireplace. There's a big chimney here." She leaned back and stared at the surrounding area. "Somebody, some time must have taken a jackhammer and knocked this down then covered it all up." She shook her head in disbelief. "Now who did a thing like that?"

No answer to this haunting question came to them. Mother Michael looked at the messy room. "This must have been quite a place at one time." Then she remembered something.

"You know those big glass doors down in the basement, the ones we couldn't figure out what they were for, I have an idea they used to be where that brick wall is now. I can't think where else they'd go in the house." Her curiosity now piqued, she took tape measure in hand, hastened to the basement and measured the windows. Back upstairs, she measured the brick wall.

"Well, what do you know?" She was all smiles. "Those doors belonged here. I wonder who took them down and bricked the wall. There'd be a great view up towards the falls from here."

The other three, fearing that their next task might be breaking down the wall and putting in the large glass doors hurried Mother Michael from the room.

"This house is amazing," Sister Margaret changed the subject from brick walls and glass doors. "We're uncovering hidden treasures all the time."

Walking through the living room, this particular mother lode of treasure held no compelling charm for them. So much needed to be done, they'd decided early on to set it aside until either their energy was restored or more nuns joined the community. The only word to describe the enormous room was "an eyesore." Wallpaper hung from walls and broken lath and plaster showed through where damp had played havoc. The desecration of the stone fireplace with pink paint angered the Sisters whenever they saw it.

The same mad hand with the same pink paint had seen fit to paint every small pane of glass in the china pantry cupboards, both inside and out. Paint on glass? There might have been method in the painter's madness but the Sisters in their wildest imaginations couldn't make sense of the crazy way pink paint was used so meticulously to cover the glass in the doors. The same old question bounced around between them, "Now, who do you think did that and why?"

Months before they purchased the house, the Sisters planned a pilgrimage to Assisi, the birthplace of St. Francis. With the strain on their meager finances, they thought about cancelling the trip. Part of July each year is usually set aside in the larger community, to meet with each other in a retreat setting. It was to Assisi most of them hoped to go in 1975. The Bridal Veil Sisters consulted Mother Guardian at the mother house. Knowing how hard they had worked since January with hardly a day of rest, she thought they had to have both a spiritual and physical break. The mother community loaned them most of the money and they managed to scrape together the rest.

Brother Jerome planned to reshingle the roof while they were gone and he promised to take care of the two dogs, Jessica and Shabar. The day before their flight, Mother Francine called at the post office for mail. The postmistress had a parcel she thought might be theirs. It was addressed to, "The Mansion, Bridal Veil." In it was a priest's stole, the kind used for hearing confessions and an incense boat. Also a note.

"I'm returning these to this place and may God have mercy on my soul."

They conjectured that the sender had taken the stole and incense boat left behind by the priests and the repentant thief, filled with remorse, felt compelled to return them. The gesture warmed the Sisters' hearts as they set off for the birthplace of St. Francis.

When they'd been away for a week, Mother Michael phoned. The first words from Brother Jerome were, "Jessica is fine."

Mother laughed, "Good, and how are things with you?" He had a strange story to tell.

"I was up on the roof a couple of days ago working away when a car drove up to the front door and a man got out. He yelled at me to come down. He said he wanted to speak to me. Well, I didn't want to climb down and then have to climb back up so I asked what he wanted.

"Then he pulled something like a small wallet out of his pocket and flipped it open. You're not going to believe this Mother. He said, 'I'm from the FBI.'"

"He said what?" Mother Michael wondered if she'd heard right.

"He said FBI so right away I came down and looked at his badge. Sure enough he was from the FBI. He wanted to know who I was, what I was doing there and did I own

the house. I told him you owned it and were in Assisi. I
said you'd all be back in two weeks."

" 'You mean nuns own this place?' You should have
seen the look on his face. Mother, he was really surprised.
Then I asked him why he was asking so many questions
about the house.

"Just wait 'til you hear this Mother! He said a report
came to their Portland office that someone was making
pornographic movies out here and he was checking it
out."

"Oh, my gosh." Mother Michael began laughing so
hard she could hardly speak. "Do you know what? When
we started to clean out the basement, we found lots of
movie film. We just bundled it up and burned it. I'll bet
something was going on and they left in a big hurry."

When she told this bizarre tale to the others, they
wondered if the sheets of black plastic covering the tall
living room windows when they first saw the house were
used to keep prying eyes from seeing what was going on
inside.

"And maybe they painted the fireplace pink and put
that awful gilt stuff on the wall sconces." Mother
Francine's sense of the absurd was ready to make much of
this revelation. "And here we are, nice, sensible nuns
fixing up our convent and foundation where porno films
were made!"

"What do you mean, 'nice sensible nuns'?" Mother
Michael's laugh was infectious. "No sensible human being
would be caught dead doing what we're doing at Bridal
Veil. Anyway porno films or whatever, we've burned the
evidence."

The trip to Assisi gave them a tremendous spiritual
lift and much needed rest. The summer months gave
three of the Sisters more free time to work in and around
the house. Mother Michael's parish work stopped for the
summer and Mother Francine and Sister Paula Jean,

employed in the Catholic system also had time off. Sister Margaret continued at the hospital.

They settled into a comfortable routine of community prayer and communal work. Their simple chapel was enhanced with the arrival of their terra cotta statue of the Virgin Mary. It had been left in safekeeping with their friends, the Macdonalds, in Vancouver. They brought it down in their station wagon and Angus, carried it in. The statue is heavy. When the library was finally restored, the Sisters made it their chapel and it fell to Angus, visiting with his family, to move it again. He vowed to be out of the country if they decided to relocate it.

The damaged floor in the living room was badly in need of attention. They'd tapped it back into place but the ugly water stains and ground-in dirt had to go. They rented a sander and went over the huge area very carefully. The quality of the fine oak showed through. With limited spare time to wax and polish it, they decided to use polyurethane to protect the wood and give it a shine. The floor glittered.

Renewing the floor made the shabby, raggedy walls look even worse by contrast. Tempted to make a start on them, they wisely resisted. Summer was almost over and the Sisters had to start back to their work in Portland.

Two Sisters expected to join the community in the months to come. With that in mind and having made parts of the house clean enough to pass muster, they felt less pressured. As Franciscans, they wanted to have their friends visit. Hospitality is part of the Franciscan call. To offer friends a cup of tea or coffee or a simple meal is to create a feeling of warmth and welcome. The Franciscan kind of hospitality as lived by the Sisters is alive and well at Bridal Veil. It permeates the house.

When friends were not expected, they kept the big wrought iron gates at the driveway entrance locked. Living in the country was a new experience. Even with two dogs running around, they thought it best to lock the gates when they were at work and after dark.

On a very dark, very rainy night, Mother Francine and Sister Paula Jean returned late from a meeting in town. They stopped at the gate and Mother Francine felt in her purse for the padlock key.

"I hope you've got your key because mine's not here." Sister Paula Jean felt in her purse. Her fingers explored every nook and cranny. "Mine's not here either."

The rain poured down. It bounced off the car roof. "Well, I guess we'll have to climb the wall." Mother Francine is not tall. The craggy, field-stone wall is about five feet.

"I guess we will." She felt in all her pockets hoping to find the key. She checked the glove compartment. Maybe a key lurked there. None did.

They sat for a few minutes deciding on their wall climbing strategy. "I think," said Mother Francine, "that if we climb up the edge of the gate by the hinges, we'll be able to stretch over and get on the wall."

"Well, we can't climb over the gate that's for sure. It's got too many twisty bits on the top."

They wore raincoats. The small veils on the backs of their heads soon clung to their soaking hair. Climbing in the pitch dark, in the rain, they made their way up the gate and managed to clamber on to the wall. The stone is not smooth. It was hard on hands, legs and feet. As they sat on the wall dripping wet, these two young women started to laugh at themselves and the spectacle they presented. That is if anyone saw them. They could scarcely see each other in the driving rain and dark.

Giggling like schoolgirls they slid off the wall into the muddy bank and skidded down to the driveway.

"Oh, good grief, I've dropped my purse," Mother Francine felt around and couldn't find it. "Never mind I'll get a flashlight from the house and look for it. Come on, let's run!"

They dashed in the back door and like waifs from the storm walked into the kitchen. Mother Michael and Sister Margaret were having a cup of tea before going to bed.

"What on earth have you two been doing? You look like you've been playing in the mud." Mother Michael wondered what was making them laugh when they looked so wet.

"Don't ask! Can you reach me the gate key, we locked ourselves out and had to climb the wall." Mother Francine looked at her dripping companion. "You know what. You've lost your veil." She felt the back of her head. Hers was there but just and was stuck to her wet hair.

"And I dropped my purse, so can you reach me the flashlight there behind you Sister. Maybe we'll find the veil too."

Sister Margaret wanted them to get into dry clothes. "Here let me go down. I'll drive the car up and you can look for your things in the morning."

"Oh, no, you're not going out in this. We'll be back in a couple of minutes." And with that they headed back into the night.

The Lawrence Villa

When Louise Buermann Lawrence purchased the Bridal Veil property in 1926, the house had been unoccupied for six years. Dorothy Jacobson continued to employ Chris Jenny as caretaker during that time. He lived with his wife and family in the gatehouse apartment above the three-car garage. The lawns and gardens had deteriorated and in the big house, some firewood had been chopped on the drain board beside the sink and wood rot was quietly invading parts of the house.

Dorothy Jacobson moved to New York after Clarence died and, in the ensuing years, married twice. When the documents were signed for the sale of the property on September 10, 1926, her name appeared as Dorothy H. Cole. The Lawrences, with her permission, moved into the house in late August of that year.

Louise Lawrence was the wife of William C. Lawrence, a well-to-do and well-respected businessman in Portland. His father, George Walter Lawrence had built up a thriving business, manufacturing fine leather goods, especially harness and saddlery. Louise had a private income. Her father owned a foundry in New Jersey that made harness hardware, bits and spurs. He invested in urban properties, mortgages and rental housing. His daughter's income came from these investments.

The William C. Lawrence company picnic at Bridal Veil,
August 29, 1936.

The Lawrences were comfortably off but were not in
the millionaire class as the Jacobsons had been. They had
two sons, William C. (Bill) Lawrence Jr., born 1905 and
Donald, born 1911. Bill was 21 and Donald 15 when their
summer home was established at Bridal Veil.

They were a close knit and loving family. Louise is
described by her daughter-in-law, Virginia, as being
"wonderfully kind and gifted at managing her home."
Louise's parents had emigrated to the United States from
Germany and Louise learned many of her household
skills from her mother. Being the daughter of a wealthy
family, she attended a finishing school in the East that
gave an added polish to her warm and friendly personality. She was loved by all who knew her.

The property at Bridal Veil was ideal for the family.
Will could drive west to Portland daily by way of the
Crown Point Highway without being blinded by the
morning sun and Louise could indulge her passion for
gardening. She was a very knowledgeable horticulturist

and an expert at growing things. Donald shared her love of plants. Early on she taught him the scientific names for the common garden plants, including trees, shrubs and the herbaceous annuals that she grew.

But there was more than a simple naming of plants going on between them. For Louise, the miracle of growth and development in plant systems in their natural habitats was the emotional core that energized her. She passed this along to Donald. Botany and ecology became his life's work. He obtained his Ph.D. at Johns Hopkins Univerity in 1936, retiring in 1976 as Professor of Botany at the University of Minnesota.

Bill loved the outdoors. Unlike his brother who revelled in the study of plants, animals and rocks, Bill enjoyed just being there, breathing the fresh air and feeling the earth beneath his feet. He was a fine horseman able to calm the most fractious animal. His skill with horses came from spending time with his Irish cousin, Robert Bassett, well known for his ability in handling and training horses.

Bill joined the family business after two years of college. He had a better head for, and interest in, the commercial world than his brother. They always remained good friends even when Donald asked Bill and his young wife, Virginia, to care for six banana slugs while he was off on a field trip.

The house was purchased fully furnished much as Dorothy Jacobson had left it. Her Chickering piano and its matching stool were given to young Elizabeth Leitzel with some delicate pieces of china and crystal going to Elizabeth's parents.

Louise Lawrence enjoyed music and played the piano well. Shortly after moving to Bridal Veil, she purchased a grand piano to grace the huge living room.

Chris Jenny had kept the house clean and dry. The grounds were a different matter. Cutting the lawns with a hand mower was a daunting task, it took hours to complete. To maintain the gardens was out of the question. They became completely overgrown with blackberries, hazel shrubs and weeds. He also had to keep the powerhouse functioning to provide electricity for the big house and the gatehouse. The Jennys always kept a supply of oil lamps on hand for times when the power failed.

Winters, with their fierce east winds, were a cruel test of endurance for Chris and his family. On days when snowdrifts were piled high around the houses and the road, he wrapped himself in sweaters and coats with a big scarf wound around his head and made his way to the village store for supplies.

None of the fountains were working by August 1926 and the goldfish and trout ponds were empty of water and filled with silt. The swimming pool needed cleaning and painting. The neat rock wall bordering the stream to the east of the house with its pretty little bridges and the rocky border of the trout pond had to be repaired. Some of the piping that fed the powerhouse was breaking apart. There was a lot of work to be done.

Louise liked to do all her own planting and spent hours putting in hundreds of plants. However, she had to call in assistance to help with major projects. A Swiss gardener, Adolph Meyer of Pacific Alpine Gardens, was hired. He specialized in creating rock gardens with little waterfalls running through them. Even with help, reconstructing the gardens was slow and painstaking work.

While clearing weedy shrubs in the summer of 1926, Louise discovered a handsome bronze Buddha. She was working in the hillside rock garden behind the house attacking a big clump of overgrowth with her hoe. It struck something hard and she was startled by a metallic clink. This was neither rock nor earth. Something solid and metal was hidden there.

She knelt down and began pulling away the covering of weeds and scrubby bushes.

"What on earth is this?" It was nothing new for her to talk to herself as she gardened but here was something that set her back on her heels. And that's what she did when she finally finished pulling away the clinging greenery.

She was staring at a two-foot-high bronze casting of the Buddha. It was standing on a square of rock. Finding it hard to take in what her eyes were seeing, she stood up and called Will. He was at the pool.

"Will, come here. I've found something." Louise's excitement at finding a new wildflower was not unusual and Will was taking his time reaching the rock garden.

"Will, hurry up. You won't believe what I've found!" As he climbed the stone steps he saw the cause of her excitement.

"Well, I'll be darned." They stood and admired the small figure.

"I think we should leave it here, don't you?" Louise was quite enamored with her treasure and didn't want it disturbed.

Will began to kick at the ground around the statue and found it soft with fallen leaves.

"Give me your hoe a minute." He began scraping around the square stone clearing leaves and earth away from it. "I think this little fellow stood in a pond and I'll wager that when we dig out all this debris we'll find a wall."

And they did. The accumulated dirt of years was washed off the Buddha, the small pond in which he stood was raked clean and water from the falls filled it. This idyllic spot became a favorite of Louise. She couldn't imagine how the sculpture had been left behind and forgotten.

Recounting the find to her sons and wondering how it had been abandoned, they decided that Dorothy (Jacobson) Cole must have left in a hurry and forgotten about it. And that is probably the answer. Grieving the sudden and untimely death of her husband, she left behind her beautiful home and its lovely gardens. The little Buddha was forsaken. Soon the pond disappeared under a burden of fallen leaves and slowly the creeping weeds and shrubs hid the sculpture from view.

The charming furnishings and the Jacobson collection of artifacts from around the world, made the house a delight for the Lawrences. Although Louise admired the Chinese room and its fine collection, her sons thought it cold and uninviting. When her brother, Henry, visited during their second summer at Bridal Veil, he was enthusiastic about the beauty of the house and the quality of the interior workmanship. The pink marble mantlepiece in the master bedroom made a particular impression. Henry enjoyed browsing through antique stores and in one of his favorite Newark haunts found a pink marble clock.

He wrote to his sister, "Louise, I've found just the right clock to sit on the mantlepiece in your bedroom. I'm shipping it by express."

Louise and Will thought it a wonderful gift. A pink marble clock on a pink marble mantle added a touch of glamor to the room.

Other areas of the house had unusual features. A unique pair of bronze andirons stood on either side of the library fireplace. Two feet tall, each topped with the head of a phoenix, they were like sentinels watching over the flames.

The Jacobson's colorful china and crystal were in constant use as the Lawrences entertained family and friends at their summer home.

In the 1920s, travel was for the well-to-do who could afford to leave their homes in the care of paid staff. The Lawrences spent most of the summer of 1924 travelling in Europe. On September 3, 1924, Louise purchased an approved copy of Raphael's, *Madonna of the Chair* at the Pitti Palace in Florence. The painting, in an exquisitely carved and ornate gilded frame, was quite lovely. Returning to Bridal Veil, the picture was hung on the west wall of the living room.

Will's sisters, Miss Sophie and Miss Mabel, also travelled extensively. On one of their trips to Japan, they brought back a Japanese stone garden lantern over five feet tall. This fitted nicely into Louise's scheme to have a Japanese look to the trout pond. A copper crane fountain sent a gentle stream of water from its mouth, rippling the pond. The Japanese lantern was placed nearby under a recently planted weeping willow tree.

Bill and Donald each had a horse. They were stabled in a small barn south of the gatehouse. Bill's was a beautiful big animal called Sea Hawk. Donald's first horse, Dick, was rented from a local dairy farmer, Fred Luscher. Dick had been at pasture without much care for years. Burdock heads so completely filled his tail that he couldn't swing it to swat away flies. Donald had to trim it down to almost nothing. The following year he was given his own horse, Tipperary. The younger of their two aunts, Miss Mabel, was also an expert rider and took advantage of her visits to Bridal Veil to take one of the horses for a run.

Robert Bassett, a second or third cousin of the family, lived on the George Lawrence family farm with its fine apple orchard at Hood River. It was Robert who picked an unbroken range horse for Donald and trained it for riding. Robert never referred to "breaking a horse." He didn't want a broken horse, he wanted an animal well schooled for riding. Robert considered Tipperary a fine example of an Irish "heavy hunter" and Tip became an excellent jumper.

When Chris Jenny retired as caretaker and moved his family from the gatehouse, Robert and his English wife, May, moved in. Robert was a big, handsome Irishman with no children of his own. He was fond of young people. Bill and Donald were favorites of his. When the Lawrence grandchildren arrived on the scene, he delighted in having them follow him around as he did his chores.

There was a lot for Louise and her sons to do during their summers at the house. She needed their help to weed and clean the flower beds. She designed her own flower gardens and each year put in a large vegetable garden behind the gatehouse. Her rows of raspberry and blackcap bushes yielded the family pounds of delicious fruit year after year.

Bill and Donald cared for their horses, fed ground beef liver to the trout in the pond and one of their ongoing tasks was to clean the screens covering the intake pipes which opened low down on the reservoir wall under the falls. Silt and debris clogging them reduced the supply of water for the powerhouse and household use.

Eventually Will asked Mr. Coopey for permission to increase the height of the reservoir wall by eight to ten feet. Mr. Coopey retained 50% rights to the water but he did allow the Lawrences to build up the retaining wall. Two wooden pipes about 12" in diameter and wrapped in stout wire were put in place near the top. The screens were now more accessible for cleaning as most silt settled to the bottom.

This arrangement worked very well. At least once a day and more often in rainy and stormy weather, someone had to walk up to the reservoir and clean the screens. The heavier sediment that fell to the bottom was dug out every spring. Donald found a drowned rabbit floating in the water one day. The water was tested occasionally for bacteria. The coliform bacteria count was a bit high at times but no one suffered any ill effects. Deer, mountain beaver, raccoons and other animals used the stream above the falls which accounted for the bacteria.

The new reservoir wall was built by men from the Bridal Veil Lumber Company. The manager of the company, Mr. Hagen, thought he had a still better idea to improve the water system. He had his engineers plan and build a large rectangular wooden, box-like water tank supported on vertical wooden timbers. This was put in place about one hundred feet downslope from the falls. It was big, some eight feet tall, ten feet long and eight feet wide. The stilt-like supporting timbers were eight feet tall at the lower end. Not a very handsome structure by any means.

The tank served as a perfect settling basin for the sediment and the system worked just fine except for one hitch. Will had not asked Mr. Coopey for permission to build the thing. It was not totally on Lawrence land and Coopey owned the property over which the pipe passed taking water to the houses and the powerhouse. He thought the tank was an eyesore and demanded that it be taken down. He threatened Will with a lawsuit. The tank was removed

Water pressure in the pipe from the base of the falls turned the powerhouse turbine which activated the generator and the resulting electricity was stored in a series of batteries kept in the basement of the big house. When the batteries were charged up, the lights were bright for a day or so, then they would begin to grow dim. That was the signal for Bill or Donald to go down to the powerhouse and turn the wheel to admit water to the turbine.

The family were pleased when a power line was run from the Bridal Veil Lumber Company to both the gatehouse and their home.

Louise encouraged her sons in their varied activities. Donald was not only interested in plants and trees, he liked to collect ground squirrels, snakes and banana slugs. He caught garter snakes and kept them in large glass containers with paper coverings, holed in several places to let in air. Handling the snakes, he recalls, "gave my hands a strange smell."

Searching through the nearby woods, he sometimes came across a rubber boa. This snake crushes its prey. It is very slow moving and not much bigger than a garter snake. Donald liked having one as a pet because they were easy to handle. At one time he had a grey digger, a ground squirrel in a cage. Not being fond of captivity, it bit his hand leaving a long scar on his right index finger.

His fondness for animals even encompassed rats. Finding a series of native wood rat families nesting in the powerhouse gave him a chance to study them.

"The air," he says, "was fragrant with their very special musky odor."

Bill married in 1932. His bride, Virginia Smith, came from the Portland area. Tall, attractive and outgoing, she was the perfect spouse for Bill. He tended to be quiet and introspective and she, the opposite. Their personalities balanced each other beautifully and their marriage was a long and happy one.

William C. (Lawrie) Lawrence III, the first of their two children, was born a year after their marriage. Eighteen months after his birth, their daughter, Jean, made her appearance. Will and Louise were overjoyed at having two grandchildren. The house at Bridal Veil was a perfect setting for the fun and games of two growing children.

Donald married in 1935. His wife, Elizabeth, also a scientist, worked with him on many projects. Although living halfway across the continent, they liked to spend part of every summer at Bridal Veil. On one of their visits,

Summer 1941. Dr. Donald Lawrence, his wife, Elizabeth, on his left and L. M. Gould, resting after a hard fought game of croquet.

Louise decided to have a luncheon so friends who had not met Elizabeth could do so. As the day was beautiful, luncheon was to be served on the terrace.

The guests arrived and after sharing some refreshments waited for Elizabeth to appear. But she and Donald were busy with their pet rubber boa. They were trying to feed it a white mouse. The snake was not cooperating.

Donald looked at his watch. "What time is lunch?" He was going to eat in the kitchen.

Holding the mouse in one hand and the snake in the other Elizabeth looked up, "Louise said one o'clock. What time is it?"

She glanced at his watch. "Oh, my gosh, I'm late."

Ever precise, Donald smiled at her, "twenty minutes, my love. You'd better hurry."

Elizabeth Lawrence sitting by the fountain pool, July 9, 1939.

She thought fast. "I'm going to take the boa with me. The ladies might want to see it and then I will tell them why I'm late." She handed the mouse to Donald.

With that, she hung the snake around her neck, ran around the corner of the house, dashed up the steps to the terrace and before Louise could say a word, took the snake from her neck and held it out.

"Sorry to be so late, Donald and I were feeding our pet snake," then smiling her most winning smile, walked towards the nearest group of women, snake in hand. "Would you like to have a good look at it. It's a rubber boa and...."

A woman shrieked, "Don't bring that thing any closer," and knocking over her chair, retreated through the doors into the living room.

"But it won't hurt you." She stroked the snake gently.

Louise intervened, "Elizabeth dear, I think it would be best to put the snake back in its cage." She was half angry and half amused. "Hurry and tidy up, we're waiting for you."

Elizabeth found Donald in the kitchen and gave him the boa then hurried to wash up. Inspecting herself in the mirror, she was surprised to see how dishevelled she looked. With her face and hands washed, she ran a comb through her hair and decided she would pass muster.

Returning to the terrace minus the snake, she found the guests interested in the creature. None of them, other than Louise, had ever picked up a snake much less draped one on her neck. Elizabeth seemed a very brave and very unusual young lady.

Living in Portland meant that Bill and Virginia were able to spend a lot of time at Bridal Veil. Virginia credits Louise with teaching her how to cook and manage a home.

"She was so kind and thoughtful. I learned my cooking skills by spending so much time with her in the kitchen. Only once was she critical of me and that had nothing to do with cooking."

"We were out there on a Sunday and I picked up some napkins I was embroidering. Louise came into the room and said quietly, 'must you do that on a Sunday?' "

Entertaining came naturally to Louise and she always had plenty of food on hand. Sunday afternoons brought friends driving from Portland fully expecting to partake of Louise's famous fried chicken dinners. She kept count of how many chicken dinners she served and proudly announced that to the family at the end of the summer.

She used the best of ingredients, many of them loaded with fat. The dairyman, Fred Luscher, knew her fondness for thick cream and brought it along regularly. It was a family joke that she liked the cream "so thick a spoon will stand up in it." Butter was used in baking and frying. The couple running the store in Bridal Veil kept some of their best cuts of meat for Louise. She was a friendly and thoughtful person, inviting some of the local people to lunch during summers at the Villa. They all liked her.

As the grandchildren grew up, they spent more and more time with their adoring grandparents. As soon as the little ones could talk, Louise insisted that they call her Louise instead of grandma.

"I'm too young to be called grandma." And although it didn't seem right to Virginia, that's what Lawrie and Jean called her. They named their grandfather, Poppy. Good manners were stressed by their grandparents and the children were expected to behave properly when adults were around. At mealtimes, they had to be quiet.

Freedom to roam around the house and grounds and get into mischief was part of growing up at Bridal Veil. The Harnan couple were the neighbors to the west. They kept goats.

Goats love tobacco so Lawrie and Jean went through the house collecting cigarette and cigar butts. The goats expected treats whenever the children appeared and rushed at them, jumping and leaping. Not wanting their sneaker-clad feet stepped on by the animal's sharp little hooves, they crept quietly up to the fence, hoping the goats were looking somewhere else, then climbing over they raced to a huge old tree stump in the middle of the field, scrambling to safety before the goats reached them. It was a game of chase that both goats and children enjoyed.

With the treats eaten, the animals were stroked, petted and talked to until they calmed down. Mrs. Harnan was fond of the Lawrence children and often had them over when she was milking. The milk was sweet and warm. Lawrie and Jean tried their hands at milking with Mrs. Harnan supervising but only managed to squeeze out a few drops. It was harder than it looked and the goats didn't much care for it either.

Their imaginations were given full rein around the house and grounds. They had heard stories about trolls that lived under bridges just like theirs and were always hoping to find a little man in a brightly colored suit waiting for them as they explored around the stream and the edge of the forest.

The house was like a labyrinth to the children when they were small. Front and back staircases, long hallways, a basement with big and small rooms, lots of places to hide and jump out with a loud "BOO" at unwary passersby. One of the basement rooms had stacks of old Sunday funnies in a corner. On rainy days they sat with their backs against the wall reading. When they worked their way through the pile, they turned them around and started all over again.

Evenings in the library were special. Radio programs to listen to, the crackling fire to peek at through the eyes of the phoenix andirons and a shelf of *National Geographic* magazines to pore over. They giggled and poked each other when they came across a native in a faraway country photographed in the semi-nude.

Louise enjoyed doing her embroidery as the family sat in the library. Sometimes she forgot to bring her materials down from her bedroom.

"Jean, I've left my sewing basket in my room. Would you please run up and get it for me?"

The last thing Jean wanted was to go upstairs alone, especially on nights when the batteries needed charging and the lights were growing dim.

"Lawrie," she whispered, "you come with me."

"No, I'm reading." He turned away from her.

"Okay, you just wait," she hissed, "I won't go with you next time," and up she got from the floor where she'd been lying on her stomach reading.

This threat moved Lawrie into action. The dim light left dark and spooky corners as they crossed the downstairs hallway, tiptoed up the stairs and along the upper balcony. Retrieving the sewing basket, they scurried back to the safety of the library. Years later, Jean recalled how frightened she was of making that little journey when she had to do it alone.

Weekend mornings with Poppy at home were always fun. Running into their grandparent's room, the children settled themselves on Louise's or Poppy's bed and listened to stories. Louise told them about her childhood and sang them German songs. Poppy's stories were about horses and the Wild West and he always finished by counting to ten in Chinese and tickling their ribs.

"Poppy, is that really Chinese?" Jean wanted to know.

"Well, sure," and he counted to ten again.

Jean especially loved watching Louise at her dressing table, combing her hair and twisting it into a round swirl which was held in place with tortoise shell hairpins.

And how they enjoyed Louise's cooking. When Fred Luscher delivered the milk, Lawrie hurried to see if the special cream was in the delivery. It had a different colored top from the other bottles. With the cream on the table, and before pouring any on his cereal, Lawrie delighted in sticking his spoon into the cream, then into his corn flakes. They stuck to it. A wonderful yummy treat just right for licking.

Poppy always said grace at mealtimes.

"Bless this food to our use and us to your faithful service.

This ritual was never neglected. Poppy liked watercress sandwiches and the children picked it fresh for him in a soggy corner behind the gatehouse. And

Louise cut the crusts off their sandwiches, something their mother never did. She said that crusts were good for their teeth and chewing them made their jaws strong. Despite the teeth and jaws admonition, they liked Louise's sandwiches best of all.

Easter brought lovely surprises. Besides hunting for eggs and chocolate rabbits in the huge living room, strings led from room to room and at the end were special treats. During the war, the treats were often $25.00 war bonds.

There were lots of family parties at the house and on one memorable occasion when Jean was seven and Lawrie, eight and a half a ball was held. A small orchestra was engaged and Mrs. Jenny and her daughter, Verna, helped serve the food prepared by Louise. The children were allowed to see the guests arriving and to greet them, then were ushered upstairs to bed.

The party was too much to miss, so putting on their robes, they crept along the hall and peered between the balcony railings to watch the dancing. They watched, that is, until their father glancing up saw them.

Bill Lawrence adored his children and was never happier than with his family. He smiled as he left the party and went upstairs.

"Come on you two scallywags, off to bed." In each hand, he was holding a small cake. "Here's a goodnight treat. Now remember to clean your teeth again when you've eaten it and then to bed." Giving them a hug and kiss, he whispered "goodnight" and left.

"Lawrie, don't you wish you were down there dancing?" Jean longed to be old enough to have high heeled shoes and a long dress.

Lawrie was disgusted, "No, I'm never going to dance. You have to dance with girls and girls are creepy."

"They are not!" Jean was ready to do battle, "I'm not creepy, you are!"

"Sssh, someone's going to hear you and you'll be in trouble." Having finished his cake, Lawrie went off to his room. He didn't clean his teeth.

At another big party when Lawrie was older, he stood up after supper to express his family's appreciation for the evening.

"When I was growing up," he said, "I thought everybody's grandparents lived in a house like this."

During summer holidays, Will often picked his grandchildren up in Portland to bring them out to Bridal Veil for a few days. He was a fast driver and the winding, narrow, up-hill-and-down-dale, Crown Point Highway, challenged his skills. Although Lawrie loved these visits, his grandfather's driving almost made him car sick. Passing big trucks on the narrow road was an adventure. There were times when the dual wheels of a truck on the side where there was nothing but a deep drop off into a chasm brushed the narrow curbstone edge and seemed ready to hurtle into the valley.

"Poppy," Lawrie's voice trembled slightly as they raced on, "don't you think one of those trucks will crash over the edge?"

"Of course not, those drivers are expert. They're up and down this road all the time."

Lawrie really wanted Poppy to slow down and had told him once or twice on their drives that he felt sick. All Poppy did was say, "Hang on, we'll soon be home," and then drove on faster than ever.

Happy days were spent with Louise in the woods and garden. A small grove of trees between the upper and lower loops of the driveway was filled with forget-me-knots. It seemed like a magical spot when they were small. In the vegetable garden, they pulled carrots from the soft ground, washed them in the stream and ate them, tasting the warmth of the earth with every bite.

But when it came time to pick green beans, that had to be done properly. Their mother and Louise canned them for the winter and didn't want broken or bitten-into beans in their baskets.

When Robert Bassett moved into the gatehouse with his wife, May, the children found another adult to play with and to tease. May was not fond of children. She liked to sit on a covered swing by the house and read and she didn't want the children to bother her. Naturally the children wanted to do just that.

There is a great rockslide on the south wall of the gorge several hundred feet from the gatehouse. Lawrie and Jean climbed to the top, certain that May hadn't seen them. Picking up a small rock, they tumbled it down so it rattled and clattered and bounced towards May and her book. Without turning her head, she called out in her high English voice, "Lawrie, Jean, stop doing that and go away."

"How does she know it's us?" Jean whispered. "Let's creep across the rocks, she's not looking up, then we'll go down and walk through from the garden just to say 'hello.'"

May always knew when they'd been up on the rockslide and they finally decided to leave her alone. She was a dead loss when it came to being playful with children.

Robert was always glad to see them. He told them stories about Ireland and horses and let them help with the chores. Doing the spring cleanup at the goldfish pond was a special treat. He rigged up a siphon using a hose to drain out the water. Catching the fish in a net, he put them gently into pails of water.

"Now watch the end of the hose," he'd tell them, "I couldn't scoop up all the little fish and they might come through." The children knelt in the grass, wet from the gushing water. Suddenly one tiny fish and then another

Front of house with pond. Note the frog fountain to the left and the spouting crane in the center.

and another came sliding out, flipping and flopping on the grass.

"Quick Lawrie, pick them up," Jean held out the pail. The slippery, wiggly fish were hard to catch.

"You can help too, so come on!" Lawrie was laughing as he scooped up a fish and dropped it in the pail.

Only one failed to make it to safety. Jean knelt on it by mistake and squashed it.

They examined the fish as they swam happily in the water. "What do you think it feels like to be sucked through a hose like that." Jean wished that Lawrie wouldn't ask such puzzling questions.

"Well, I think I would have a headache," she spoke in her most positive voice, "and I would be scared that no one would save me."

The bottom of the pond was covered in silt. Taking off their shoes and socks, in they went with small shovels. Robert did the real work but let them know how much he liked having their help. When the dirt was out and everything washed clean, the pond was refilled with fresh water from the creek. A small ornamental frog fountain sat on the edge. To bend over and drink from its spouting mouth without falling into the pond was much more fun than drinking from a tap in the house so the children thought.

World War II brought changes in the family. In 1942 Donald joined the Army Air Corp as a teacher. He was stationed first in Texas, later in Orlando, Florida and finally in New York City. Elizabeth was able to join him during his tour of duty.

The Bridal Veil visits continued for Bill, Virginia and the children. Bill's health problems precluded him from active service and he was needed at home to work with his father in the family business. War bonds as gifts were now expected although Lawrie did receive a red racing wagon, with a speedometer, for his tenth birthday. He was now in the big leagues of wagon owners. His special run was down the curving driveway at Bridal Veil, screeching to a stop and making a quick turn at the bottom near the gatehouse. Jean sat behind him when he wanted a passenger and down they flew. More often than not, she was scared but kept coming back for more.

As she had with her sons, Louise taught her grandchildren the names of the plants including shrubs. She let them carry her flower basket when she was cutting blooms for the house. Her gardens were glorious. The wall and columnar Thuja hedge that bordered the "bowling green" lawn provided a spectacular backdrop for her colorful display. The lawn was perfect for games of croquet. She had two cutting gardens, one near the swimming pool and another down the slope. The rock garden behind the house was eventually rehabilitated and filled with unusual trees and shrubs, including a Japanese double-needle pine, Japanese maples, rhododendrons, short-stemmed flowers and attractive ground cover. The sculpture of Buddha stood in this splendid setting as though meditating.

The swimming pool was filled every year and used on hot summer days. It wasn't heated although a steam pipe ran underground from the huge house furnace. Starting up the furnace to heat the pool seemed wasteful. As a result the water was never very warm; in fact, it was very, very cold, usually 40 to 50 degrees F. However, a refreshing dip in the pool after a drive in from the city on hot summer days was more than welcome for family and friends.

The cold didn't bother the children. They frolicked in the water whenever there was an adult to watch them. One of their morning tasks was to check the pool to see if any wandering night creatures had fallen in. Once they found a rat, another time a mouse, then a mole, a nasty scorpion and a poor drowned rabbit.

For the happy Lawrence children, loved by their parents, grandparents, uncle and aunt, life was perfectly satisfactory. It was the sudden death of their beloved Poppy that jolted them into the dark world of grief.

Louise and Will spent a long holiday with Donald and Elizabeth in Florida during the winter months of 1944–45. On their return to Oregon, they drove immediately out to Bridal Veil. Will complained of feeling unwell and before Louise could summon a doctor, he died. His death from a massive coronary on March 4, 1945, at the age of 75, marked a turning point in the life of the family.

Louise stayed on during the summer of 1945 but without Will coming and going, she felt terribly alone. Bill, Virginia and the children visited as before. Lawrie and Jean often stayed out with their grandmother to keep her company. But without Poppy even the children felt desolate. Their games, their wagon runs down the driveway, their evenings in the library, their gardening work with Louise were edged with sadness.

Louise decided to sell the house as she had found it, leaving it beautifully furnished and with the surrounding lawns and gardens exquisitely maintained. She kept a few pieces for herself, the pink marble clock, the phoenix andirons and some of the china she particularly liked. Donald and Elizabeth wanted little but did admire one of the Chinese tables with white marble top. It remains with them still.

She sold her Raphael painting, *The Madonna of the Chair,* to a family friend, Henry Day Ellis. He, in turn, presented it to the Marylhurst Provincialate, near Oswego, Oregon, as a semi-official remembrance in honor of Sister Miriam Theresa Gleason of the Holy Name Sisters. This exceptional woman had won laurels in the Oregon labor movement with her efforts to obtain a minimum wage for women. She also helped create a first rate sociology department at the college. The bronze Buddha went to Fred Ellis, Henry's brother, and now graces his home on Shaw Island, Washington.

The Japanese stone lantern standing by the trout pond eventually made its way into Jean's garden in Portland after her marriage. The marble clock, the phoenix andirons and some pieces of china came to Bill and Virginia upon Louise's death.

The Bridal Veil property was purchased on January 20, 1947 by Kathryn Reynolds. Bill Lawrence acted as his mother's attorney in her absence. Louise was off on a trip to Peru. She tried apartment living for a few months and decided it was not for her. There was no opportunity for gardening. She bought some property on Council Crest in Portland and built a house with a garden. Summers were spent in her new home. Most winters found her either in California or South America.

Louise's love and interest in her family never wavered. In 1954, Virginia was hospitalized and underwent serious surgery. Louise had a wonderful plan for Virginia when she was up and around.

"I want you to get well," she told her, "and this is my plan. I want to send you, Bill, Lawrie and Jean to Europe for a long holiday. How does that sound to you?"

Virginia was overwhelmed, "Why, I think that's wonderful." She found it hard to speak. A trip to Europe!

Lawrie had completed three years at Stanford and Jean was in college. Summer was close at hand and the trip was planned when Lawrie and Jean were free. They spent eleven weeks traveling on the continent. It was the trip of a lifetime. Virginia was refreshed and totally well upon their return.

Two years later, Louise gave a similar European trip to Donald and Elizabeth.

In 1961 Louise had a totally disabling stroke. She had round-the-clock nursing until her death in 1963 at the age of 85. She and Will brought much joy into the lives of their children and grandchildren. For Lawrie and Jean, their Bridal Veil memories remain vivid. Their own father died in 1983.

The house at Bridal Veil was a true family home. It left its impact on every member of the Lawrence family. Louise was the hub of the Bridal Veil universe. The warmth of her presence, her delight in preparing wonderful meals, the artistry of her gardens echo down through the years.

Lawrie has a beautiful memory of how his grandmother greeted him and Jean.

"She would hold my face in her hands, bend down and give me a kiss. It was so nice to feel that gentle touch and see that loving smile."

Kathryn Reynolds and the Reynolds' Health Studio

January 20, 1947 and Kathryn Reynolds, the "woman with the healing touch," bought the property at Bridal Veil from Louise Lawrence. Rumor has it that a grateful patient helped with the purchase price since neither Kathryn nor her son, Keith, had much money. Nor did they have the necessary formal training required to operate a health studio. Kathryn had sublime faith in herself as a healer using natural foods, colon therapy and massage to treat the sick who came to her for help.

Her formal education was limited. First daughter and fourth child of a Swedish family of twelve living on a Nebraska farm, she had to help out in the house and on the land at an early age. Babies arrived every couple of years and Kathryn was kept busy cleaning, cooking, caring for younger siblings, besides weeding the vegetable patch.

She married at twenty. Her husband, David Reynolds, was a young farmer. Shortly after the marriage she became pregnant but before the birth of their son, Keith, David was struck down by influenza. This terrifying illness raged throughout the United States in 1918-19 taking the lives of hundreds of people. Keith never knew his father who died before he was born.

All her life Kathryn was plagued with severe
headaches and other health problems. Determined to find
the cause of her poor physical condition, she took herself
and Keith off to Rochester, Minnesota, home of the Mayo
Clinic. She told her parents she was going to the place
where "the learned ones of medicine practiced."

With no money to pay doctor's fees, she found employment in the kitchen of the famous clinic. She also did
some practical nursing for a Dr. Pemberton. Kathryn was
intelligent and a keen observer of everything happening
around her, learning much about food preparation by
watching the work in the kitchen. When her sister, Peggy,
joined her in Rochester, they opened a boarding house for
patients requiring special diets. Three years of this specialized work and exhausted from the grueling seven-day-
a-week operation, the two young women decided to try
something else.

They moved to Denver and Kathryn found a job in a
physical therapy salon. She credits her experience there
as a major turning point in her life. As she learned her
craft, her hands became more and more skilled at easing
pain. It was as though some mysterious power flowed
through her fingers.

Wanting more independence, she left the salon after
six months. With Peggy, she opened a reducing salon
which they ran successfully for seven years. Although
working hard, Kathryn still did not feel physically well. It
was her good fortune to meet and later marry, Dr. Gerald
Stahl. He was an organic food chemist, one of the few in
the country at that time. It was he who suggested that
Kathryn's health problems might be caused by the foods
she ate.

Ready to try anything, she had him prepare a diet
relying completely on natural foods. This was to be strictly vegetarian. Although a coffee drinker from childhood,
she stopped drinking it, "cold turkey" and substituted

large quantities of herbal teas and lemonade. Her health improved dramatically. Experimenting with various diets and going on short fasts, she began her lifelong learning in how foods affect body chemistry. She read everything she could on the subject but in the late 1920s this was not the vast and entertaining topic it has since become.

With Dr. Stahl, Kathryn worked out a program which included physical therapy, colontherapy and diet. They opened a clinic in Denver but pressure from what she refers to as "unfriendly sources" forced them to leave the city. They moved to Eugene, Oregon in 1929.

This was a temporary stopping place. They settled in the Portland area two years later. It was here that Kathryn joined the Seventh Day Adventist Church. Always a deeply spiritual woman, she found this church satisfied her spiritual needs and she was comfortable with its proscriptions against certain foods and drinks.

The clinic that she and Dr. Stahl opened in Portland was immediately successful. Named, The Health Studio, it was reported that people came to them "in a dreadfully rundown condition." The Health Studio was a last resort for some very ill patients. Restoring the sick to health became the passion of Kathryn's life. There was a quality about her that brought comfort and strength to those who sought her help.

Her marriage to Dr. Stahl ended in divorce and he moved to California. With the Health Studio now her own, she and Keith joined forces. They bought the Columbia School of Massage and combined it with the Health Studio. This new enterprise was known as "Reynolds' Nature and Therapy School."

They gave courses in colontherapy, massage and nutrition. It was Kathryn's firm belief that overcoming chronic and seemingly hopeless illnesses, meant dealing with the patient in a holistic way. She used colontherapy or colonics to cleanse the colon. For the uninitiated, these

Reynolds
HEALTH
STUDIO

●

Health
T H E
PRICELESS
POSSESSION

by

Kathryn Reynolds, D. M., C. T., H. T.
Nutritionist

P. O. BOX 83—BRIDAL VEIL, OREGON
Phone Coopey Falls No. 2   Via Portland

are "high" enemas using pure water. Before undergoing this treatment, her patients were put on special diets to build healthy body tissue and increase muscle tone. Gentle massage was part of the total therapy, offering restful relaxation to bodies being nurtured back to health.

The school ran smoothly for two years. After many successes in healing the sick and easing pain for others, she ran into problems with the medical profession. She acceded to an order from the Board of Medical Examiners and left Portland.

Kathryn's determination to continue her work brought her eventually to Tigard, Oregon. She and Keith opened a health studio which met with such success that they were forced to find a location with more space. It was to Bridal Veil they came in 1947 with patients ready and willing to follow them there.

The beautiful grounds, the waterfall, the streams running by, the fresh air, the feeling of being close to the natural world and the lovely house created the perfect atmosphere that Kathryn craved for her patients. She had a brochure printed detailing the healing properties of natural foods, the importance of a balanced diet, the clearing of body waste, as required, through colontherapy and the importance of massage for healing relaxation. She also created an exercise program for those in her care.

It was the summer of 1946 when Kathryn began a correspondence with Lois Fabian, then living with her husband and three children in San Diego. Hearing about the New Vita Health Food store in Portland from a friend, she wrote to its owner, Harry Ross, for information about diet. He put her in touch with Kathryn and thus began a correspondence that lasted until the Fabians moved to Gaston, Oregon the following year.

It was on their move north that their youngest child, Janis fell afoul of poison oak. With her face swollen and her eyes completely closed, she was in pain and in need of expert attention. Her parents decided to drive straight to Bridal Veil and see what Kathryn could do for Janis. It was well they did.

Kathryn filled a small bath with cool peppermint tea and lifting her gently, put Janis in to soak. She bathed the child's face with the soothing tea. The painful sting of the poison oak subsided and within a few hours, the swelling had disappeared. For fair-skinned, fair-haired Janis, Kathryn was a miracle worker.

From that initial meeting, the Fabians and Kathryn became close friends. She invited them to stay a week. Frank and Lois became so enthused about her vegetarian diet that they determined to make changes in their family food habits.

Much to the dismay of Frank Jr., Gordon and Janis, their parents turned them into vegetarians overnight. That was bad enough but since Kathryn used no milk or dairy products, those had to go as well.

On their return home to Gaston, Lois opened their refrigerator. Out went the eggs, milk, butter, meat and soft drinks. Out went the tea and coffee from the kitchen cupboards. Things looked bleak indeed for the three children. Instant vegetarians by parental edict!

Soya milk was substituted for regular milk. Frank Jr. tasted it first. He gasped. He clutched his throat. He staggered around the kitchen.

"Mom," he cried falling into a chair as if to die, "this is awful stuff. Do we really have to drink it?"

Gordon and Janis tried some tentative sips. "I don't like this stuff," Gordon announced, "and I'm not going to drink it."

"Neither am I," echoed Janis holding Gordon's hand.

Their pleas fell on deaf ears. It was soya milk or nothing, "unless you'd rather have herbal tea?" Lois was a determined woman. She was going to follow the diet plan carefully laid out in Kathryn's recently published cookbook.

Kathryn was meticulous in her food preparation. She was in her element in the big Bridal Veil kitchen. All her meals were built around the very best natural foods. Nothing was wasted.

All the leftover vegetable scraps went into what she called "the broth." It could be drunk hot or cold and was used as a base for many of her soups. If, by chance, any was left over, Kathryn used it as a natural fertilizer in her garden. When she was writing her cookbook, she put in the recipe for the broth, calling it "Min-Vita Broth." The Fabian children loved this tasty concoction as did all her patients. She was hard put to make enough and usually kept a big pot brewing on the stove. (Min-Vita Broth recipe at end of chapter.)

Using no dairy products nor eggs, soya milk was used in her diet preparations. Herbal teas were a specialty. Red Clover Tea, Princess Pine Tea, Sage Tea, Parsley Tea, Peppermint Tea and Oat Straw Tea, were some of her creations. She encouraged her patients to drink copious quantities of these teas to cleanse their bodies. This was an article of faith with her. In the introduction to her cookbook, she wrote:

"Keep step with the times and take more of the foods that promote health; take gymnastics daily; drink plenty of pure water; breathe fresh air and take sun baths. These are indispensable and outstanding measures adopted in the effort to replace old bodies with new. Hippocrates, the Father of Medicine, said that the best remedies are good food, massage, baths and gymnastics.

"If we realized how precious are the minerals in our daily food, we would value them more than gold for the building of health, disposition, character, vitality and loveliness."

Her teas, soups, nourishing main dishes, fruit desserts and puddings were all carefully created to build health and vitality. The special dietary needs of every patient were studied in detail. Kathryn developed a watermelon diet, also a grape diet for certain patients. These diets were only used under her strict supervision.

She notes in her cookbook, "We may study books for food facts but to get the proper nutritional knowledge, we must closely watch the effects upon the sick as a test." Despite her lack of formal training in nutrition, her care for the patients at the Health Studio was beyond reproach.

Huge bowls of fruit were kept on the dining room table and everyone was encouraged to help themselves. The atmosphere of warmth and tenderness that Kathryn brought to those who had come for help was like a healing balm. Soft spoken, she seldom raised her voice. She loved what she was doing and her enthusiasm for her work drew people to her.

The great heartbreak of her life was her son Keith. Although a gifted massage therapist, he had begun drinking at an early age and was now on the way to becoming a full-blown alcoholic. When he married, she thought he might mend his ways but even his lovely wife, June, was unable to influence him. June's two year old son, Michael Collier, from her first marriage became a loved grandchild of Kathryn's. In 1950, Linda Kathryn was born to June and Keith. She was welcomed into the warmth of the family circle and adored by her grandmother.

Two of Kathryn's brothers, Emil and Dan, both carpenters, came to Bridal Veil to give her a hand. She wanted a small house built near the gatehouse where Keith's family lived. She needed some privacy and a break from the twenty-four hour demands of her work.

Able to survive on little sleep, she did require some uninterrupted down time.

They built a neat little frame house and painted it brown. It's interior walls were lined with knotty pine and a field-stone fireplace in the living room made it a warm and cozy haven for the hard working Kathryn.

She brought her mother to live with her. This dear old lady had to have her coffee and "dunkers." She could abide the vegetarian diet but absolutely had to have her coffee. Another family member also came to stay.

This was Ellen, one of the younger sisters in the family of twelve. She had been married off very young to an old Swedish farmer. When he made his weekly visits to town, he locked her in a closet. Over the years, Ellen began to lose her grip on reality. Unable to cope with her strange husband and his demanding ways and without the emotional strength to leave him, she retreated into her own private, pain-free world. He had her placed in a mental hospital.

This was more than Kathryn could bear. As soon as she was settled at Bridal Veil, she brought her sister to live with her.

Gentle, harmless and childlike, Ellen loved to play with Michael and Linda. In the winter when the snow was piled high on the driveway, she'd find a trash can lid, sit on it and go shouting and laughing down the slope.

The house and its surroundings were a family place. As Michael and Linda grew up, they spent much of their time in and around the big house. Linda was a special favorite of her grandmother and followed her everywhere. On summer mornings, she ran up from the gatehouse into the big kitchen knowing that's where she'd find her grandmother. Sitting on a high stool, elbows propped on the table, she watched Kathryn preparing food for the day.

This was a woman who knew the value of carrot tops, beet tops and dandelion greens among a host of other vegetable cuttings that otherwise might be thrown away. Linda was curious about what she was doing.

"What are making, Grandma?"

Looking up from her chopping and mixing, Kathryn smiled, "Oh, it's a little of God's magic we're doing here." Then reaching for a small bowl, she scooped some of her mix into it and handed it to Linda

"Here, you have some too and you can do magic with me."

Although her mix didn't look particularly magical, Linda stirred and added bits of this and that. Sticking her finger in, she had a taste. "Maybe I'll make a wish while I'm stirring," she thought to herself. She did and didn't tell a soul hoping her magic wish would come true.

Another treat Kathryn prepared for her was a special and delicious drink. Made with honey, soya milk and flax, Linda sipped it slowly to make it last.

"Grandma, that is the best drink in the whole, wide world."

Michael liked to be out with Emil and Dan as they worked on various projects. One day when he was three, he wandered away to explore on his own and found his way into some thick shrubbery. Tall and close together they made a tight green wall. Suddenly he began to feel lost and wanted out but couldn't find where he'd come in.

"Uncle Emil, Uncle Dan." He was shouting as loud as he could, "Come and get me!" He began to cry. Maybe no one will come. His tears turned to sobs, "Uncle Emil, Uncle Dan, where are you? Come and find me."

"Michael?" Dan's voice sounded close by.

"I'm here, in the bushes." With his uncle so close, Michael felt better, "I can't find the way out."

Dan was tall and looking over the shrubbery saw the little boy. "Well, well, what are you hiding in there for?"

Michael was indignant, "I'm not hiding, I'm lost and I want to get out of here."

Dan guided him out of the maze. "Now next time, don't you go in there alone. You were lucky I was close enough to hear you." He put his arm around Michael's shoulders, gave him a hug and whispered in his ear, "I don't want you to get lost because you're my special helper." And off they went to repair a door at the gatehouse.

Slowly the reputation of the Health Studio as a place of healing spread. Kathryn turned no one away who came for help whether they could afford her treatments or not. If they were unable to pay all their expenses, they helped out around the house as they regained their health. In one case, the sister of a patient worked for several weeks, full time, to pay for her sister's treatment. This was Olive Holloway. Olive's sister Nellie Harwood, came to the Health Studio in April 1953, very ill after the birth of her first child.

Here is how Nellie describes her treatment in a letter to the author, dated July 3, 1990:

"In April of '53 after giving birth to my first child, I began to lose weight, dropping from 152 lbs, to 117 lbs. in approximately two months. My husband and I were ahead of our time in living as hippies and therefore, refused drugs and medical attention. Someone told us of Mrs. Reynolds at Bridal Veil and so I was taken there unable to walk but for a few steps.

"I was put on a rigid diet and treatment plan after she discovered I was just short of gangrene of the uterus. With packs and treatments, I started gaining back my strength. In the mornings, (early) I was brought a tea to drink and encouraged to move as much as I could. As soon as I was able to walk a ways, we (patients and staff) walked to the falls where the beauty of God in nature lent a helping hand in regaining health. We were encouraged to walk barefoot in the dewy grass when it was warm enough.

" The food was excellent. No one could miss meat, eggs and so on with such attractively prepared meals, abundant amounts and tasty. Mrs. Reynolds was under a lot of stress because of the closing of her health resort but gave we patients talks of encouragement and always a smile.

"I don't remember any of the patients but one elderly lady befriended me and took me under her wing. My clothes were huge on me because of my weight loss and she took them, cut them down to fit me and resewed them by hand. I'll always cherish that memory of her kindness.

"I was a 19-year-old young mother and not too learned in the ways of the world but thanks to Kathryn Reynolds and her knowledge of health, I'm still here to help others in the health search.

"The atmosphere was cheerful, positive and up and helped to keep patients' attitudes good. It was a perfect setting in God's beauty and also in the building itself. I enjoyed the early morning worship time. Everyone who joined in seemed to draw from each other. I'm thankful for the privilege of having had a place such as that to go to when I would have died without it.

"I realize that God gave our doctors knowledge for us to use but still feel places such as Mrs. Reynolds ran have their place too." Signed, Nellie Harwood.

Other patients, grateful for their own recovery or the recovery of a relative paid, not only for the treatments but offered financial assistance to Kathryn as well. Those who had been in her care knew the value of her work and wanted to keep the Health Studio functioning.

"Kathryn never had a dime," her daughter-in-law June declared. "Whatever money she managed to put together was spent on keeping the Studio up to state standards."

State Licensing Board Inspectors made regular visits to Bridal Veil to check on the Studio. Kathryn was ordered to install fire doors, to have two fire escapes on the north side of the house with access doors cut into the second storey wall, to have the place rewired and to put in a water purification system. With her own meager resources and help from grateful patients, all these changes were made. One patient on his own paid for the fire escapes. This mysterious person was rumored to be a count or a baron.

Frank and Lois Fabian became regular helpers at the Health Studio. They spent many weekends and school holidays there. Lois became as expert as Kathryn at food preparation while her husband worked around the grounds. They asked nothing from Kathryn in return. It pleased them to be there.

An appreciative patient donated a large piece of land near Latourel Falls for Kathryn's use. She was now able to grow much of her own food. An organic gardener before the words were in common use, she knew exactly how her vegetables and herbs were grown and who cared for them.

Her brothers prepared the soil and planted it under her supervision. The Fabian boys, Frank and Gordon, were sent out to weed and till around the growing plants. At harvest time, they helped with the picking, then down to the big kitchen to clean and prepare the vegetables. It gave them a great sense of achievement to see the end result of their work being bottled or dried. Even more, they loved to eat the delicious food Kathryn prepared from the carefully nurtured plants.

A cousin of the Fabian children, Linda Moss, stayed with them one summer. She was then eight years old, the same as Janis. The two girls were delegated to household tasks. Dusting and polishing the furniture and all the railings and bannisters upstairs and down kept them busy.

"Janis! Linda! I can see finger marks on the bannisters and railings in the front hall." Lois was calling from the far end of the great living room. She saw the girls kneeling by the balcony railings above the fireplace, giving the wood a high shine.

"Okay, Mom, we'll do them again when we come downstairs." Janis wished her mother wouldn't look at everything so closely.

"Janis, do you think Aunt Lois has magnifying eyes?" Janis sat on the floor to think this over. "Well, I don't know about that but she sure sees every little thing. In fact, I heard her tell Mrs. Reynolds the other day that a mother has to have eyes in the back of her head." The idea that her mother had extra eyes hidden under her hair made Janis start to laugh.

"Linda, let's peek the next time Mom's sitting down. I'll hug her and put my face against her hair. I'll be able to feel any eyes."

The oak floors in the living room, now the Health Studio communal room, had to be polished to a high gloss. The girls did their best. Even with much of the floor carpeted, there was a lot of wood. Patients resting in soft chairs cheered them on. Having happy, chattering children around the house added to the family atmosphere that Kathryn encouraged.

Not all patients at the Studio recovered. Some arrived having had surgery for cancer with little hope for recovery. Kathryn believed that surgery caused cancer to spread. Although admitting these very ill people, she was strictly honest about what she could do for them.

Sitting close beside a hopeful patient, she took a thin hand in hers, holding it gently. "I must be honest with you. I don't think I can cure you but I can keep you free from pain." She paused a moment, looking into the other's eyes, "Will that be enough?"

Kathryn never used drugs. She made special teas for relaxation, others to restore restful sleep. Her foods for the very ill were prepared for ease of digestion. Tired, aching bodies were soothed by her gentle massage. Reputed to have "magic fingers" that alleviated pain, she used her skills to keep those in her care as free from pain as possible.

When one of these very sick patients died, there was, inevitably, a hassle with the medical authorities. Only one doctor came to Bridal Veil to write out the necessary death certificate. Dr. Shiomi was Japanese. Even some years after the end of World War II, he was shunned by his medical colleagues. To him Kathryn turned. Only he was ready to prepare the necessary documentation.

For her to have taken in such terminally ill patients was, perhaps, an error of judgement. It made her vulnerable and suspect in the eyes of the medical establishment.

Despite these difficulties, she continued to nurture and heal. A trip to the local farmers' market before she had her own garden, was a treat for her two grandchildren, Michael and Linda. To them it seemed that she bought mountains of food, then having made her purchases, visited various farmer's stalls who kept their carrot tops, beet tops, turnip tops and other "throwaway" items for her. Driving home, she'd spot some clover at the roadside, stop the car and with the children helping, pick all she could find.

Carrot juice was always in big demand at the Studio. There was a huge juice extractor in the basement and one of Frank Jr.s' jobs was to make the juice. He was given big sacks of washed carrots to dump bit by bit into the machine. Every last drop had to be squeezed out.

"I made gallons of carrot juice for Kathryn. Her patients enjoyed it. I think she used the leftover pulp for garden fertilizer. I was big enough to operate the machine but my Dad cleaned it up afterwards. Who knows, maybe the pulp went into the Min-Vita broth."

But it wasn't all work and no play for the Fabian children. When the boys were in their early teens, they decided on a hot summer day to fill the swimming pool. Asking permission to use the water, Frank and Gordon went to the basement to turn the big iron wheel that controlled the water line to the pool.

"Janis you stay outside and tell us when the water starts going." Running out the back door, she raced to the pool. Suddenly she heard a whooshing sound and looked back at the house. A great fountain of water was gushing up through the lawn.

"Mother," she screamed, "there's water coming up through the grass!" Lois dashed outside, calling back to the boys, "Frank, Gordon, turn that water off right now!"

"But Mom," Gordon yelled up the stairs, "we haven't filled the pool yet." He saw their chance for a cool swim disappearing.

"Don't argue with me. Just turn it off!" The pitch of their mother's voice had changed. They knew that tone. It meant trouble. Turning the heavy wheel as fast as they could stopped the flow.

"What's the matter?" Frank wanted to know. Lois had calmed down, realizing the boys weren't at fault. "Come and see."

Water was gurgling up from a sagging hole in the lawn. "Boy, oh, boy, that pipe down there sure must be rotten." Frank was on his knees poking his hand into the wet grass. "I'll bet it's got holes all through it."

The water pipes from the reservoir under the falls were beginning to cause problems. Water pressure dropping in the house meant someone had to go up to the falls and investigate. Small holes appeared regularly in the wire-wrapped, wood piping letting water spurt out. Frank Jr. and Gordon were expert at cutting bits from small trees and whittling them down to plug in the holes.

Unwilling to give up on the idea of having a cool swim, the boys decided to divert water from the stream running behind the house and down the hill near the pool.

With considerable skill, they built a small dam with rocks and dirt. The stream, diverted from its course, began trickling into the pool. Too much was still going into the stream so they built the dam bigger and soon had the diversion they wanted.

Leaves and twigs that had collected on the pool bottom floated to the top began pouring over the side and down the grassy slope.

Gordon put his feet in the water. "It's freezing." Janis tested it and decided it was too cold. Her brothers changed into their bathing suits and racing back from the house, dared each other to be first in. They hit the icy water together. Within minutes they were out, shivering in the hot sun and running around to get warm.

Kathryn wasn't overjoyed at seeing their dam. Water was flooding towards her little house. She told them to put the stream back where it belonged.

By the end of 1952, her problems with the medical authorities and the State Licensing Board were beginning to take their toll. Although still providing her usual high standard of care, she realized that her days at the Health Studio were numbered. Fewer and fewer patients were admitted.

Keith and June decided it would be best for them to move to Portland with the children. He found immediate employment as a masseur with the Multnomah Athletic Club. Whenever they could, they came out to Bridal Veil. Her two grandchildren were a comfort to Kathryn during this stressful time. However, the marriage of Keith and

June was in trouble and ended in divorce. Having an alcoholic spouse does not make for a good marriage.

Always devout in her faith, Friday evenings were devoted to a religious service. Family, friends and patients gathered around the big fireplace. Sometimes Kathryn, sometimes another member of the Seventh Day Adventist Church led the service. A lesson was read and a short talk given. There was a lot of singing accompanied on the big grand piano by whoever could play.

All the Fabians participated during their visits. When it came time to pick a song, Gordon knew exactly which one Kathryn would pick. It was a favorite of hers and she always asked for it. "I'd like to have us sing, 'Is Your All On The Altar?' " It seemed to reflect her life. She gave everything she had to anyone who needed her.

A man came knocking at the door in the early summer of 1953. He introduced himself and asked if he could look around. "My sister-in-law is very ill and I wonder if a stay at your Health Studio, having your treatments might help."

Always pleased to talk about her methods, she took him over the house, showed the treatment rooms, introduced him to Lois working in the kitchen on some of the special diets and gave him a copy of her cookbook. Then he dropped a bombshell.

"I'm a physician and what you are doing here is practicing medicine without a license." His voice became strident, "I'm going to report you to the authorities and have this place closed down!"

Kathryn was speechless. She had been threatened before but this man seemed ready to ruin her.

"Stop, wait a minute," she hurried after him, "I'm not practicing medicine, I'm healing people. I don't prescribe drugs." Pulling at his arm, she pleaded with him, "Come, talk to some of the patients and hear what they have to say.

He reached the front door ahead of her, then turned and fired his last salvo, "You are practicing medicine and I am going to clear you out of here." With that, he walked out, slamming the door behind him.

Open and honest in all her dealings, Kathryn was devastated at the man's devious behavior. She would have been pleased to show him around, had he identified himself in the beginning and acted in a civil manner.

He was as good as his word. The Oregon Medical Association had Kathryn charged and brought to court. She faced a charge of practicing medicine without a license. Her family put up the necessary bail so she didn't have to spend time in jail.

Despite her plea of "not guilty," she was told that she had to leave the state peaceably or be prosecuted. With no heart for legal battles, nor finances to pay legal fees, there was no alternative but to close down the Health Studio. This took time since there were forty-two patients in care when the ultimatum was handed down. Kathryn had to leave Oregon but continued to counsel her staff by phone. Even this was not to be tolerated by the authorities. Patients had to be sent home with no further treatment.

Unable to sell the Bridal Veil property at such short notice, Kathryn asked Frank and Lois to stay on with their children until a buyer was found. Leaving only the furniture that was necessary for the use of her friends, she took everything else with her. Dorothy and Clarence Jacobson's beautifully crafted furnishings and unusual artifacts went to California with Kathryn. She was determined to continue her healing work in a new setting.

The Fabians remained at Bridal Veil until July 1954. When they left, the property had not been sold. A buyer was not found until early 1955. With the proceeds and help from friends, Kathryn purchased a beautiful facility in Desert Hot Springs. This fine location was once owned by the Roosevelt family. Calling it "Mirage Isle" she ad-

vertised it in a brochure as "An Adventure in Fun, Rest
and Relaxation." Anyone staying at Mirage Isle found just
that and also were offered Kathryn's nutritional high
road to health, the same program she had provided at
Bridal Veil.

Although never licensed in Oregon as a physical
therapist, she is listed as licensed in her California
brochure. She also signs herself in the brochure as Dr.
Kay Reynolds, Nutritionist. Her patients there called her
Dr. Kay.

As with her previous efforts, this one met with success
as witnessed by numerous letters of thanks from grateful
patients. Then, as night follows day, the pattern of her life
began to play itself out once again. Word of her treatments eventually reached the medical authorities and
she was ordered to close Mirage Isle. Tired and beginning
to feel her age, Kathryn decided to give up the work to
which she felt called.

Driving to town one day shortly after receiving this
last blow to her life's work, she was killed instantly by a
speeding car as she entered the freeway.

The story of her life is kept alive by her two
grandchildren, Michael and Linda and their mother,
June Reynolds Cusack. Frank, Gordon and Janis, the
Fabian children, now in their middle years, remain
devoted to her memory. Having known her well and
watched how she worked with the sick, each of them will
maintain that she was "years ahead of her time."

Frank loves to tell this story about Kathryn. "She
usually was in wonderful health but sometimes was
plagued with sinus problems brought on by the cold and
damp of the gorge winter weather. The cure she used on
herself was unique. She sniffed cayenne pepper up her
nose! This remedy was for her alone. No one else dared,
wanted to or was allowed to try it."

The effect of diet on health was not high on the teaching agenda of many medical schools when Kathryn was doing her work. Therefore, her persistent efforts to teach the basics of sound nutrition through the model of her work and the printing of her cookbook, met with a complete lack of understanding by those in authority who sat in judgement on her.

In their defense, licensing authorities protect the public from charlatans who may do great harm to vulnerable people seeking help for a variety of illnesses. There was no way they could legitimize Kathryn Reynolds' work. Without a medical degree nor a license to practice as a nutritionist or physical therapist, she was without legal standing in both Oregon and California. Skating on thin legal ice most of her working life was dangerous. That she managed to continue her healing work for so many years, speaks of great courage and devotion of a high order.

Kathryn was a remarkable woman. Devout in the practice of her faith, she felt called by God to do His work on earth. Not given to preaching, she modelled what she believed. She was, in her own mind, a true medical missionary, teaching health, a life-enhancing life style and making daily prayer a way of giving thanks for the gift of being.

Min-Vita Broth

Taken from *Health Recipes, Books 1 and 2*, by Kathryn Reynolds.

     2 bunches celery, leaves, outside stalks, roots
          (save hearts for eating)
     1 lb. spinach, roots included
     1 green pepper
     5 dry onions, or green onion tops
     3 bunches carrot tops
     1 bulb garlic
     2 bunches beet tops
     ½ lb. fresh red clover (in season, blossoms and leaves)

You may add potato peelings, outside parts of cauliflower, watercress stems, parsley, outside leaves of artichokes, hard ends of asparagus, turnip, radish or any green tops that you have on hand. Cut fine.

Pour over the above enough cold water to cover. Let stand one hour or overnight. Set on stove, bring to a boil, simmer for five minutes and then let stand one hour. Press through a colander, adding a little hot water while pressing, and strain juice through a cloth. Add about 4 pints of tomato juice. Bring to a boil and seal in sterile jars or store in refrigerator. If not sealed, the tomato juice may be added when used. Salt to taste.

Throw away the vegetable pulp from which the juice has been extracted as this is no longer of any food value. Makes about ten quarts. Cut recipe to any amount desired.

Not without an artistic touch, Kathryn liked to make her food attractive to look at as well as healthy to eat. Her recipe for Candle Salad is an example.

Candle Salad

Place stub end of half a banana in center of pineapple slice. Put a dash of mayonnaise on top of banana and let it run down the side to imitate melted wax. Place cherry on top for a flame. The base of the candle may be garnished with lettuce or parlsey.

The Columbia Gorge Nursing Home

With a fourth change of owner, the house at Bridal Veil lost its strong female orientation. Dorothy Jacobson, Louise Lawrence and Kathryn Reynolds had each brought her own unique style to the house. For the Jacobsons and the Lawrences, this was a family summer home. They used and cherished it as such. Kathryn Reynolds although using the property as a commercial venture, made of it more of a family place. Money was not her great motivator, healing sick human beings was.

Each of these women loved the house and the grounds. Each of them enjoyed meeting and being with people. Each found the gorge area with its sheer rock cliffs, waterfalls and river views a constant delight.

With Kathryn Reynold's departure in 1953, her friends, Frank Sr. and Lois Fabian agreed to stay on at the house until it was sold. On her move to California, Kathryn had taken all the furniture except for what the Fabians needed for their own comfort. Intending to stay until the house was sold, Frank and Lois found that after one year with no buyer in sight, they had to move on. They left in 1954. From then until 1955 when it was sold to Lester C. Vanetta, the house was vacant.

Or so it seemed. According to Vanetta, there were two women in the house trying to run a nursing home and were totally incapable of doing so. Who these women were and where they came from and disappeared to, remains a mystery. Vanetta is said to have reported them to the State Board of Health for various violations of the health code and the place was closed down. Whatever the rights of the story are, he bought the property himself. He was going into the nursing home business as a strictly commercial operation.

With the ownership now safely in his hands, Vanetta hired Jack and Madge Nepper to run it. They were an ideal choice. Jack had experience in such a facility, Madge was a bookkeeper and would also be able to assist with patients. Their reputation as honest, responsible and caring people suited the new owner well.

Distressed at having a family member addicted to alcohol, the Vanetta's financial plans included accepting many alcoholic patients for treatment. The location of the home out in the gorge area was deemed ideal for treating alcohol problems. There were no taverns within miles to tempt patients. Isolation from the demon drink seemed as good a way as any to help during recovery.

The Vanettas kept a close eye on their nursing home, driving to and from Portland in a gold-colored Cadillac. Although reputed to be millionaires, the couple lived simply in a small apartment in town. To visit them in the winter was to sit shivering in chilly rooms. They did not believe in overspending on fuel bills.

The Neppers moved to Bridal Veil in 1955. "The house was in terrible shape," Madge recalls, "it needed to be painted inside and out." With their two small children, Carol and Ronnie, they moved into the upper gatehouse. Madge's father was a painter, unemployed at the time. Her parents and fifteen-year-old sister, Annette, moved into the small house built by Kathryn Reynold's brothers and Madge's father was hired to paint the house. The work took six months. The family then moved into

Portland. For Annette though, visiting at Bridal Veil and helping out where she could was always fun. She would take Carol and Ronnie on little adventures, leading them up a trail that would bring them to the top of the gorge overlooking the house and grounds and the magnificent Columbia River to the north.

The great rock fall that edged part of the gorge wall on the property was a perfect climbing place. They would go as high as they dared then sit at the top laughing and calling out to anyone passing below.

For Jack and Madge there was a lot to be done to make the house ready for patients. Staffing and furnishing were Jack's first priority. A registered nurse on staff was a requirement by the authorities. The woman he hired was not young, she is reported to have been "elderly." Her qualifications were excellent and she was pleased to be part of this new facility. An attractive room with knotty pine walls was built for her in the basement. It was warm and comfortable and was a favorite place for Annette to visit and gossip with Helen, the nurse.

"Oh, how I loved that room," Annette will recall, smiling at the memory, "I decided that when I grew up I would have a room with walls just like that."

A woman who lived nearby came on staff as cook and two young women were employed to assist in the kitchen, help with the patients and make themselves generally useful. Grace Hanks was hired to work in the basement laundry. She wasn't interested in taking care of patients.

Jack Nepper did not have the necessary certification to operate a nursing home. He did, however, have a friend who was a physician. This doctor had some influence with the State Board of Health and assured them that Jack was capable of supervising patient care and maintaining requisite operating standards.

There is an echo here of Kathryn Reynolds, and her lack of formal education resulting in her being unable to receive the necessary certification to operate her Health Studio. Unfortunately for her, she had no influential friends to speak out on her behalf.

Determined to make the nursing home a financial success, the Vanettas accepted welfare patients and those with private means. It was soon evident that more bedrooms would be required on the second floor.

The beautifully designed ballroom with its soaring ceiling, elegantly designed windows and the balconies that gave it such charm was to be forever changed. To have seen this room as Morris Whitehouse designed it was to have seen a masterpiece. It says much for the integrity of the design that after the desecration wrought by the lowering of the ceiling, the room is still a thing of beauty.

And the flooring, according to Phyliss Clark whose mother worked at the home and who helped out during school holidays, was light weight and sagged. "I hated seeing that beautiful room changed. When the workers had finished the balconies had disappeared. All that was left were those curved oak supports. And the stone chimney that used to go right up to the roof was covered up. Upstairs, part of it went through one of the new bedrooms."

The library became a four-bed ward for men. To make room for patients, every nook and cranny was utilized. The large ballroom, except for the ceiling change, remained intact. It was used as a dayroom for the patients. What had been the Chinese room was set aside for visiting relatives and friends.

Young Phyliss Duncan, the daughter of Grace Hanks enjoyed meeting some of the patients. One of them, Jack, who was being rehabilitated from a skid row past, taught her how to play different kinds of solitaire.

"He was such a nice man, a real gentle man. I often wondered what happened to him." Phyliss remembers the day when one of the patients, tore off her clothes and began running down the drive to the main gate. "Jack and Madge ran after her along with my mother and managed to catch her just before she ran on to the road."

"She was such a sad woman. Evidently she had a baby that died and she became so emotionally distraught that she had to be put into care.

"They took her upstairs to her room and mother told me to get some sheets and bring them up to use for restraints.

"I remember going up those big front stairs wondering if I'd have to help. I was a bit scared!

"When I came into the room, the poor woman was lying on her bed with her teeth out and she looked up at Jack Nepper and with a big, toothless smile called out 'Kiss me honey.'

"I guess she needed more treatment than the nursing home could give her because the police came and took her off to the State Hospital."

Finding space for Madge to have for a small private office was proving difficult. Finally they hit upon the idea of walling off that part of the hallway just above the front entrance. It led past the French doors overlooking the ballroom to the door of the once Chinese room. Wallboard was installed floor to ceiling, covering the fine railings which had been visible from the front door. It was a dark, narrow office but it gave Madge a place for her desk, chair and a filing cabinet. The Vanettas wanted the accounts kept in meticulous order.

Difficulties with the authorities began almost from day one. Water from the falls was deemed unsuitable for a nursing home and Jack was told to have a chlorination system installed. This was easier said than done. Having the equipment designed specifically for their needs was the simple part, having it built and installed was the hard part.

The only factory making the system they needed was in New York. The order was placed there.

Days went by. Weeks went by. A month or two rolled on and still the equipment did not appear. Jack Nepper, being the nursing home manager, soon had the health inspectors breathing heavily down his neck. He was given an ultimatum. Get the equipment in and soon or the place would be shut down.

The Vanettas were away travelling and Jack was left to handle this frustration on his own. Telegrams and phone calls to New York finally brought some action. The chlorination system arrived, installed and the pressure was off, at least for the time being.

But not for long, the system kept breaking down. Silt coming down over the falls found its way into the equipment. Jack became an expert at repairing and maintaining it. It was another burden added to his already heavy work load.

Finding and keeping quality staff in such a remote location became a constant challenge. There was a regular turnover. Young women would start then find the remoteness of the home and the work not to their liking and would quit. Even family and friends coming to visit patients found the distance from town a barrier. Winter months, with snow and ice sometimes closing the roads, meant isolation for patients and staff alike.

As part of their job, health inspectors dropped by unannounced to keep tabs on the home. Madge answered the door one day when they had been operating the home for a couple of years. One of the women inspectors came in. She and Madge had met many times before and liked each other.

As they walked into the large main room, they noticed one of the library doors open and there in full view was one of their women patients snuggled up in bed with one of the men. This was Elsie, not as stable as she might be and refusing to be ignored.

"Hi Madge," she called out "look where I am."

"I thought I would die," Madge smiles at the memory, "the last thing we needed was to have a bad report about patient care. Elsie was really rather harmless, she just liked to stir things up a bit. Fortunately the inspector understood and we were able to laugh about it over a cup of coffee."

There never seemed to be hours enough in the day for Jack to keep on top of the work and the supervision of the staff. His budget for staffing was tight so he had to find time in the summer months to cut the vast lawns and keep the gardens in some kind of trim. Winter months meant that the winding driveway had to be kept clear of ice and snow.

Soon a demand came from the authorities to have a sprinkler system installed. Considering the remoteness of the site with no handy hydrants nearby should a fire break out, a sprinkler system was a must. Once this was installed, Jack asked himself, "What else will have to be done before we're running without problems?"

He soon found out. Being an honest and trustworthy person himself, he expected others to be the same. It was a shock to find that the staff, according to Madge, were "stealing him blind." Food and cigarettes were disappearing. He was forced to padlock all the storage cupboards. "Is Madge the only person other than me that I can trust with the keys?" he asked himself.

Little by little, hardly noticeable at the time, the stress of operating the home began to tell on Jack. Money was tight for hiring more staff. Then when he was feeling pushed to the limit, their nurse, Helen, began to abuse the patients. At first he and Madge thought she was overworked and gave her more time off. When this made no difference, they had to conclude that she had lost her desire to work with difficult patients. With complaints ringing in their ears, they had to let her go. They valued her for her years of service but could not tolerate the change in how she was treating vulnerable patients.

By 1958, Jack was so completely burned out that he collapsed, mentally and physically. He had to be hospitalized. When he returned to Bridal Veil, he was unable to work and just lay around their apartment day after day.

With Jack's collapse and prolonged absence, Madge was hard pressed to run the nursing home. She called in Jack's brother, Bud, to come and help but it fell to Madge to take on many of the tasks that had been Jack's. She had to hire a couple of young women to replace two that had left. When they turned out to be unsuitable, she had to fire them.

With her change in status and unable to keep the books herself, Madge turned the financial affairs of the home over to an accountant. She instructed him to send the two women she had fired, their termination checks. For whatever reason, he failed to do so and before Madge knew what was happening she was called before the Labor Commission. The women had reported her for not sending them their checks.

Called up before a staff person, Madge was thoroughly reprimanded for failing to pay her ex-employees. Her explanation as to what had happened fell on deaf ears. No one wanted to hear her side of the story.

"It was a terrible experience," Madge frowns as she relives it. "I was humiliated and treated as though I was a cheat. Honestly, they seemed to think I was some kind of of a criminal."

Madge stuck it out for another year. By 1959 she was close to the edge of despair. Worry about Jack. Worry about the home. Worry about staff. Too many things were pressing in on her. The Nepper's contract with Lester Vanetta was about to expire. It was an opportune time to leave. Bud Nepper stayed on at the home for several months at the Vanetta's request to wind it down. The property was once again put up for sale.

"When we left Bridal Veil, I felt as though a huge burden was lifted from my shoulders. We had a tough time there." Madge recalls, "The place is beautiful I guess but for me, what I remember is all the work and the frustration and when Jack got sick, I just wanted to get away."

Empty for a year, the house was finally sold in early 1961. The new owners, a male religious order, the Redemptorists. The property was to become a novitiate for young men being prepared to enter the Roman Catholic priesthood. A year of study and meditation at this new facility would be required before they took temporary vows.

The Redemptorists

With the purchase of the property by the Redemptorist Fathers on February 23, 1961, the house took on a wholly new character. It was now to be a novitiate, where young men preparing to enter the Roman Catholic priesthood would spend a year of study and meditation before going on to a major seminary.

The house had been unoccupied for two years. Brother Oliver was sent ahead to make the house ready for the novices. One of his first tasks was to make the kitchen fit to use.

"It was in a terrible mess," he recalls. "There was a hole in the floor that I had to fix and then walls and ceiling had to be scrubbed clean before we could bring in any appliances. Everything had to be in some kind of order before the novices arrived but a lot of the work had to be left until I had more help."

The Novice Master, Father Fitzgerald, arrived shortly after Brother Oliver and between them, they had the house ready for the arrival of some twelve novices, four of whom were brother postulants. A report in the *Catholic Sentinel* dated July 27, 1961, states, "On the second floor of the large building, 20 small monastic cells have been constructed."

Besides Father Fitzgerald and Brother Oliver, other staff were Father Nicholas Missen, Father Joseph Nuttman and Brother Hubert. The novices were young, between the ages of nineteen to twenty-one, although the brother postulants tended to be an older group.

The property was declared a "Novitiate" on June 17, 1961 and named St. Alphonsus College after the founder of the Redemptorists, St. Alphonsus Liguori. Investiture of the twelve members of the first class at the college took place on August 1. It wasn't long before the men found themselves outside with rakes, clippers, lawn mowers and spades. Two years of typical Gorge weather had taken its toll on the abandoned property. When not busy with their studies, the novices were outside working.

The white stucco walls surrounding the terrace were in bad shape from the black mould growing there. All the stucco had to be scraped off and replaced. The red brick floor of the terrace and the steps that circled around the fountain set in the wall all had a blanket of thick green moss. The various garden fountains were choked with weeds and the handsome carved faces of ancient Greek gods were dark with mould and dirt.

There was much to do. Scrubbing mould and scraping moss were not favorite tasks. It was Brother Oliver's mandate to make the house liveable and the grounds attractive. However, it was apparent that more help was needed than he could expect from the students. Replacing the white stucco of the terrace needed a skilled tradesman. Painters and carpenters were hired. The twenty monastic cells were created by partitioning the large bedrooms. The house was painted inside and out.

Father Fitzgerald, the Novice Master, soon realized that the remote location of the college and the lack of recreational amenities for his students were going to be a problem. The first winter was a bad one. It rained a lot. It snowed a lot. There was no place on the site to play sports. The ballroom was the college recreation area and table tennis was set up. On the worst days of rain and snow, the crack of the racquets, the ping of the balls hitting the table and the laughter of the players brightened the gloomy atmosphere. Being stuck indoors while the rain poured outside made for much grumbling. The men from California found the lack of sun hard to take.

"It never seemed to stop raining," Brother Oliver recalls, "it just went on and on. When I think back on our years there, mostly what I remember is the rain."

The rain, at least, kept the fire hazard low when the warm weather came around. The Redemptorists filled the swimming pool, not for swimming but to have a good supply of water should they have a fire.

The pond at the front of the house was cleaned out and filled by their second year at Bridal Veil. Water lilies were planted in boxes. Goldfish were added. Hardly had this been done when the pond sprang a leak. To repair it meant catching the fish, putting them in the swimming pool, emptying the pond and repairing the break. All went well until it was time to return the goldfish to the pond.

They were now swimming happily in an eight-foot deep pool.

"Anyone want to volunteer to go in after them?" This from one of the Californians who thought someone might be crazy enough to go into the icy water.

There was nothing for it but to empty the pool and catch the fish before they disappeared down the drain.

"We lost some of the little ones but only a couple of the big ones got away." Brother Oliver was teased mightily about the goldfish caper. Some lessons are learned the hard way. After this, when the pond had to be cleaned the fish were put into buckets of water.

Father Fitzgerald's concern for his students well-being kept him thinking up ways and means of balancing their religious studies with physical activities. He liked the outdoors himself so when he had the opportunity to buy two kits for making canoes, he jumped at the chance. The beautiful Columbia River right at their doorstep was too tantalizing to leave alone.

The canoes didn't take long to build. They were painted dark green inside and bright red outside. One was called Morningstar and the other, Star of the Sea. Launching them into the river was a big event, paddling them provided hours of fun.

But Brother Oliver soon became concerned about how far out in the river the men were going. "Father Fitzgerald was a bit of a daredevil. I thought he was taking those kids too far out where there were dangerous whirlpools. I had a picture of them being swept right downriver to Astoria. Well, Father just laughed at me. 'they're good paddlers and they can all swim. Besides they all have their life jackets.'"

One of Brother Oliver's duties at the college was to cook. When Father Fitzgerald had the novices out canoeing, Brother Oliver packed up a picnic lunch and took it down to them.

"Usually when I arrived with the food, everyone was laughing and having a good time. Well, I came down this one day and everyone was sitting around real quiet and subdued. Hey, what's the matter? I asked, aren't you interested in what I've brought. I'd never known them not ready to eat or at least to ask what I'd prepared.

"Father came over to me and said 'I guess I had it coming. You were right.' Right about what, I asked. Then he told me.

"Four of us were in one canoe and we headed out into the river. Suddenly we capsized. The water was about eight feet deep, down we went and even though we could all swim, we had a few minutes of panic before getting to the top. That's when we saw the paddles and our life jackets floating away. The canoe stayed pretty close. We took off after the paddles and jackets, brought them back and pulled the canoe to the shore."

" 'I hate to say, "I told you so" but I told you so. And how come none of you had on life jackets?' One of the kids, still wet from his unexpected dunking said they're too bulky for canoeing. I spread out their food. I knew they'd soon forget what had happened once they had eaten.

"I ate lunch with them and just when I was going to leave, Father wondered if I'd like to go out in the canoe.

"Are you crazy Father, you wouldn't catch me in one of those things."

The Chapel

The library became the chapel for the college. The stone fireplace was taken down and covered up. The book shelves were also boarded over. When they had occupied the house for a year they realized the chapel was not large enough for their needs.

Pews similar to those in churches were installed with the altar area at the south or falls end of the room. As part of the ritual associated with their status as novices, the students were required to prostrate themselves at the altar to be invested with their habits. Cramped for space, the Redemptorists decided to take down the French doors and extend the room out towards the falls, about nine feet. The glass doors were put in the basement to be replaced by a brick wall. It then was covered with wallboard. What had once been the graceful library created by Morris Whitehouse, was now a very simple room, severe in its simplicity.

Kneeling students and staff faced the altar with its crucifix, tabernacle, candles and votive light. There was nothing to distract the novices from their prayers and meditations.

As the next year or two went by, it became very clear that the college was poorly placed. Father Fitzgerald made valiant efforts to keep the young men in his charge physically active. When the winter was very cold, he got up at 4:00 a.m., drove out to backwaters of the Columbia to see if the ice was thick enough for skating. Most of the time, the skating was uneventful and enjoyable, albeit a bit rough in places. However, one of the students hit a thin spot in the ice and went through into the water. He was pulled out quickly and hustled back to the house to get out of his freezing clothes and into a warm shower.

Apart from the changes made in the library, the house remained as the Redemptorists had purchased it. Although they found the upstairs rooms created by the lowering of the ballroom ceiling useful, they were saddened at the desecration of a beautifully designed room.

Altogether they spent some $50,000.00 on the house and grounds during their four-year tenure. They increased the electric power coming into the house, put in a new pipeline to the pool and a settling tank below the falls with new filters.

It was while digging at the back of the property for the pool pipeline that Father Fitzgerald's shovel banged against something hard and metallic. Scraping away, he uncovered a length of pipe, about 3 inches in diameter. It was stamped, Transcontinental Cable. He called on Brother Oliver to have a look. He was puzzled.

"I've never seen cable in this kind of pipe before. Maybe I'd better phone them and find out what it is."

Sure enough, Transcontinental had run cable through strong steel pipe close to the gorge wall. The fine for breaking it was astronomical. It was covered over and left alone.

As St. Alphonsus College entered 1965, changes were made by the Oakland Province of the Redemptorists which left the novitiate at Bridal Veil without students for a year. They were altering the study schedule at the seminaries creating a hiatus at the college.

The decision was made to close the novitiate and put the property up for sale.

Given its lack of facilities for sports, its remoteness from town and the challenge of coping with the Gorge weather, the sale of the college was a blessed relief to the staff. Brother Oliver was delighted to be sent to a less rainy environment while Father Fitzgerald went off to work in the middle of Brazil where he has ministered to the local population for the past twenty years.

Now it was the turn of another male religious order to buy the house. The Fathers of the Divine Word made the purchase on September 27, 1965.

The S.V.D. Fathers

The sixth owners of the house, The Society of the Divine Word had a vision. It was to create a minor seminary at Bridal Veil. Following is the S.V.D. record of how the property came to be purchased:

"Our attention had been called to the property by a benefactor of the house, a Martin Deragisch, in July of 1965. Very Reverend Francis Humel, S.V.D. Provincial Superior of the Western Province came to see the property and the S.V.D. Generalate in Rome was sounded out on the matter.

"Approval was given on condition that the Archbishop of the Portland Archdiocese would allow the Society of the Divine Word to establish a foundation in his province. Most Reverend Edward D. Howard D.D. gave his approval on September 20, 1965. The property was purchased on September 27, 1965.

"The first Superior of the place was appointed in September of 1965 - Father Edward D. Borkowski.

"The house was officially named St. Martin's by the S.V.D. Generalate on November 13, 1965."

Father Ed Borkowski was transferred from Denver to develop and staff the minor seminary. He wasn't long in the area before realizing that the house was not suitable for a college type of institution. It was too remote and a seminary that had been operated by Franciscan Fathers in Troutdale, a nearby town, had just closed down.

Becoming aware of the shortcomings of the house as a school and the closing of a nearby seminary seemed to indicate that the Bridal Veil property, now called St. Martin's, was not a viable proposition. It was for Father Borkowski, at least, a "white elephant."

However, there he was and there he had to stay to see what he could make of the place. He was joined in 1966 by Brother Nick Carlin. Also, a caretaker, his wife and two teenaged sons came to live in the gatehouse. They were hired to help with general maintenance and upkeep of the land.

Brother Nick recalls how pleased he was to work with Father Ed. "We worked as a team and I was happy to be able to be with him. Wherever Father Ed works he always puts a missionary flavor in it, that's why I liked working with him."

Brother Nick acted as cook and did janitorial work in the house but he especially enjoyed working "on the beautiful grounds." With the caretaker and his two sons, Father Ed and Brother Nick spent hours outside digging, planting flowers and weeding to keep the grounds looking attractive.

"I furnished the house as best I could," recalls Father Ed. This was a troubling task. The future of St. Martin's was in doubt from the beginning. The original vision was impractical yet he felt compelled to make his stay of value to his order and the church.

A minor seminary being out of the question, he decided to open the house for women religious, offering one day retreats or a day of recollection. He would give talks and an opportunity for meditation. Counselling was also available if requested. The success of these ventures depended to some extent on the weather. Spring and autumn were fairly busy times for Father Ed but there were many days with empty hours to fill. He went out from Bridal Veil to preach parish renewals, to assist in parishes and conduct retreats in Portland and on the coast. In this way he was able to support the house financially.

Winters were especially hard and harsh. The reservoir below the falls often froze and Father Ed, Brother Nick and the caretaker had to get up the icy path with crowbars and axes to smash the ice. With the cold weather and frequent ice and snow storms that make driving a nightmare on the Interstate, the house was a very lonely place. Sometimes a priest came out to make a private retreat but these were few and far between in the winter months.

During the summer, Father Ed elicited the help of local boys to work around the grounds. He put the swimming pool back in order and for a half hour of work on the land, the boys could swim for an hour. This worked well. Occasionally he asked them to bring in a gallon of chlorox to clean the pool. The youngsters thought this a fair enough deal and enjoyed jumping into the cold water after working in the gardens.

But for Father Ed, the house had become a burden, both financially and physically. His personal efforts to make the Society of the Divine Word known in the Portland area were successful, still that didn't make the house at Bridal Veil a going concern.

"I felt from the beginning that the handwriting was on the wall and that what we were attempting to do would not bear fruit, and there were some major repairs needed and I did not have the finances to make them." He thought back, "The roof was in really bad shape and some of the plumbing was causing problems.

"The area is recreational and scenic but also lonely. One has to have some special job to enjoy it." As he recalls his efforts to make St. Martin's a viable entity he smiles

"I had time on my hands between parochial assignments. I had run down every opportunity to find ways and means of making our place a success. So I decided that between my parish work I would take up a hobby. I went into antiquing old furniture. One of the basement rooms was ideal for my workshop.

"I don't like giving up on a project but this one was a no-win situation from the beginning. Finally my superior agreed that I should leave and I moved into a parish in Redland. I also was responsible for the mission church in Estacada."

Neither Father Ed nor Brother Nick had any regrets about leaving Bridal Veil. Hard as they had worked, the lack of S.V.D. personnel had made it impossible to carry on. Early in 1968 they vacated the house.

The caretaker stayed on for a short while. When he and his family left, the property was now unprotected. The gatehouse and its immediate area became a handy garbage dump. The grounds deteriorated.

Huge pack rats finding the big house to their liking moved in. Creeping blackberry bushes began to lay waste the lawns and gardens while moss and black mould slowly covered the terrace, the steps and the fountains. Leaves falling year after year filled the trout and goldfish ponds. Great trees crashed down during winter storms. And out of the woods to the east came weedy alders until they were lined up and pressing against the east wall of the library. Silt and rocks coming down from the falls buried the rock-walled stream bed. Within a few years an overburden of green hid walls, ponds, lawns and gardens.

With no human hands to love and care for it, the once beautiful house stood alone. Abandoned. Empty. The only sounds the whispering of the winds, the creaking of the walls, the scratching of rats and mice scurrying around. Then with the rains came the steady, drip, drip, drip of water seeping through the broken roof.

The S.V.D. Fathers put the house on the market. Months and years went by with no offers.. Then the Golden Peacock Inn Inc. expressed an interest in the property, their purpose to put a restaurant in the house. An appraisal indicated that the house was unsuitable for such a venture.

However, a company, U.S. Enterprises Inc., entered into a leasing agreement with the S.V.D. Fathers on August 15, 1974 to extend to August 14, 1979. A Mr. Shaw was their representative. What happened to break the lease is not clear. By the time the Franciscan Sisters presented their offer to the Fathers, there were no legal entanglements. U.S. Enterprises had disappeared from the scene.

A postscript to this part of the Bridal Veil story concerns Frank Fabian. On a trip to Oregon to visit his brother, Gordon, in the summer of 1970, he decided to take a run out to see the house where he had spent so many happy days.

Driving through the gate and up the winding roadway he looked around at the neglected lawns and gardens. An air of desolation hung over the once immaculate grounds. Parking the car by the house, he stepped out to look around and perhaps walk up to the falls.

Within minutes of his arrival, a car drove up and parked behind his. A man got out.

"What are you doing here?" he demanded.

"Why I used to live here many years ago and I just wanted to have a look around." Frank didn't like the man's attitude but wanted to know more about why the property was in such bad shape. "Is the place empty now? It looks pretty bad compared to the way it used to be."

The man's demeanor now changed, perhaps realizing that Frank might be useful to him. "Would you like to see inside?" And with that, he produced a key and unlocked the front door.

"I'm going to buy the place," he boasted, "and turn it into a fancy supper club. When I have it open and operating, I'll invite you."

As they walked through the empty, echoing rooms, Frank pointed out changes made to the house. He was horrified to see the devastation in the huge living room. With the ceiling lowered, the elegant balconies, the soaring stone chimney had been obliterated. The library had pews in it.

"Why the fireplace has been taken out!" Frank rapped at the wallboard, "it used to be right here," then walking the length of the room, he leaned against the brick wall.

"There were French doors here so you could see the gardens and the path to the falls." He felt sad as he looked around the library. It seemed ugly to him as he remembered how it had once been.

"The walls used to be covered in gold silk. I remember one time when the wisteria vine that grew up the wall worked its way under the tiles and rain ran down one part of the silk staining it. I wonder who covered up all the book shelves."

Frank suddenly realized that his companion had taken out a notebook and was busily jotting down everything he told him.

Going upstairs and into the bedrooms, Frank pointed out little wires coming up under the window sills.

"What are those wires for?" the man wanted to know.

"Why those were the wires for the house telephone system and they were in just about every room. The phones were the old-fashioned kind with a receiver and a crank. Each had a set of buttons." He smiled to himself as he recalled the fun and games that Gordon, Janis and he had calling each other from room to room. "What you had to do, was turn the crank and press the button for the room you wanted to call."

"Good. I'll have that restored," announced the alleged new owner.

When they walked through the basement, Frank pointed out the shelf covered with dozens of wires, "That's where the phone system was hooked up to the batteries that ran it."

Every new bit of information was carefully written down. When they finished their walkabout, Frank handed his business card to his new acquaintance although none was offered in return.

He waited long and fruitlessly for the invitation to the "fancy supper club." It never materialized. And we are left with the mystery of who the stranger was. He had a key. He knew his way around the house. What kind of club was he proposing to open? Local gossip has it that he wanted to open an exclusive men's club with young women on display in scanty outfits, a la Playboy.

Making Progress—1975

Between taking down walls, hacking through blackberry thickets, moving rocks from the holding reservoir below the falls and creating havoc in the rodent population, the Sisters took time to sit around the kitchen table and assess their progress. Slow it was and happy they were, knowing deep within themselves that their decision to purchase the property was right for them.

With so much to do, there was scarcely time to think, yet within each of them, unspoken, was a sense of purpose. An ill-defined and not quite clear vision of what the future held was enough to anchor them firmly to their task of building a viable Franciscan community.

For Mother Michael, her call was to make it a home. "The mother of a center always has the call to stabilize the place so the Sisters can live intensely and go out into the community." Recalling those early days. "I was still going out to work then but eventually was to stay home, centering the whole community."

Living a healthy life as Franciscans was Mother Francine's vision. "We wanted to be self-sustaining on the land. That's one level. On another level, we'd be relating to people in a way, in which together, we'd be restoring ourselves by the work we'd be doing."

"I never really had a goal about how the place might look nor how we'd develop our community." Sister Paula Jean went on, "Our commitment to live as Franciscans sustained me. I knew this place was special when we found it and although we weren't sure, we knew we were going to create something life-giving not just for ourselves but for others as well."

Mother Michael smiled as she listened. "I doubt if St. Francis knew exactly where he was going when he started out so we haven't let him down. And he knew how to work hard. One of the differences between him and us? We have to sit down and rest now and again."

"Don't ever visit Franciscans." Sister Margaret's gentle warning belied the smile on her face. "They'll always find some work for you to do. You know, I thought we might have retreats here and have families and children come. We wanted to have children around. We just weren't sure at the beginning what this place would be. I knew one thing, I wanted some chickens as soon as we had some money and a place for them to live." As the community nutritionist and expert in meal preparation, she remembers how poor they were. "It's God's truth. There were times when we couldn't afford to buy an egg."

By the fall of 1975, Brother Jerome was gone, recalled to his community. His help had been invaluable. There was still more than enough work to keep everyone busy. The smell from the room at the back of the house, even with the door closed, seeped into the upstairs hall and into the nearby bedrooms. Something had to be done.

One Saturday afternoon, a group of parishioners from Portland, friends of the Sisters, came out to help clear heavy pieces of junk from the basement. Mother Michael was working with them. "Do any of you have crowbars in your pick-ups?"

"Why sure," a couple of them replied.

"Well when we're finished here will you bring them and come upstairs with me. We need help." Leading the way and carrying her own hammer, she opened the door to the room. "Isn't this awful?" She hurriedly opened a window.

"We took up the old lino that was glued to the floor thinking it was rotten, but it wasn't." She tapped the wall. "That's a partition. It doesn't belong here. A previous owner made small bedrooms out of the original big ones by putting up these walls. We've taken down the others. Do you think you can get this one down?"

"No problem." One of them picked up his crowbar and started working on one of the corners. The others followed in different places. The smell was even worse as the wall opened up to reveal its secret.

Two partition panels had been put back to back with a space between, leaving an opening at the top into the attic. The space was a rat and mouse graveyard. Rodents of various shapes, sizes and varieties could and did fall in. Unable to escape, they died leaving bodies in a state of stinking decay.

"Don't let Mother Francine see this or she'll freak out! I'll run down and get some boxes and garbage bags to put this mess in." She wanted out herself to breathe some fresh air.

Containers were filled, taken out and burned. The partitions were burned. "We just had to burn stuff although we found out later, we should have had a permit. There were so many overgrown trees around here than no one saw the smoke.

It was a few years later when Sister Patricia was burning trash down by the gatehouse that the fire rangers with the forest service came hurtling down the road, sirens blaring, to charge her with setting a fire without a permit.

During all their long days and evenings of work, their prayer life continued. Morning and evening prayers and daily attendance at Mass always were and always will be part of their lives as religious. Their little chapel in Dorothy Jacobson's Chinese room served them well.

In the spring of 1976 Sister Mary Gregory arrived. A professional hospital administrator, she was hired by Providence Hospital in Portland to manage their nursing department. Her talents, however, went far beyond those professional skills. As a child she had followed her father around as he worked in the building trades. Bright and inquisitive, she asked endless questions about what he was doing and why. She learned how to take apart lath and plaster walls and put them back together again. She also did wallpapering.

Sister Mary Gregory was a godsend to that broken down old house. A precise and exacting worker, she took upon herself the task of repairing the walls and ceiling of the living and dining rooms. This, of course, was weekend and evening work. Sister Paula Jean offered to help. Having no illusions about her plaster and decorating skills, she did whatever jobs came her way. They rented a steamer and got rid of several layers of wallpaper. Now the damage to the plaster wall was plain to see. It was extensive. Years of neglect and seeping moisture broke the plaster down. Crumbly and soft, it had to be scraped away.

With that done, some new lath was purchased. Now the real work started. With Sister Paula Jean as "go-for," Sister Mary Gregory replaced the lath, then mixing the plaster to her liking began the exacting and delicate job of laying it on thickly and smoothly.

No one was allowed to help with this tricky bit of business. When the two rooms were finished, her work would have passed the critical eye of a first class tradesman. The other Sisters stood in awe of this achievement. While the plaster dried, they decided on wallpaper.

"If you think that nuns are all sweetness and light," laughed Mother Francine, "you should be around when we're trying to decide on a wallpaper pattern. That's when we're at our very worst!"

Money was the main constraint in their choice but finally they found something both cheap and acceptable. With expenses for the materials needed to repair the house mounting daily, the Sisters were barely scraping along financially.

"We'll have to find a way to raise some money." Mother Michael had an idea. She dropped this on the other four weary Sisters one evening after prayers.

The Benefit Ball

"I have an idea that might work." She had their attention. "We have that great big living room which is really a ballroom. Why not have a benefit ball?"

"A ball!" Sister Mary Gregory's tired eyes snapped open. She'd just finished the plastering and the wallpaper had to wait for it to dry out. "Who'd want to come into a place that bare?"

"Now just take it easy," Mother Michael enthused with her brainwave, wanted the others to think about it. "I'm sure we'd be able to make the room okay for one night."

Mother Francine, usually ready to get involved in mad schemes, shook her head in disbelief. "Don't you think people will be shocked at nuns putting on a ball. I honestly don't think that's such a good idea."

Sister Margaret not so quick to dismiss this novelty, asked. "What kind of an event did you have in mind? I could put on a really nice dinner before the ball actually started. Why this might be fun." Used to preparing meals for large numbers of people at work, she thought it would be a treat for her to do something special.

"Sister Paula Jean, what do you think?" Mother Francine hoped for an ally to shoot down this whole crazy business.

"Well, it might work. I mean it will be a dignified kind of ball, won't it?" Sister Paula Jean leaned towards the others. "After all the people who come will be friends."

"Okay, okay. What about music?" Mother Francine felt uneasy.

"Well, we'd have to hire a band. It's no good having a ball if people can't dance." Mother Michael smiled happily at the others. "I think we'd have a great time."

"A band! At a convent? We can't do that." Sister Paula Jean was wavering. "Has this been done anywhere else? I mean is this a precedent or what?"

"Let's think about it. We don't have to make a decision tonight." Ever the diplomat, Mother Michael knew when to back down and when to bring her pet idea back to the table.

She recalls, "We had more donnybrooks over that first ball. It's a wonder we put it on at all."

But put it on they did. Mother Francine persuaded the others that the music be provided by a chamber orchestra. She knew of a small group that didn't charge too much.

Invitations were printed and sent to relatives and friends. The cost was $25.00 and that included dinner. There was a tag line on the invitation. The invitee could become a patron for the small additional sum of $50.00.

Everything was rented; dishes, glasses, cutlery, tables and chairs. They bought candles for each table but had no money for flowers. Without much in the way of decor, the ballroom looked a bit bleak.

When the great day arrived, Mother Francine enthused and ready to make the ball a success, decided to pick flowers growing by the roadside. Queen Anne's Lace bloomed everywhere. In her mind the tiny flowers in a circular mass around a strong center, symbolized their community. Each was an individual strongly connected to a core.

Armed practically with scissors, and spiritually with her thoughts, out she went. She cut hundreds of white blooms. Every nook and cranny of both ballroom and dining room was filled. Well pleased with herself, she walked around admiring her arrangements.

Their neighbors, Don and Kay Gibbon, dropped by to see if the Sisters needed any help. They were coming to the inaugural ball and knew the amount of work involved in putting it together. Don looked around at the flowers.

"My God, why have you brought cow parsley into the house?" He started laughing.

"What do you mean, cow parsley. That's Queen Anne's Lace!" Mother Francine beamed fondly at her decorations.

This was too much for Don who laughed even harder. "Do you know what you need? You need a botany lesson. That's cow parsley. It's not Queen Anne's Lace."

"Well, cow parsley or not, it's here to stay. I don't suppose for a minute anyone will know the difference and I'm sure not going to tell them, and don't you either!"

The Sisters were all laughing now. They'd been feeling a bit tense as the minutes ticked by to zero hour and the arrival of their guests. Thinking about Queen Anne's Lace a.k.a. cow parsley lightened their spirits. Now they were ready and eager for the party to begin.

The dinner prepared by Sister Margaret was simple and superb. A salad to start, a choice of two meat dishes and vegetables, her special dinner rolls and the *piece de resistance,* a cheesecake for dessert. Red and white wines accompanied the meal. Their guests were delighted.

It was the music that put a damper on the proceedings. "I told the Sisters we had to have music with a beat." Mother Michael came from a family where singing, dancing and theatrical events were a part of their daily lives, "I mean you can't dance to chamber music," and with heavy emphasis on every word, "this was inner chamber music. It was awful."

Even Mother Francine who had insisted on chamber music cringes at the memory, "I know the musicians did what they were supposed to do but talk about dreary stuff for a ball!"

Fortunately their guests took it all in stride. No one even remarked on the unusual flowers. Having made some money and liking the idea of a ball, the Sisters decided to make it an annual event. This is their Annual Benefit Ball and is always scheduled for the third Saturday in June. The music is now danceable.

With a little money on hand, they bought the wallpaper and Sister Mary Gregory set to work. She didn't want any help just someone to clean up after her.

"She wasn't about to trust us with that wallpaper and truth to tell, she didn't need us. She was better working alone." Sister Paula Jean followed along doing the clean up.

Even with the new wallpaper, there was still a lot to be done in the living room-ballroom. The stone fireplace with its pink paint, the light sconces with their cheap gilt, the steel girders supporting the ceiling and the low hanging chandeliers were totally at odds with the design of the room.

Sister Mary Gregory had a proprietary feeling about the room after the work she'd done. "I'll clean that paint off the fireplace. It looks awful." Whoever had covered the natural grey stone with an oil based pink paint never intended that it be removed. Eighteen gallons of solvent and numerous pairs of rubber gloves later, the stone was clean. In some small crevices around the intricate carving, bits of paint still lurked. In certain lights, a faint blush of pink remains. The stone had absorbed some of the color and there it stays.

With that done, Sister Mary Gregory and Sister Paula Jean turned their attention to the china pantry. With meticulous care, the mad painter with the pink paint, covered every inch of glass in the cupboard doors.

"I think," said Sister Paula Jean as she spread solvent on what seemed the thousandth pane and picked up her scraper, "whoever did this should be stood in a tub of solvent and melted down!" Her arms ached, her back ached, she was tired of smelling solvent, her natural good humor and generally cheerful outlook on the human race, didn't extend to the pink paint perpetrator.

"Working around here is like trying to put out a forest fire. Everytime we turn a corner, there's something else to do." Mother Michael and Sister Margaret were investigating the devastation wrought by years of neglect and rotting garbage at the gatehouse.. The mess was long gone but the lower level still smelled.

"We can't leave this place like this, it's just going to rot away." Sister Margaret looked at her companion, "What do you think we should do with it?"

"I agree that something has to be done, but what?" She ducked into what had been part of the Jacobson's three-car garage and looked around. "I think this place would make a small apartment or a couple of small rooms. What do you think Mother?"

"I know who we could ask. There's a man at my parish who offered to come and give us a hand. He's a carpenter. Maybe he'd figure out what to do here."

It is Mother Michael's credo in life that if you need something, you ask. For her, nothing is gained by sitting back, biting your tongue, waiting for someone to guess what you need. With that in mind, she spoke with her parish friend. Out he came, looked at the site, made some suggestions and gave them an estimate.

The five-member community met and decided that somehow they'd find the money to have the lower gatehouse remodelled into a small apartment. When this work was completed and the inside freshly painted, the seven-year smell of garbage disappeared. The Sisters now had two apartments for relatives and visitors to use and for Sisters when chapter meetings were held at Bridal Veil.

The Wild Steer Caper

Kay Gibbon phoned on a sunny Sunday morning and asked them for lunch. "I'm sure you need a break and Don needs your help to round up one of his steers." Mother Francine hung up the phone and turned with a big smile to the others having breakfast after returning from Mass.

"How would you like to go over to the Gibbons and round up some cattle?" She put on her best cowboy drawl as she relayed Kay's message.

"You have to be kidding!" Mother Michael had never been on a horse and had no intention of starting now. "We can't ride his horses."

"Well, Kay never said a thing about riding horses, just that Don needed some help. Come on. I don't know about you, but I need a break."

They drove over, had a nice lunch, a relaxing visit, then Don laid out his plan. It was simple in its concept.

"I have a steer, tagged 92 and every time we round up the animals he always escapes. He's ready for market now. And this is what I'd like you to do."

Mother Michael interrupted, "If I have to get on a horse, forget it!"

Don sat back and hooted. "I can just see you on one of my quarter horses. You wouldn't last a minute." Then he described what he wanted them to do. "I'll ride out with one of my boys and head 92 toward the corral. All you have to do is stand in a line down from the corral gate. He'll see you there and turn into the gate."

The Sisters wore their long jean work skirts with the small black veils on the backs of their heads. With Kay Gibbon leading the way, they crossed the fields to the corral and as instructed stretched in a line straight away from the gate. They stood about ten feet apart. Don had warned them to be still and quiet not to spook the steer.

In minutes Don and one of his hands headed toward them with 92 galloping ahead. Suddenly the steer, seeing the corral, changed direction and came charging straight for the women.

Don kicked his heels into his horse and raced after the animal. He saw trouble ahead. "Yell, you bloody fools, yell!" he shouted at them. By then it was too late, 92 was almost on them and coming straight for Sister Margaret. Instinctively she began moving backwards and sideways to get out of the way. With no time to think or look behind, she didn't see the small gully and with the grace of a gymnast tumbled backwards head over heels as the steer leaped over her.

In a flurry of dust and grass, Don pulled in his horse and jumped to the ground. The others rushed over.

Sister Margaret picked herself up, brushed the dust from her skirt, straightened her veil and smiling benignly on her friends remarked, "I guess I didn't watch where I was stepping." Her gift for understatement had them laughing with relief. Except for Don.

"Are you sure you're alright?" Still shaken by what might have been a very serious, if not fatal accident, he blamed himself for involving the Sisters.

"I'm just fine Don, now don't you worry. I didn't hurt myself one bit."

"I don't know about you, but I need a cold drink." Kay wanted her heart to stop racing. This near disaster was too close for comfort.

As for the Sisters, this was a break away from the house and the endless chores. With no harm done, they teased Sister Margaret about how she looked when she did the back flip.

"How about a repeat performance when I find a camera?" Mother Francine put her arm around her, "But without the steer of course. I don't think he'll be ready to do that stunt again."

One of the Gibbon children came to say "Hi." "Do you know what, Sister Mary Gregory, I was down at the creek and saw Beavie. He even flapped his tail at me when I called."

Beavie is a baby beaver. The children found him when he was small and brought him home. They fixed up a nice cage with a big bath of water and small logs to chew on. He quickly adapted to his new environment and enjoyed being petted and played with.

The news about Beavie was relayed especially to Sister Mary Gregory. She was visiting a few weeks earlier and picked up Beavie. He snuggled happily into her lap. Being neither house broken nor toilet trained and relaxing with the gentle stroking, his bladder began to empty. Before she could lift up the little animal and jump from the chair, her skirt was soaked through.

The children fell on the floor laughing. Sister stood holding out Beavie. "Okay kids, you can have him," and putting him down, pointed in the direction of the children, "Go." Beavie detoured to a nearby chair leg and began to chew.

When he began chewing at the house, he was returned to the creek. Eventually he found a mate, built a beaver lodge and raised a family. Sometimes when called, he'd come out, look around and dive back to the safety of the lodge.

Sister Mary Gregory was wearing the brown habit the Sisters had adopted a few years after Vatican II brought so many significant changes to the life of the church. At that time, they began wearing simple suits and blouses. The move into "civilian" clothes was a change but after awhile the Sisters became more aware of the need to have a stronger visible sign of their commitment and to identify themselves as Franciscans. With that in mind, they had simple, brown habits made, mid-calf in length with long sleeves. A few months after wearing this new, comfortable habit, they added a small black veil that sat at the back of the head, held in place by a very small black frame. The clothes were practical, washable, made mostly of polyester and the cost was minimal.

They wore a simple cross on a cord around the neck. It was made from nails reclaimed from an old barn they tore down.

A little money was coming into their slender bank account from renting the ballroom for meetings. A priest from a Portland parish asked to bring his parish council to the house for a daylong retreat. These were Saturday meetings, of course, when the Sisters were home. Word soon spread around the Catholic community and the Sisters had a small source of revenue. They also took on office-cleaning jobs after their regular work to bring in extra money.

Although every Sister who joined the small community was a fully qualified professional in her field, each was also used to tough physical work.

Perhaps Mother Michael says it best. "To touch the earth, to come to know who we are and who God is." As followers of St. Francis, the Sisters are responding to his teaching. "Watch how you live it. Don't preach it."

Once when St. Francis was revisiting his birthplace, Assisi, one of his companions said, "We must go out in the streets to preach and tell them about the Lord."

Off they went and walked through the city without a word spoken. When they reached the far limits, the friend asked, "But when are we going to preach?" and Francis replied, "We have."

In mid-1976, Mother Francine was asked by the Providence Sisters to take over the administration of their Montessori school. Their administrator was ill and unavailable for many months. The school was for children age 2½ to 5 years. Although working as an educator all her professional life, she had never been satisfied that children were receiving the best possible education. She had some knowledge of the Montessori system but had never been fully exposed to their methods.

She was impressed. So much so that she suggested to the Providence community the need for continuity. The parents wanted their children to continue with Montessori teaching. The Providence Sisters and their Board of Directors decided they couldn't go beyond the what they were doing.

"I never wanted to start a school," Mother Francine recalls, "but the need was there and it's part of our Franciscan philosophy to create something new. I gave this a lot of thought before bringing it to our Bridal Veil community. It meant starting a school right from scratch, and remember, we were broke. We hardly had a dime to our names.

"The Sisters supported my decision to quit my job, and they'd support me while I put a school together. I'd never felt in all my years as an educator that the system provided for children to grow independently and to move at their own pace. This opportunity fell into my lap and scary though the whole project seemed at the time, I didn't want it to slip away."

Mother Michael, founder of the Bridal Veil Center, became co-founder of the school with Mother Francine.

Calling upon Portland colleagues in the Catholic School system, she rented an empty classroom at St. Rose Elementary School and a small office.

"The community loaned us $7,300.00. I don't know where they got it. I contracted to hire a Montessori-trained teacher to start in September 1977. Seventeen students were recruited. I bought the necessary materials and put it all together."

Mother Francine failed to mention as she described the stresses and strains of starting a brand new school, that the life of dedicated work at Bridal Veil continued. No one was spared. The black and white marble-floored solarium was scrubbed clean. Friends gave them house plants. As they cleaned, so they painted. A creamy white color suited the interior. It contrasted nicely with the handsome oak floors, the dark wood of the bannisters and railings and brought the lovely house back to something like its original striking appearance.

Early in 1977 Sister Mary Coleman joined the Sisters and was their youngest member. She had an under-graduate degree and planned to earn her master's at the university in Portland, then take Montessori training to enable her to teach at the new school.

All this cost money so she went looking for a job. What she found was work in a clothing factory. Not a comfortable office job but in the factory on the production line. She sewed shirts. Skilled with her hands, (she was a potter in her spare time) and highly intelligent, she was a valued and popular worker. A Sister wearing a habit, doing factory work, caused something of a stir but she insisted on being treated like the other women and was.

Within months, her supervisor wanted to promote her but Sister turned it down. She knew she wasn't going to make a career as a factory worker. Replacing her on the line would be fairly easy, it might be more difficult if she accepted a promotion to a higher level.

Working in the factory through the summer heat and winter cold allowed her to earn enough to cover her fees at the university and her Montessori training. There was even enough cash left over to add significantly to the funds at the house. Sister Mary Coleman, like the others, a devoted Franciscan, was able to work all the hours that God sent, keeping her finely honed sense of humor through it all.

With the extra money contributed by their factory-working Sister to the household expenses, Mother Michael resigned from her pastoral work to become the secretary at the new school. She looked after money coming and going, wrote letters, the usual things. At the end of three years when the school relocated to larger quarters to cope with increased enrollment, the demands on her time at Bridal Veil also increased. She moved out of the school, still supporting it as co-founder and stayed at home, full time, to center the community.

A School Is Born

To have some chickens, to have fresh eggs was a priority item on Sister Margaret's wish list. The Gibbons were well aware of this. A friend of theirs moved out of Oregon and had to find a home for his five chickens. If the Sisters wanted them, they were theirs. He couldn't bear the thought of having them slaughtered.

The birds arrived early in 1977 when the weather was still cold. The barn that once housed the Lawrence family horses, was falling down but, with their usual confidence, the Sisters thought there was enough space for the five chickens.

"The place just wasn't right for them," Sister Margaret laments. "It was cold and drafty and one day they just put their little feet up to the sky and died. So that was the end of our chicken venture for several years."

With some money coming in, the Sisters kept a small stock of food on hand for friends who dropped in. Hospitality was and is high on their agenda. They enjoyed sharing what little they had so even a simple cup of tea or coffee was an occasion to celebrate.

Their friends, appreciating the work going into the house and grounds did what they could to help. One brought out some good used furniture, another, having new broadloom put down, rolled up her area rugs with a lot of wear still left in them and sent them out.

"I'm having my kitchen remodelled, do you want my old appliances?"

"When do we ever say no to a gift like that!" Mother Francine, like the others, was delighted at seeing their once empty, sad looking house, becoming like a comfortable home.

She was spending more and more time at St. Rose's School in Portland fixing up the basement room that was to house the seventeen students in the new school. What to name this fledgling waiting to spread its wings gave the Sisters something to think about. Montessori had to be in the name and they wanted Franciscan as well. Because of their strong connection and spiritual feelings for the land, they wanted that to be part of the future school curriculum. They chose well. The Franciscan Montessori Earth School says it all.

With school plans well in hand, Mother Francine held an open house at the school early in August 1977. This day of celebration for the Sisters was stiflingly hot, the thermometer pushing 100 degrees with humidity to match.

I, the teller of this tale, celebrated with them. Why I was there and not at my home in Toronto, Canada is part of this story. Through my acquaintance with a Jesuit seminarian, Craig Boly, now Father Boly S.J., whose family home is in Portland, I heard that a community of Sisters in that area accepted one or two people wishing to make a retreat.

This was a new venture for me. As a recent convert to Catholicism, I hankered after a retreat experience since it seemed the thing that Catholics did on a regular basis.

Craig was a volunteer at Distress Center in Toronto where I worked as coordinator of volunteers. One of his fellow Jesuits, Father Frank Costello, is Mother

Michael's brother. A long-distance call to Bridal Veil was all I needed to make the necessary arrangements. Leaving my husband to fend for himself for two weeks, I flew to Portland.

Craig picked me up at the airport and did his best on the way to Bridal Veil to calm my nervousness. I was thinking that I might not like these Sisters and even worse, they might not like me.

As he drove slowly up the winding drive, my nervousness disappeared to be replaced by a tremendous feeling of anticipation, a sense of wonder at being where I was. When we arrived at the front of the house, I was awed by its beauty. This was love at first sight.

My arrival was timed for a Saturday when the Sisters were at home. A ring of the bell brought Mother Michael. This moment remains vivid in my memory.

With a huge smile and her arms outstretched, she welcomed me. "Come in, come in," and holding my arm walked Craig and me to the back of the house and into the kitchen. Five of the Sisters were there. Sister Paula Jean was away visiting family. By the time introductions were made and we sat around drinking coffee and getting acquainted, I felt right at home. The feeling has never left.

My two weeks at Bridal Veil were low key and totally satisfying. I worked on the land. The garden plot behind the gatehouse was overgrown with weeds and the ever present blackberries. When the Sisters were away on their three-week retreat in July, the jungle moved in. Potatoes, huge squashes, beets and cucumbers appeared as if by magic when I got rid of the overburden of weedy growth.

The weather was hot and dry. Although the gardens and lawns were parched, the Sisters had no sprinkler to water them. I bought a sprinkler. They had very little of anything in the way of gardening tools. At Christmas I sent them a garden fork, courtesy of Craig who carried it, don't ask how, on a flight from Toronto to Portland.

Alone every weekday while the Sisters were in Portland, I did some hard physical work, strolled the grounds, sat by the falls savoring the coolness and stared at the abandoned swimming pool, wondering. Wondering about the people who had lived in the house and walked the grounds. Who were they? I couldn't let go of the feeling that the place was alive with memories calling out to be heard.

Mother Michael, bless her patient soul, was my spiritual guide. After evening prayers in the small chapel, we sat together going over the day's events, reflecting on certain biblical themes. These meetings soon became less formalized as she, in her wisdom, realized I was plumbing my own spiritual depths. Either that or she concluded I was a lost cause!

Being with the Sisters, sharing in their lives, having fun and helping out was a profoundly satisfying experience. As a temporary member of the F.S.E. community, I attended the open house of the Franciscan Montessori Earth School.

Like the story of the Little Engine That Could, this small school with its humble beginnings has overcome obstacles, kept on going and now is a vibrant and resounding success.

Mother Francine was anxious for September to arrive. Everything was in place. Although she had her community behind her, full responsibility for the success of this venture fell on her shoulders.

With September, the seventeen students of the Franciscan Montessori Earth School began their education.

"We got it off the ground," Mother Francine recalls, "and within weeks I knew it wasn't right. It just didn't feel right." Although she was not Montessori-trained, her instincts were ringing alarm bells. This was not the school she imagined. Deeply concerned and worried, not sure where to turn for help, she was leafing through a Montessori publication and came across the name of a Montessori consultant living in New York. Her name, Margot Waltuch.

Why she chose this particular consultant? Mother Francine is not sure but into their lives came Margot Waltuch and into their lives she has stayed.

"I will never forget going to the airport to meet her." Mother Michael's memory of this event finds her at her story-telling best.

"She told us on the phone that she'd wear a purple hat. That's so we'd recognize her. Well!" Her voice takes on extra dramatic tones. "She was wearing a full length fur coat. Her hat was gorgeous. It was purple with a kind of wide brim and there was a big silk flower off to one side. I tell you Mother Francine and I were awed by this vision walking towards us."

Margot Waltuch and her husband settled in New York after leaving Germany, their birthplace. Both were well educated, sophisticated Europeans, fluent in several languages. Margot had trained with Maria Montessori in Italy. A gifted teacher, she was also a first class Montessori resource person. And to the two Sisters, vaguely intimidating.

Taking her to the fledgling school the following day, Mother Francine left her to observe the teaching in the basement room. Within an hour she was back in Mother Francine's tiny office.

Raising her arms and her voice she gave vent to her feelings. "Disaster!" She cried out. "Disaster!"

To have her lovingly created school labelled a disaster was shattering but Mother Francine remained reasonably calm and reasonably collected.

"That bad, huh?" She forced herself to smile and gestured to the only other chair in the room besides her own. Margot's initial reaction to her observations was now replaced by her cool, professional appraisal. With meticulous care she detailed what had to be done to bring the school up to Montessori standards.

These two women, different in so many ways, one Jewish, the other a Roman Catholic nun, found a common ground in their unshakeable belief that every child deserves the best education possible. Mother Francine shared her concerns about the school and what had been worrying her. Within hours, they made decisions about needed changes and how to make them happen.

"I felt as though a huge burden was lifted from my shoulders. Margot was wonderful."

It's the policy of the Association Montessori Internationale to issue Certificates of Recognition to schools that meet their rigorous standards and show evidence of commitment to growth and development.

Schools in the United States are expected to seek consultation at least once every three years through AMI/USA. For Mother Francine, a once every three years consultation was not enough. Professional to her fingertips, she appreciated the value of yearly consultations with someone of Margot's experience and wisdom.

Early in every school year, usually October, Margot Waltuch comes to Portland. As the school has grown and moved into its own buildings, she values more and more the quality of Mother Francine's leadership. The innovative programs developed at the school, the quality of the staff and the phenomenal increase in enrollment reflect the dedication of the Sisters in their role as educators.

Instruction in the Roman Catholic faith is available to students. Following the model of St. Francis, the Sisters live their faith without preaching it. A quality of love and caring permeates their work at the school. Following the Montessori model, the children learn not only to be responsible for themselves and their studies, they are encouraged to assist younger students.

The Flood

The winter of 1977 was cold with lots of snow and ice. Little wonder the first lot of chickens decided to pack it in. For the small Bridal Veil community, it wasn't just snow and ice on the driveway that gave them trouble, part of their house was flooded.

Ice had built up in the stream behind the house. They'd been chopping away hoping to clear it. They were all home one evening having dinner in the kitchen when a sudden whoosh of water sent them running to the dining room. The water dammed up behind the ice had overflowed and now pushed under the back patio door. A steady rush of water swept across the dining room into the solarium.

"I can hear water downstairs!" Sister Mary Gregory racing ahead of the others dashed down the basement stairs. "Oh, dear God, the place is full of water."

Pulling off her shoes, she plunged ankle deep into the icy flood. Splashing across the slippery floor, she reached a drain cover and pulled it off, then pushing farther on near the huge furnace, she found the second drain and opened it. The water had a place to go and their precious furnace wasn't damaged.

"Terry is down at the gatehouse! Get him on the phone and tell him we need help." As Sister Paula Jean picked it up, Mother remembered something else. "Tell him to put on his coat and big boots."

Terry Falls was on a retreat for a few days. The frantic call from the Sisters sent him racing up the hill at a dead run.

By the time he arrived, three of the women, their coats and boots on, had picked up a shovel and axe at the back door and were frantically trying to move the ice jam.

"Here, give me that axe." Terry smashed at the ice and as big pieces broke away, the Sisters pushed them to one side. The dam gave way and the water fell back into its usual channel.

Shivering in the wet and freezing cold, they dragged themselves into the house and took off their icy coats and drenched boots. The Sisters in the house were in the dining room with brooms and a couple of mops pushing water from the dining room through the solarium and out into the garden through the solarium door. The marble floor was streaked with wet mud and gravel. Cold air pouring in through the open door added to the general misery.

With the water cleared away and the door closed, a modicum of heat began to filter through the house. It hadn't been very warm before this latest disaster. The thermostat was set low to conserve fuel. They were all shivering.

"Look, we have to get warm. I'll light a big fire in the living room." Terry was as cold as the women. They had to get themselves warm in a hurry.

The thought of a fire cheered them considerably. "I'll put on some coffee," Sister Margaret headed for the kitchen. The dinner of beef stew was still on the table where they'd left it. Returning it to a pot, she reheated it and calling for some help to carry dishes, the food, steaming hot, found a rousing welcome from the shivering group at the fireplace.

With food inside them and a fire to comfort them, they sat around wondering what to do about this latest threat.

"I know what we're going to do as soon as spring comes, we're going to put in a well and do something about the water. We can't go through this again?" Mother Francine stood by the fire warming her cold hands.

Hours were spent cleaning up the mess left by the flood. With the coming of spring, they hired a well digger. The well provided water for the house. He also recommended that a holding pond be dug in the stream bed.

Calling on friends with strong arms and shovels, a pond was excavated. The Sisters worked along with them. The two older Sisters, Mother Michael and Sister Margaret were excused from this labor. Both were used to hard work but digging out mud and stones from the icy water was deemed a bit much for women in their early sixties. They did take their turns though in moving wheelbarrows of stones out of the way.

Changes

Early in 1978, Sister Paula Jean moved to a community in Cloquet, Minnesota, to become Director of Religious Education in a parish. A new arrival, Sister Patricia, stayed with the Bridal Veil community for a couple of years while she completed her training as a mortician in Portland. The F.S.E. community at large wanted to have one of their own Sisters as a mortician. She would then be available to assist when a community member died. Blessed with a warm, caring personality and an open, friendly face, she was an asset to the funeral home that hired her. Assisting the bereaved to cope with the loss of a loved one became an important part of her work.

It was Sister Patricia driving back and forth to work who found another source of income for the Sisters. Passing a health food store, The Daily Grind, she noticed a sign in the window. "Wanted. Fresh Watercress. Top Prices Paid." The stream behind their house was thick with watercress. When opportunity knocks, the Sisters answer quickly.

After dark, when their work days were finished, they parked the two community cars facing the stream, switched on the engines and turned on the lights. They picked watercress.

"We picked tons of the stuff," Mother Francine winces at the memory. "Then we had to wash it and pack it in boxes ready for delivery in the morning. The Daily Grind was delighted with our produce."

"I'll take everything you can bring me." The owner paid cash. So they picked and picked night after night until the watercress ran out.

"Boy, was I glad when that was over!" Mother Michael's back ached from bending, kneeling and slipping on the watery edges of the stream, "but we made some money. Wasn't that great?" Her joyful loving presence is a constant source of delight to all who know her. Even those who have just met her soon fall under her spell. Her brother, Father Frank Constello, S.J., remembers meeting her at the bus station in Spokane. She travelled from Portland for a visit.

"She got off the bus and everyone, including the driver got off with her. I hardly had time to say hello when she began introducing me to everyone on the bus by their names. 'This is Mrs. Price and she's going to visit her daughter, and this is Jim Harris and his mother is sick,' and on she went. I couldn't believe it."

"Finally she managed to say goodbye to everyone and we got in my car. How on earth do you know so much about all those people?"

"Well," she said, "It's a long trip and we had rest stops along the way and sat around drinking tea and coffee and talking. So I got to know them."

"She tossed this off quite casually as though it was something everyone did on long trips."

The Bear

The school in Portland after Margot Waltuch's consultation and follow-up changes went well. For it to be Franciscan as well as Montessori, the children had to be in touch with the earth and growing things. At the close of the first year, Mother Francine arranged for the students to come to Bridal Veil. This was planned as a camping experience on the land. Tents were borrowed and the children brought sleeping bags. Several parents came along to assist and food was prepared for the big event.

Saturday morning of the camping day, Mother Francine was out of bed earlier than usual to make sure everything that could be organized was organized. She walked down to the garden behind the gatehouse to see what kind of work the children might do there. Lost in thought, she sauntered around the house and met a bear.

"I looked at the bear and the bear looked at me and I don't know which of us was more scared. Anyway, he looked about eight feet tall so I wasn't about to stick around." As she tells this story she holds up her arms to show how big the bear was. "I turned around and ran up to the house. Shivers were running up and down my spine and I was almost afraid to turn round in case he was coming after me. But I did, and he was going in the other direction."

Bursting through the back door, she screeched to a stop at the kitchen, "There's a bear in the garden!"

No one blinked. "I'm not kidding. There's a bear in the garden and he's eating a squash."

"Oh, sure." Sister Mary Coleman thought a squash-eating bear was a bit far fetched, but decided to go along with the joke. "Okay, come on and show us."

Down they all walked to the garden. Mother Francine tramped into the squash vines and picked up a squash. "Just look at this." The claw marks of the bear were plain to see.

Now the significance of a bear wandering around hit home. Mother Michael reacted first, "We can't have those children out here in tents tonight. What if the bear comes back?"

The question hung in the air as they hurried back to the house to phone the ranger station. The ranger told them that a young bear had been seen around The Chinook Inn, a few miles west of Bridal Veil. Probably the same bear. He promised to be out within two hours with a trap.

What to do about the children? Knowing how much they were looking forward to camping out, the Sisters didn't want to disappoint them and cancel it. On the other hand, what if the bear returned and charged into a tent? A quick decision had to be made. Cancel or not?

Sister Mary Coleman thought they should go on with it, "Look, I'll take turns sitting up all night with you. We can bang pot lids or something if the bear comes back." Having heard it was a young bear and not quite the monster described by Mother Francine, she felt confident about scaring it off.

"Should we tell the parents who are coming?" Mother Francine put the question to the others. "Personally I don't think so. There's no need to alarm everyone. The ranger was sure the bear wouldn't return with a lot of people around. He said he'd put the trap away from our property."

Although a Franciscan through and through, a lover of the land, animals and growing things, she was not fond of sleeping in a tent. For her students, she was prepared to make the supreme sacrifice. Convinced even before the bear appeared that she'd be awake all night, sitting up with pot lids at the ready, was as good a way as any of passing the night time.

Their plans went ahead. The ranger arrived with a huge cage. The bear, he told them, would not be harmed but taken some distance away and released.

The children had a wonderful time. They weeded and raked the garden, played around the grounds, got as close as they could to the falls and slept uneventfully in their tents. Two wide awake nuns sat outside. Every twig that snapped, every bird that twittered, every night sound had their adrenalin pumping. The bear stayed away.

Two days later, he walked into the trap and the door slammed down behind him. He was a half-grown, young male and hungry. To him a squash tasted good.

"I thought you said the bear was eight feet tall." The Sisters had a look at the captive and Sister Mary Coleman was laughing.

"Well, at six o'clock in the morning and without a cup of coffee to wake me up, he looked like a monster!" Mother Francine was feeling quite heroic about scaring off the bear. What with poisoning rats in the crawl space and tangling with a bear, she began to wonder what else might be in store for her.

Adjusting constantly to changing situations is part of the lives of these Franciscan Sisters of The Eucharist.

Although there are only seventy-five of them in the United States, they interact with one another regularly. Mother Michael is in daily contact with their Mother Guardian in Meriden, Connecticut. The bookkeeper for their school is in Minnesota.

"We involve ourselves in each other's projects. When we came here and there were only four Sisters, we did have the community as a whole behind us. They couldn't offer financial help but just knowing they were there helped to keep us going," Sister Margaret remembers the tough first year.

For an outsider trying to understand the differences
in religious communities and what makes the Franciscan
Sisters tick, a simple and uncomplicated explanation was
given by one of them.

"Whereas the Dominicans give you a sermon, the
Jesuits protect the Holy Father, the Benedictines are
cloistered, Franciscans live and work in the
marketplace."

Pursuing the topic, Mother Francine added. "We live
the principles of social justice by the work we do and the
people we work with. We make sure, for instance, that our
staff at the school have full medical insurance, a just
salary and a good place to work. But there is so much
more than that to our call as Franciscans.

"Deep in the heart of our tradition is a reverence for
the body of Christ and living the reality of the Eucharistic
call. It's hard to articulate in spiritual terms but our
commitment is to that part of our faith that talks about
the Eucharist. This devotion is very important to us
which is why our prayer lives are as intense as our professional lives." She smiled as she continued, "The struggle
of living a life in a community is that it can look all
peaceful and lovely and glorious yet be filled with ten-
sions and struggles and personality differences.

"What we believe and what is central to our community is that we pledge ourselves to work through the
struggles. That can be terribly painful and also filled with
a lot of ecstasy.

"As a community, we make a strong effort to be
physically together for prayer and our regular meetings.
It's important for the F.S.E. that we stay put and draw
people to us. How that happens, none of us is really sure
for we certainly don't go out and preach and we don't try
to change anyone."

A friend with a slightly irreverent wit, already taken in by Sister Margaret's fine cooking remarked. "Maybe you lure people in by feeding them so well."

This brought whoops of laughter from the Sisters before Mother Francine continued, "Sometimes lay people wonder about that phrase, 'the Body of Christ', for us it means our Church of which Christ is the head and we are all parts of His church. The mystery of the Eucharist is what we celebrate daily at Mass."

The Community Develops

By the time the Third Annual Benefit Ball rolled around, it had become a well-run social event. No more chamber music. The music, provided by two men playing accordion, drums and a couple of wind instruments as needed, was danceable and fun. My husband and I travelled from Toronto to attend.

"You just have to meet these women!" My enthusiasm for the Sisters was contagious. My non-Catholic, somewhat skeptical husband agreed to come. What he didn't know and I didn't tell him is that visitors to the Bridal Veil community find themselves involved in work almost the moment they set foot on the ground.

"Bill," said Mother Francine in her most innocent voice the day after we arrived, "the eavestroughs and downspouts on the roof over the back of the house are blocked." She paused to let this piece of information sink in. "Do you think you could get up there and clean them out?"

What could he say? He, who studiously avoided climbing on roofs at home, found himself up a ladder, cleaning eavestroughs and trying not to fall off. Having accomplished that task, he was asked to drive Mother Michael to Gresham to pick up all the dishes, glasses and cutlery required for the Ball. Only too happy to escape more roof climbing, off the two of them went.

The rented items were neatly packed in boxes and to Bill's eyes were perfectly clean. Not quite clean enough for the Sisters. Everything had to be washed and dried.

Mother Michael's brother, Father Costello, made the mistake of arriving early enough to become Bill's assistant at the dish, glass and cutlery washing. Bent over tubs of hot detergent water, cleansing rinses and final clear water rinses, the two men were encouraged to keep going by various Sisters hurrying by. Everyone was busy preparing food, polishing windows, doing last minute cleaning and setting up tables for the evening.

Out at the goldfish pond, Mother Francine and a young friend who had come by to help, were catching the fish, draining the water and digging out the silt that had collected over the winter. The pond was to be spanking clean for the party. The two women working in the muddy water were a sight to behold. Splattered with dirt, their clothes soaked through, they were enjoying themselves as though mucking out the pond was the best fun in the world. Finally finished, they hosed down the last of the silt and left the pond to fill.

"Why, it's like playing mud pies and getting dirty!" Mother Francine has never lost sight of the child she once was. One of her strengths as an educator is the ability to put herself into the mind of a child, to remember what it's like to feel dumb when something is hard to understand, or to feel out of place or to be so full of energy, it's hard to sit still.

Two new Sisters arrived in 1979 and 1980. Sister Janet came to teach at the school. One of the younger Sisters she is an asset to the staff. Her quick and lively sense of humor keeps spirits from flagging when too much work becomes, too much! Sister Bernice, a phar-

Spring cleaning up of the fish pond at the front of the house. Sister Kathleen Ann, Mother Francine bending over and their friend, Ramona Gilbert, helping out. Ramona's baby is in the playpen.

macist, was invited to Bridal Veil when the small community of which she was a part, dispersed.

Gentle, quiet and a thoroughly competent professional, she works in the pharmacy of a large Portland hospital. The two newcomers were scarcely settled when they added extra work hours to their already busy days. They cleaned offices.

"Oh, cleaning offices isn't hard," Sister Bernice remarks with a big smile. "We finish in a couple of hours and then we go home." What she forgot to add, is that more work awaits them at home.

And getting home during the winter months has its trials and tribulations. In bad ice and snowstorms, the freeway is closed. One ice storm laid a slick of black ice on the road and the state troopers were out diverting traffic and urging people to stay at home. Mother Francine and two Sisters were at a meeting in Portland after school and were late leaving the city. They were turned back by the troopers. The freeway was closed.

"Mother Michael was at home and I knew she'd be worried about us because of the weather. I decided to try our luck on the Crown Point Highway," This is daredevil driver Mother Francine tempting fate.

For those unfamiliar with it, this beautifully engineered, two-lane road twists up hill and down dale between stands of giant trees, with some sheer drops over rocky cliffs at many turns along the way.

"We prayed as I headed down the road. It was icy! And I wondered what on earth possessed me to try this. We crept along. No other motorist was fool enough to be out. We slid around corners. I tried to keep the car close to the side of the road away from the sheer drops into oblivion. When we finally got to our place, we couldn't get up the drive. It was like a skating rink."

Sister Mary Coleman chimed in, "So we slithered and slipped up to the house, got some pails of sand and salt to spread on the drive. I wished it hadn't been so dark because I'd like to have tried sliding down."

A Pilgrimage

Late in 1978, the Sisters were asked by a group of women friends from Portland and Seattle to organize a pilgrimage to the Holy Land. Two Sisters of the F.S.E. community were already working there. Arrangements for the trip were made through them. March 1979 found Mothers Michael and Francine heading out from the West Coast with their small group. At their stopover in New York, Father White joined them as their spiritual mentor and I flew in from Toronto to make the journey with them.

It was an unforgettable experience. In ten days we visited most of the holy places of the Christian church, entered and appreciated a mosque and of course, being with Franciscans found work to do! In Emmaeus, Franciscan priests purchased an abandoned Arab Christian boys' school. It badly needed to be cleaned and refurbished. What we pilgrims did was wash windows and remove what seemed to be centuries of dirt. Ancient germs found their way into our North American lungs. Two other women and myself on returning to our homes became very ill with bronchitis, a condition new to me and to them.

The pilgrims from the Portland area determined to keep the Franciscan spirit alive by creating something new. They proposed to the Sisters that they sponsor a Valentine's Day luncheon every year on the Saturday closest to February 14th, at Bridal Veil. The first luncheon in 1980 attracted close to one hundred people. Eleven years later, luncheon is provided for over four hundred and now there are two sittings.

This money raising event is a boon to the Sisters. The work involved in putting it on strains the resources of the kitchen to the limit but Sister Margaret and her helpers rise to the occasion and according to her, "We just have a ball."

One of their neighbors, Connie Grenfell, sees this as her big effort of the year for the Sisters, "I work two days before the luncheon, twelve-hour days and I love it."

Gregarious, attractive and bubbling with energy, Connie with her sense of fun, dresses as a waitress to serve the guests. She is also the creative genius behind the crazy skits acted out by other neighbors whenever there is a celebration of any kind at the house.

In preparation for Valentine's Day luncheon, 175 2lb. French breads baked in 1½ days.

The pilgrims are all active in preparing food for the Valentine Day luncheons. Sister Margaret provides home baked bread, the others bring in salads of all kinds and whatever else Sister Margaret requires to round out the menu.

"Now don't forget to keep me on your mailing list." The enjoyment of the guests and their appreciation of the fine food, finds expression in the request to let them know about the luncheon the following year.

In the five years since they moved into the house, the Sisters have managed to bring back much of its original charm. With the library turned into a chapel by the Redemptorists, the Sisters decided to change its appearance to reflect the beauty of the house and their community.

Having removed the wallboard panels and uncovered the gaping hole left when the elegant fireplace was torn down, they thought to restore the room as nearly as possible to its original design. To have a stone fireplace meant hiring a stonemason skilled in the art and that was beyond their slender means. Brother Jerome came back to help. He found a length of wood at a local lumber yard and from that he created an attractive and simple mantlepiece.

The next major effort was the removal of the brick wall and the return of the French doors back where they belonged. Sadly, the framing had deteriorated through years of basement storage. Moisture damaged the wood. Some of the glass was broken.

With Brother Jerome supervising, friends of the Sisters took down the wall. The French doors were repaired and installed. Light flooded into the room. In the following weeks and months, with a table for an altar, a tabernacle for the hosts and various mementoes of their lives and those of their friends placed on the newly painted shelves, the chapel became the focal point for their morning and evening prayers. A varied assortment of fine wood chairs, all donated, completed the furnishings.

It is a beautiful place of worship. Friends are welcome and visiting priests celebrate Mass for the community.

Starting with nothing, only themselves and their resourcefulness, the Sisters took a dying house, breathed new life into it and created a home. Its family atmosphere is heightened by the constant comings and goings of friends, many with their small children tagging along. The laughter of these little ones echos through the house. Not only do adults enjoy the company of the Sisters, children adore them.

In late 1979 Sister Mary Gregory left to take up a new position in Duluth, Michigan. Her skillful work on the walls of the ballroom and dining room live on. Her prodigious feat of plastering and papering those rooms is now part of the lore surrounding the house. She was a gifted fixer of things that went bump in the night, taps that dripped or a heating system acting up.

The enormous furnace presented her with a real challenge to her fixer skills. More than once she put it back in working order when it threatened to die in the middle of a freezing cold wintry day.

The Earth School was attracting an increasing number of students. With no room to expand in their present location, the Sisters decided to go for broke. With their usual courage and belief in nurturing what they begin, they leased a vacant school building. Montessori-trained teachers joined the staff. Then with their uncanny ability at doing the seemingly impossible, the Sisters equipped the new classrooms with all the materials necessary to create a fine learning environment.

Their Montessori consultant, Margot Waltuch, returns every autumn. Thinking back to those early days, Mother Francine has the greatest praise for her.

"She was absolutely splendid. I often wonder how we could possibly have achieved what we have without her guidance along the way."

Apart from her annual consultation at the school, Margot has become a close and loved friend of the Sisters. She stays at Bridal Veil and as with all other visitors, has work to do, usually on the land. All this is light years away from her sufferings at the hands of the Nazis and imprisonment in a concentration camp. Now in her late seventies, she has the same sense of style and *joie de vivre* that impressed the Sisters when she first walked into their lives.

The Goats

1980 and Mother Francine is celebrating her twenty-fifth year as a Sister. It's usual in their small community to mark these special occasions with a gift. Driving through Portland one day with Mother Michael, this particular celebrant spotted someone walking on the street, leading a goat.

"Look at that!" She poked her companion in the ribs. "See that goat. That's what I want for my jubilee."

Mother Michael winced, not from the poke but from the thought of a goat. "Now, what will we do with a goat. Get serious. We don't have a stall for one." She hoped she was throwing cold water on the goat idea.

But Mother Francine's busy mind was already in high gear. "We can put it in part of the chicken coop. It won't take much room. Besides it'll be out in the field most of the time."

Repairing the old Lawrence horse barn and turning it into a chicken coop was a project of a young friend of the Sisters, George Zifcak. He and his wife, Isabelle lived in Seattle and George travelled down on weekends to work on the barn. A skilled carpenter, he soon had it shipshape and ready for chickens. This delightful couple and their children moved from Seattle to Gresham, a town not far from Bridal Veil. Here Isabelle set to work building up her small business as a designer and maker of fine, handmade silver jewelry.

Sister Margaret now had her chickens housed to her liking and the clucking hens, free to scratch the earth and move around, began laying eggs.

It was to this revitalized barn that Mother Francine proposed to put her goat. That is if a suitable goat was found.

As luck would have it, she mentioned to a friend that she was on the lookout for a goat.

"I have an aunt that raises goats. I'll bet she'd have a goat for you." He gave her the name and phone number of the goat-raising aunt.

When Mother Michael and the others heard that the goat was a distinct possibility, they decided to go along with it. An appointment was made to view the goats. Mother Michael went with her to make sure Mother Francine didn't get carried away. The idea of having a goat now firmly rooted in her mind, she was bursting with enthusiasm to own one.

"Well, you should have seen the goat lady's place." Mother Michael's dramatic gifts are in full flight and she laughs as she recalls their visit, "It was really something! Why she had goats right in the living room. I guess she really loved those animals and didn't mind them wandering around the house."

"Now, come on, don't exaggerate! She only had little ones with her and she had beautiful pedigreed goats. Actually she had three tiny goats, four weeks old, and she was bottle feeding them," Mother Francine's face was wreathed in smiles as she remembered the pretty baby animals.

"She told us that she'd bring them out in a week so I could decide which one I wanted."

She turned up on a Saturday morning, driving her big old Chrysler. Beside her on the front seat, sleeping in a big basket were the three babies. The Sisters were entranced. These tiny goats, like most baby animals were hard to resist.

Mother Francine looked at them, then looked at the others and in as wheedling a voice as she could manage said, "I'd like them all."

They accepted the three goats. A space in the chicken coop was cleared of birds, a partition put in place, beds of straw laid down and as with all new parents, so with the Sisters, bottle feeding the new arrivals became a part of their daily routine. Two of the goats were female and named Rosa and Dosa. The male was Antonio.

The animals thrived. When Antonio was old enough to be a virile billygoat, the Sisters asked the Gibbons to keep him at their ranch. Rosa and Dosa had a fenced field near the barn to run and jump in. One morning when they were just over a year old, Dosa died. They found her dead in the field. The Sisters were at a loss to discover what caused her death and wondered if she'd been poisoned by someone coming on the property.

Then another shock hit them. Their good friends, Don and Kay Gibbon were divorced and the ranch sold. The new owner offered to keep Antonio for them but suddenly he packed up and left, taking Antonio with him.

"He was a goatnapper!" Years later Mother Francine underlines these words with heavy emphasis. "He stole my goat and he was such a nice goat too. Do you think goatnapping is a crime?"

Crime or not, Antonio disappeared and Rosa was their lone goat. Believing that one goat wasn't enough, the Sisters added three more. Alice May, Israel and Ami. Israel and Ami were neutered. Ami didn't mind but Israel took it to heart. His temper frayed, he is not to be trusted. He likes to butt. The Sisters manage him but friends are warned not to go in the field with him. Even a hand reaching through the fence with some tempting, prickly blackberry bush, is fair game. He crunches the branch, thorns and all, then butts the hand that feeds him.

Besides being a banner year for Mother Francine, 1980 was the year the Sisters realized that the lawns, gardens, fields, woods, everything other than the house, was too much for them to handle on their own. They had no money to hire gardeners. What to do?

They mulled the problem over. "I have an idea," Sister Margaret is always worth listening to. "Our friends love coming to visit and enjoy helping out. Do you suppose we could find a nice group of people who'd like to come out, maybe once a month to work on the land? I'd make a nice lunch for them and there'd always be coffee and sweet rolls to start the day."

"Sure that's a great idea but how do we find these people?" Sister Janet echoed the thoughts of the others.

"Hey, wait a minute." She taught at the Earth school and parents are encouraged to take part in school activities. "What do you think about this. We send home a letter with the children asking their parents if they'd be interested in a day at Bridal Veil. Of course, the children would come too."

She had barely finished speaking when Sister Mary Coleman broke in, "I think that just might work. It's worth a try anyway."

A letter was written. What it offered was a chance to spend a day in the fresh air, do some yard work, have a delicious lunch, plus refreshments morning and afternoon. The third Saturday in the month was suggested. This to become a regular work day if the offer was accepted.

To the delight of the Sisters, a group of parents and children arrived on the designated day. Into the kitchen they trooped for coffee and sweet rolls, with milk or juice for the children. After this welcome, out they went with the Sisters to see what had to be done. Assignments were given, tools handed out and everyone, including the Sisters went to work.

The Saturday Work Days were an instant success. A community feeling developed among the workers as they met once a month. Many of them left their own yard work at home to drive out to Bridal Veil. A sense of being part of something bigger than themselves kept them coming.

Work Day

When the second work day came round, more parents and children arrived to take part. One of them was George Erdenberger, whose daughter attended the Earth School. George and his wife, Georgia, had known the Sisters for some time but had never visited the house. George, a landscape architect by profession, worked with a group during the morning. At lunch he sat next to Mother Michael.

"Can I see your plans for the grounds?" He was fascinated by the estate and sensed its potential.

Mother Michael laughed at this question, "Plan, we don't have a plan. We don't know how to draw up a plan and can't afford to pay somebody to make one. We just work away trying to keep on top of things." She knew that George did some kind of landscape work but didn't know he designed gardens.

"Will you let me draw up plans for you? I know how hard you've been working. I can tell you've put a lot of effort into what you've been doing. I think if the work was better organized you'd get more done."

Mother Francine was listening, "George, if you want to organize us, go ahead. We've been going from one thing to another. There's so much to do! Sometimes it's overwhelming."

George drew up plans for the gardens and lawns and in every minute of his spare time, supervised the work. He waxes eloquent about the Sisters, the house and the grounds.

"There's a magic about the place and the Sisters are ideal clients. Their mission as Franciscans is to preserve the area. They are in it for the long haul and whatever is planted will survive the present time.

"All the people who come out here to work are touched. They are involved in a creative act that will survive as a living monument. As we develop the grounds, there's a therapeutic value or catharsis with nature that everyone will enjoy.

"Hiking or walking in a forest is an enjoyable experience but for the uninitiated, it needs to be interpreted. A garden is more human-sized, call it 'formalized nature' and people can relate to that more easily. Unless you understand the forest and look for all its complexities, you miss a lot. But look here and there in a garden and it interprets itself to you."

George Erdenberger is neither a Catholic nor a churchgoer, yet he expresses his love of the land and the people who work on it, with a spiritual quality that begs to be heard.

"When I arrived and was given *carte blanche* to supervise the outside work, I realized that the first thing we had to was," and he pauses to emphasize what he says next, "to preserve and protect the land, then restore it and finally enhance and maintain it. And that, takes a lot of hard work.

"I am constantly amazed at the power of the human hand. In this highly technological world, I think we have almost forgotten that. What we have achieved out here has been done with good old-fashioned stoop labor."

As a landscape architect and designer, George has the greatest admiration for the way Morris H. Whitehouse, designed the house, the grounds and the winding driveway.

"He placed a formal architectural structure with a wild natural setting on the perimeter. The further you go from the house, the less formal are the grounds. This is not unintentional. It was designed that way. There is a mix of formal and informal. A meeting of man and nature."

With a plan and a vision of how the land will look in the future, the Work Days became a little more structured and just as much fun. First on the list to be reclaimed was the trout pond. It had to be cleaned out by hand. A machine would have destroyed its fine rock wall. The combination of decaying leaves and silt created a slick, slimy, greasy mess.

Cleaning the pond was stoop labor on a grand scale. The Sisters in their long skirts and their helpers were up to their knees in the sloppy, slurpy, slippery goop. They filled five-gallon pails, passed them to another group who took them away to be dumped in a far corner. To hear the Sisters tell the tale, "We had a ball. Everyone was covered in mud and we were laughing so hard, it's a wonder we did so much work."

Rome wasn't built in a day nor was the pond cleared of its greasy, smelling muck. Two more Saturday Work Days were spent before the trout pond was clean. The attractive stone wall showed up well when the years of dirt were washed away. In the center of the pond was the rock base on which the Lawrences had placed their spouting crane fountain.

The Sisters realized soon after they bought the property that water, lots of it, was essential in case of fire. To fill the trout pond meant clearing out the stream that marked the east boundary of the land. Like the pond, it was lined with a skillfully laid rock wall. Some rock had fallen into the stream creating a natural dam that eventually blocked the natural flow of the water.

The Sisters and their Work Day friends dug out the stream bed. By hand. Men, women and children all pitched in. One tired woman was heard to remark, "I'll bet when God created the world, she didn't have to do the work herself."

Water now ran freely, under the pretty stone bridges and into the trout pond. When it was filled, the Sisters had an emergency water supply.

What kept and still keeps these workers coming back? Bernard and Bethany Franceschi and their children are next door neighbors of the Sisters. When asked why he comes over to help, Bernard put down his shovel, leaned on it and asked himself the question.

"What keeps me coming? Some form of addiction! I've known the Sisters since 1976 and have seen lots of changes here. There's a chance to do physical work on the land. It's kind of wonderfully mindless. I give myself over to the experience and it's a nice contrast from the workaday world of business and being in the office most of the time.

"Then there's the connection with the Franciscan spiritually to the work and the land. This connection is unspoken but it's there. And I like the real communal aspect with the people who come here and work on Saturdays.

"So there's a lot of pleasant sharing and it all happens around a constructive project. We're not just sitting around jabbering at one another.

"The work becomes a place to focus your energies. The work we do brings the lay and religious life together in a very nice way without a lot of theory."

On one memorable Work Day, Bernard and some of the men were working down at the gatehouse. His wife, Bethany, and some of the women with their various children gathered in the kitchen planning their schedule. Bethany needed something at home for her baby and drove over in their new Volvo rather than walk and get soaked in the rain. On her return she parked the car by the front door and ran in.

Sister Margaret was upstairs picking up an extra sweater. She glanced out the window and saw the Volvo resting half in and half out of the goldfish pond. In her usual quiet fashion and understated sense of the absurd, called Mother Michael from the kitchen.

"Do you think Bernard knows their car is in the pond?"

"Oh my gosh, that's their new car. Bethany must have left it in gear. She'll have a fit when I tell her."

Sister Mary Coleman grabbed her raincoat and ran down to give Bernard the bad news. They phoned for a tow truck and it was with considerable difficulty that the car was pulled from the pond. For Bethany, it was awful. She couldn't believe what she'd done. The tow truck driver gave her the impression that no woman was to be trusted behind the wheel of a car, especially a new Volvo.

The saga of the Volvo, Bethany and the tow truck driver didn't end at the goldfish pond. Driving into Portland on the Interstate a couple of weeks later, the car began huffing and puffing, it lost power and she managed to pull on to the shoulder. A passing motorist offering to help called in a tow truck. Sure enough it was the same company and the same man.

"Why," she asked herself, "is this happening to me?" She looked him in the eye with self-confidence. "The car began making funny, kind of clinking noises and then just stopped."

Catching what she thought was 'another poor dumb woman probably out of gas' look on his face, she lowered her voice a notch and growled, "The car is not out of gas!"

"Okay lady, I never said it was." He raised the hood and looked around. "I think I know what's happened. It won't take long to fix." With some minor adjustments, he had the engine running. Then. "I guess when you dropped it in the pond, it didn't do it any good."

Bethany's usual gentle manner deserted her. Through clenched teeth, she snarled at him, "I didn't drop it in the pond. Now how much is this costing me?"

She wrote a check. Grateful for the service but smarting at his macho attitude, she smiled as she got back in the car, the look on her face giving lie to the words coming from her mouth.

"I hope I never see you again as long as I live!"

The Villas

In 1984 Sister Margaret retired from her position as Food Service Supervisor at Park Forest Care Center in Portland. She was sixty-five years old. With hardly time to catch a quick breath, she and Mother Michael, now sixty-eight, embarked on a new project at the house.

"Well, we kind of grew into this thing." The 'thing' she described in her casual way were luncheons they catered at the house.

"I guess it really started when a priest we knew came and asked if he could bring his parish council out for a whole day. He wanted us to provide luncheon and coffee breaks. Before we knew it, we had other churches calling us to do the same thing, then Protestant churches and then people wanting to bring groups."

When the two women realized they had something going, they decided to name what they were doing. *Villas* had a nice sound and was associated with the past history of the house. They prepared a brochure describing what they had to offer. Because Sister Margaret was the main mover and shaker of this venture or foundation, as the community calls it, she was given the designation of Mother.

The Villas have proven so successful that a limit was put on the numbers they could handle comfortably. Three and four phone calls a day bring requests from individuals or groups to book a Villa.

"Why we have people booking six months ahead." Mother Margaret has specialties that are favorites of some groups.

"Every time they come they ask me to do my Emerald Chicken. I'd really like to give them something different but that's what they want." (See end of this section for Emerald Chicken recipe.)

Their brochure describes their venture this way:

"Within the tradition of Franciscan hospitality and centering, the Franciscan Sisters of the Eucharist of Bridal Veil, Oregon, have opened their Villa to meet a variety of needs.

"Located in the beautiful Columbia River Gorge, forty minutes from downtown Portland, the Bridal Veil Franciscan Villa provides a unique alternative for group gatherings.

"A perfect spot for: Business Meetings, Luncheons, Parish Staff Meetings, Executive Planning Sessions, Management Workshops, Days of Recollection, Scripture Study Groups, Seminars, Sessions tailored to your needs."

To watch these two women at work is to wonder at their energy. In some contexts, they might be called "elderly" but no such description can be applied to Mother

Mary Michael and Mother Margaret. The money they earn from their activities goes to maintain the house.

"Any tips we get, we put in a separate account and that's to help maintain the grounds." Mother Michael's gregarious and outgoing personality makes her the perfect welcoming hostess. Because the story of the house and the Sisters' activities are fascinating to all visitors, she is called upon to give short talks to some luncheon groups on the history of the house and their community.

Franciscan hospitality as practiced at Bridal Veil requires dedication and lots of hard work. The numbers of social events held at the house are mind numbing. The Benefit Ball, the Valentine Luncheon, the twice and three times a week Villas, Thanksgiving dinner for all the Saturday Work Day friends, a huge Christmas celebration for their friends and their children, keep the place full of life. Then there are friends who come from afar to visit and stay awhile. Groups of Sisters arrive for meetings from their communities. And so it goes.

Yet for all their giving out and sharing what they have, something mysterious continues to happen.

"I don't understand this but whenever we give something, we get something back," Mother Michael seems honestly baffled by this phenomenon.

"Just look at what happened last November. We had the Work Day volunteers come for Thanksgiving dinner. There were sixty I guess. It's one of the ways we show how much we appreciate their help.

"Well, that was on a Saturday and the very next morning, one of the parishioners from the church we go to, came knocking at the back door. He had a couple of boxes of potatoes, carrots, rutabagas and several packages of frozen beef. He wanted to know if we could use them.

"Could we! He came in, of course, and had some coffee. Mother Margaret had made some sweet rolls and put some in a bag for him to take home. It was her way of expressing how much we appreciated what he had brought, and her sweet rolls are really good."

Baked Chicken Breasts In Emerald Barbecue

Serves 6

6 Chicken breasts, split
½ cup flour
1½ tsp salt
⅛ tsp. black pepper
1 tsp. poultry seasoning
½ tsp. paprika
¼ tsp. granulated garlic
¾ cup butter, melted

Emerald Barbecue Sauce

1½ cups dry white wine
1¾ cup favorite barbecue sauce

Combine flour and salt, pepper, poultry seasoning, garlic and paprika. Coat chicken with flour mixture.

Dip chicken in melted butter. Place chicken, skin side up in an open baking pan. Bake uncovered 25 minutes at 400 deg.

Reduce heat to 325 deg. and continue baking uncovered for 20 minutes. Baste once or twice with natural juices. Baste each piece with Emerald Barbecue Sauce.

To make sauce. Simmer wine for 5 minutes. Add barbecue sauce and cook 5 minutes longer.

Serve with a rice pilaf and a garden green salad.

(Note from Mother Margaret. For anyone on a low salt diet, reduce salt to taste. Also, substitute cholesterol-free margarine to replace butter as required.)

Postscript from the Author: The Emerald in this recipe comes from the brand name of the wine used. Any dry white wine will be fine.

Magic Margaret

Mother Margaret has a nickname, one that follows her wherever she goes. She denies having any magical powers but the name, Magic Margaret, sticks. Stories abound of her culinary tricks that mystify the beholders.

The first at Bridal Veil happened shortly after the Sisters moved in. They had beds to sleep in and enough odds and ends of furniture plus second-hand appliances to make do. Three Sisters from another religious community dropped by to see how they were getting along. Although very little had been done to the house and grounds, the Franciscans were delighted to show their guests around and persuaded them to stay for lunch. The new arrivals had some shopping to do in Gresham but decided to return to spend more time with their friends.

Nothing would do but they must stay for dinner, evening prayers and since it was dark and the rain was pouring down, spend the night. The Franciscan Sisters gave up their beds and bundled up in sleeping bags.

When they came down for breakfast, one of the visitors took Mother Michael aside.

"It's Sister Marie's birthday and we bought her a purse in town. Have you any wrapping paper?"

"All we have is brown paper sacks." These clearly wouldn't do. The purse was already wrapped in brown paper. As they sat down to breakfast, the purse was produced and Sister Marie, delighted with her surprise gift, didn't notice the lack of pretty paper.

This was the first moment that Sister Margaret knew there was a birthday. She got up, went into the kitchen to pick up the coffee pot and was gone all of three or four minutes. When she returned, she was carrying a small cupcake, iced, on a plate, with a lighted birthday candle in the middle.

"Happy Birthday Sister." She put the cake down. The visitors thought this was a lovely gesture and thanked her.

The three Bridal Veil Sisters looked on bemused but said nothing. If the visitors thought they had iced cakes and birthday candles lying around, all well and good. They knew better.

When they were alone and back at their chores, Mother Michael decided she had to know how the cake and candle trick was done.

"Okay, Sister Margaret, how did you do it?"

"Do what?"

"How did you produce that cake for Sister Marie? I know," she paused, "well maybe I don't know what's in this house but how did you do it in a couple of minutes?"

"Oh, I just had a few things to play with. It was nothing really." And that's a typical Magic Margaret answer implying somehow that anyone can do the same.

Among her many accomplishments, she has a special affinity for animals. Small children adore her and follow her around. Over the years, birds and animals took up residence at Bridal Veil. Peacocks, geese, ducks, chickens, goats and dogs settled in. The peacocks roamed freely. One day when Mother Margaret was working in the garden, she stood up to watch one of the peacocks fanning out his beautiful tail feathers.

"Why there's something wrong with him," she thought. Unable to put her finger exactly on what that was, she relied on her intuition. It signalled something to her. She called Sister Paula Jean to have a look at the bird as he strolled on the lawn.

"He looks fine to me. What do you think is wrong?"

"I'm not sure but I'm going to call the vet." He came out the following day. By then, the bird was showing signs of distress and Sister Margaret put him in a large pen by himself.

"There's definitely something wrong, Sister. I'd better take him back to the clinic with me."

The peacock died. The vet called Sister Margaret. "I'm not absolutely sure but I think that bird was poisoned."

When the Sisters digested this bit of news, they decided to build a big enclosed pen for the peacocks. With their property accessible to anyone bent on injuring their birds, they'd be safer in a pen with a secure catch on the gate.

The birds thrived and their numbers increased. So it was on a November morning years later that a visitor staying in the upper gatehouse looked out to see peacocks, peahens and all their various half-grown off-spring out of their pen, wandering around the grounds.

She phoned up to the main house. "The peacocks are out!" The Sisters were dressed ready to leave for Mass and hurried down. The gate was open. Somehow the lock hadn't been closed properly.

Mother Michael raised her voice, "Come on and get back in your pen. We have to go to church!" Her words rang loud and clear reaching the half-grown birds now perched high on the barn roof and their parents scattering hither and yon. Nothing happened. Mother Margaret came to the rescue.

In her usual quiet way, she asked the Sisters to stand back, then she spoke to the young birds on the barn roof. "Come on down now. Come back to your house." With her arms spread wide and her voice soft, she spoke to them again. "Come on. That's right." They flew down at her feet and walking quietly with them to the pen, she gentled them along. "You're doing just fine." And when the last young bird was in, she shut the gate.

Turning to the Sisters who were watching this performance without making a sound or a movement, Mother Margaret smiled, "There. Now the older birds won't leave while the young ones are inside so we can go to church."

And sure enough, when the Sisters returned over an hour later, the adults were waiting to rejoin their young and walked sedately through the gate into the enclosure.

Mother Michael is still astonished when she recalls the scene, "If I hadn't seen it with my own eyes, I never would have believed it. She just talked to those birds and they did exactly what she wanted."

Mother Margaret is thoughtful of her chickens. When they have finished laying and are to be slaughtered, she insists they be traumatized as little as possible.

"I found a very kindly man who takes the chickens. I went to see how he killed them. I just wasn't going to send them to one of those awful places where they hang the poor things upside down on a conveyer belt and move them along until their heads are chopped off. He handles them very gently like my father used to on our farm."

There are lots of Magic Margaret stories. I have watched her make jam from blackberries we've picked together. While seeming not to be doing a lot, she moves around the kitchen, chatting to those of us who've come in for a break, pouring tea, offering cookies, all the while cooking up the berries, sterilizing jars, checking the jam for doneness and finally ladling it in jars. Everything is done gracefully and with what seems to be a minimum of effort.

As one admiring Work Day volunteer remarked, "She knows exactly what she's doing all the time and knows just how much time it takes to get things done. I remember coming over to help on the afternoon of the Ball one year and at five o'clock she was out in the stream behind the house in her rubber boots and work gloves, pulling weeds. I thought she had lost her mind! The guests were due to arrive for dinner at seven and there she was out mucking around in the stream."

"Well, by the time the first guests arrived, there she looked fresh as a daisy, smiling as though she didn't have a care in the world."

For Connie Grenfell who volunteers her help at the Valentine Luncheons and the annual Ball, she is convinced that she and Mother Margaret are soul mates. Two more disparate personalities as soul mates would be hard to find. Connie, young, married, attractive, gregarious, vibrant, funny, with a crazy sense of humor that has everyone in the kitchen laughing and Mother Margaret, quiet, gentle, unobtrusively energetic, creative, given to rare witticisms that bring a double take from listeners.

"If I don't see Mother Margaret for a couple of months, I almost hurt inside." This is the serious Connie Grenfell. "In a way, I come here for replenishment, for a kind of therapy I guess. Yesterday although I had so much to do at my house, I came over to see if the Sisters needed any help. I leave here feeling good. Even when I'm exhausted after the Valentine Luncheons, I enjoy it. I'll work ten and twelve hours days with her. I set those days aside on my calendar and no matter what else is going on in my life, they have priority.

"When I'm doing dishes after the luncheons are over, I keep trying to think of ways to make them even more successful. It's not so much the money we earn, it's what the money goes for. Like 'this is for the rose garden and we got it from this event', things like that. There is really something to show for all the work we do."

And Magic Margaret keeps doing her thing. In 1989 the kitchen and two pantries had to be scrubbed down and painted. Anyone who has taken a kitchen apart knows the turmoil it causes and the disruption in family routine. It's a time when meals are thrown together, the toaster goes missing, buried at the bottom of a box filled with pots and pans and the smell of paint fills the house.

The Sisters and some helpers worked day and night on this project. Tempers were frayed and muscles fatigued. On a day when the job was almost completed, the weary workers looked forward to sitting down and having a cold supper. They were totally dumbfounded when Mother Margaret emerged from the basement carrying a roast turkey followed by all the trimmings, right down to pumpkin pie.

A chorus of wondering voices greeted her. "When did you do all that?"

"Oh, it was nothing. I just used that old stove we have in the basement." The happiness she felt at bringing a good dinner to the tired crew was evident by the big smile on her face. "We'll just go into the dining room and sit down. I'm sure you're ready to eat now."

One of the volunteer crew is still puzzled as to how Magic Margaret pulled this off. "We thought she was out working in the garden or down at the barn with the animals. When she appeared with that turkey dinner, I wondered if she'd conjured it up with a magic lamp."

Geese and a Wheelbarrow

The community goats outgrew their space in the chicken coop. An animal barn was built for the four goats with proper stalls. A large part of the field behind the gatehouse had been fenced and they had access to it from the new barn. From the Earth School came five geese.

Actually the geese were hatched at home by one of the students and soon became a problem for the boy's family. Five growing geese need space. Sister Janet, the boy's teacher, hearing of their dilemma offered to give them a place of their own at Bridal Veil.

There were two ganders and three geese. Free to wander the grounds, they became a familiar sight. Richard, the boss gander was pure white. He strutted ahead of his little flock, neck stretched, head high. The very picture of a gander very much in charge. The females followed behind with the other gander taking up the rear.

Geese are reputed to be wonderful "watchdogs" giving loud hisses and honks when intruders enter their space. They have been known to chase, hiss and flap their big wings at unwary passersby. The Bridal Veil geese sometimes hissed and honked, especially Richard but they never gave chase. The Franciscan spirit pervading house and grounds, had a calming effect on the fractious geese.

Sad to say, after living happily in their pleasant surroundings, tragedy struck just before Thanksgiving 1989. Richard was stolen. He disappeared without a trace and without a sound on the eve of Thanksgiving, perhaps to end up as a thief's dinner.

Losing their leader threw the geese into disarray. The lone gander didn't know what to do. He wasn't a leader, just a good follower. The females wandered around, bewildered and listless, a sorry sight. The Sisters, too, missed Richard. He had such style, such a way of arching his neck, of taking his flock to find the best grass for eating.

"I guess this is the price we pay for living in the country. It's really too bad though that someone would sneak in and steal him." Sister Janet's feelings about thieves were evident in her voice. "Poor Richard, whoever stole him must have had a struggle because he was a big bird. But, you know, we didn't see any signs of feathers or anything by the barn."

The Wheelbarrow

The Sisters never seemed to have enough tools to do many of the jobs they tackled. Bits and pieces were added as money was available. Sister Mary Coleman had a birthday coming up and was asked what she wanted.

"A wheelbarrow. We really needed another one when we were cleaning out the trout pond."

It fell to Mother Michael to go to Gresham and buy the wheelbarrow. As luck would have it, one of the stores in town had a sale on. The advertised price for a wheelbarrow was too good to miss. Knowing she'd need help to wrestle a wheelbarrow into the car, she asked their neighbors, the Franceschis, if they'd drive her in.

Mother Michael has presence. She also has determination. With Bernard and Bethany, she walked into the store and they searched around for the "on sale" wheelbarrows. Finding none, she went up to a clerk.

"I want to buy one of those wheelbarrows you advertised."

"I'm sorry, Sister, but we're sold out. Not one left."

She looked around and spotted a wheelbarrow chained up on a side wall. "What about that one up there?"

"Oh that's not for sale. That's for display only."

"Well is there anything wrong with it?"

"No, M'am, but it's not for sale."

"What do you mean it's not for sale? If there's nothing wrong with it, I want to buy it." She was half laughing at herself and the clerk but was being firm and positive.

The clerk began again his litany of, "I'm sorrys" and she cut him off, "I'd really like to speak with your manager." Turning to her friends she whispered, "Did you ever hear of anything so silly? There's a wheelbarrow there and they won't sell it."

The store manager arrived. "I'm sorry Sister but that wheelbarrow is not for sale, it's chained to the wall for display only."

More determined that ever to buy the thing for Sister Mary Coleman, she tried again, "Is there a padlock on the chain?"

He fell unwittingly into a trap. "Oh, yes, to keep it from being stolen."

"Have you got the key?" she asked innocently.

"Of course."

"I really have to have that wheelbarrow. If you'll give me the key, Bernard will climb up and bring it down. I guess you have a ladder somewhere."

Out maneuvered, he was gracious in defeat and produced the key. A clerk was asked to unchain the wheelbarrow and lower it to the floor. It was examined and found to be perfect. Exactly what Sister wanted for her celebration.

"I'm sorry to give you all this trouble but one of our Sisters has a birthday next week and this is what she wants as a gift." They shook hands both having enjoyed the little contretemps.

"A wheelbarrow for a birthday present! My wife won't believe this when I tell her. Well, I hope she enjoys it." The manager went off smiling to himself. He'd always pictured nuns as pale, thin creatures who looked holy all the time. The one getting the wheelbarrow must have muscles because it was a heavy model.

With George Erdenberger overseeing the work on the ground, chaos began to give way to order. To get a better sense of the land, a huge task was to rid it of blackberries.

The lawns and gardens were covered. It was difficult to work on the site until they had been removed.

As he walked the land, George felt the integrity of its design. The underlying structure of the lawns and gardens had been laid so well that he had little trouble visualizing where Dorothy Jacobson and Louise Lawrence had their flower gardens. To check the accuracy of his thinking, he wrote to Dr. Donald Lawrence in Minneapolis asking for help. Drawing from memory, Dr. Lawrence sketched the whole site, detailing gardens, ponds, woods and driveway, including the main house and gatehouse.

Landscape architecture as a profession is one hundred years old. There were very few in Portland in 1916. Architects in Morris Whitehouse's time tended to be more broadly educated in site relationships and setting than they are today. There are many site sketches in his original drawings.

The lawns and gardens on the north side of the house are perfectly aligned. Looking straight out on an axis from the living room doors leading to the terrace is to see the beauty of the design. Everything falls equally on either side of the axis.

Although he has been working in and around the site since 1980, George's enthusiasm for the place never wanes. "The quality of the landscaping, the quality of the building materials and, of course, the presence of the Sisters makes being here a joy." He recalls a special find.

"I was doing some work up near the falls and found a brass valve from the old water system. I took it apart, cleaned it up and it's in perfect condition. The Sisters saw something in this place when they first came here. It was so well built, they knew instinctively it shouldn't be lost. It has quality, wonderful craftsmanship and restoring it has given them tremendous pleasure."

The Third Saturday volunteers continue coming each month to help out. Some are from the original group, others are recent recruits, some come every Work Day, others manage three or four times a year. What keeps them coming?

Nancy is an old hand. "I come out because of the Sisters. They are the most warm, friendly, loving and non-judgemental women I've ever met. They know how to work, to love, to laugh and to cry and they do it all so beautifully." Nancy continued her leaf raking as she talked.

"I feel so good after I've been here. No matter how tired I am, I feel good when I go home. It's got something to do with the land. I'm a nature lover and just being out here is a lot of fun, there's a sense of community, everybody getting in and doing a job with the Sisters then looking back and seeing what they've accomplished.

"I've watched over the years the people who come here, including myself, who've had some emotional therapy that's been accomplished during these work projects. We didn't realize anything particular was happening until suddenly we knew we were feeling better.

"The Sisters make us feel good about who we are and what we're doing. It's that simple. We're never aware of any particular thing they do and that's what's so beautiful about it.

"Somehow they help people become more centered so they are at peace. Working together is part of it. I could never go anywhere and find a nicer bunch of people than come to these work parties, just genuinely fine people who care about others, who are unselfish."

Nancy is given to loud peals of laughter when something amuses her. "And here we are with dirty houses and dirty lawns at home, helping these women and happy to do it. I've never brought anyone out here who didn't feel comfortable and content as soon as they arrive. The

Sisters put them at such ease when they walk in the door."

In 1983 Sister Kathleen Ann, a Sister of St. Joseph, Third Order of St. Francis, was attracted to the Franciscan community. The F.S.E. community was on their annual retreat at Meriden, their mother house.

"I always looked forward to working on the Franciscan land whenever possible. During the retreat, I met more and more Sisters. Two of them, Mother Michael and Mother Francine were working in the same area as me. Mother Francine was raking the lawn and mentioned that she administered a Montessori school in Oregon.

"I'd read about their philosophy and was interested in hearing more. She filled me in on what her school was doing as we worked. When we'd finished the raking, I walked up the hill to see what else had to be done. Mother Michael was working and when she saw me in a clean blue skirt, white blouse, veil, nylons plus a rake, she fell on her knees and said, 'Oh my God, I'll need to pray for this one' and we all burst out laughing."

Sister Kathleen Ann, although a religious for many years, was on a personal search. It happened that one August evening in the course of a conversation, Mother Suzanne said to her, "How would you like to go visit our Sisters in Oregon?"

"WHAT FOR?" Sister Kathleen Ann gave this a real socko delivery. "School is only two weeks away and I still have to find two teachers."

Mother Suzanne smiled, "We have a school there and I think you should see what our Sisters are doing in an educational setting since you are an educator."

Recalling this, Sister smiles, "I gave every reason why I didn't think it would be possible and then, and I can only think the Holy Spirit took a hand in this, said, 'okay, I'll go.'"

Back she went to her community and told the others she had an opportunity to visit a school for a week. "The Franciscan Sisters in Oregon have a Montessori school. It will be helpful for my professional development to see how it functions." Her community being educationally minded not only agreed that she go but also paid her plane fare.

Sister Mary Coleman and Sister Patricia met her at the airport. Her arrival at the house affected her deeply.

"I knew right away this was special. Then instead of having me stay at the main house, I was given space at the gatehouse. With time alone, in the evenings, I walked the land, reflected, prayed and with tears did much soul searching. Why am I here? What does God want from me?"

During the days, Sister Kathleen Ann visited the school. "I loved it all. The day-care program was in operation and I was sent to observe. I sat with one young fellow and asked him if he wanted me to read to him. Well, he gave me such a look. 'I can read!' He didn't need me."

This watershed week in Sister Kathleen Ann's life was a busy one. She spent hours with Mother Francine discussing Catholic education, education and the needs of children and their families. Both found they shared many of the same ideals, aspirations, dreams, and visions about education.

"I was deeply moved by this experience. I knew I must search to find where God was leading me and how I could best serve Him."

She returned to Meriden and continued administering a school. The year was one of soul searching, hours of prayer, reflection and consultation with her colleagues. With the direction and guidance of both communities, she responded to her call.

"I chose freely to transfer to the Franciscan Sisters of the Eucharist with the blessing of the Church, following the three-year process as outlined by the Church and the two religious communities."

She found it extremely difficult departing from the Sisters of St. Joseph and it was hard for them when she responded to the promptings of her call from the Holy Spirit. This was a whole new development for the F.S.E. community.

Upon entering the Bridal Veil community, she became the Associate Administrator of the Franciscan Montessori Earth School, bringing her special skills and talents to the already well-established educational program in progress.

She wasn't long at Bridal Veil before she realized the need to raise funds for their various projects. "I took eggs to school and sold them for a dollar a dozen. Then one day working in the peacock pen, I thought that maybe I could sell some of their beautiful feathers and make a bit of money. I picked up about twenty and next day started on my journey as a salesperson."

She thought florists might be a place to start. In and out of five different shops she went. Opening the door of the sixth, she walked in and began her sales pitch. This time she was successful. "I sold five feathers! At $2.00 each. I'd discovered a small but useful way of adding to our income."

She happened to turn a corner and there right in front of her eyes was, The Peacock Cleaners. "I just knew that our feathers would add to their decor." The cleaners didn't need or want the feathers. She kept on with the fifteen remaining feathers, now losing something of their allure.

"I know, I'll try the Oregon Craft and Floral Company." She wasn't talking out loud, just keeping herself company as she walked the streets. Into the Oregon Craft and Floral Company she strode, looking purposeful. As purposeful as someone can clutching fifteen peacock feathers.

The receptionist greeted the visitor. It's not everyday a Sister in a brown habit walks in selling feathers. "I don't think we're in the market right now," she said.

Nothing daunted, Sister Kathleen Ann pitched her best line, "We have a peacock farm and we could supply you with feathers."

A man came from one of the back rooms. "I have feathers for sale from our peacock farm. We'd like to supply you."

He looked at the fifteen feathers. "M'am we buy those by the thousands and we've just received a big shipment. Sorry we're not buying."

"Well, here is my card. Please call if we can be of service." With that, she decided that there wasn't a big market for peacock feathers and so ended that line of work.

Sister Kathleen Ann fits in well at Bridal Veil. With her boundless energy and exuberant personality, she's a true Franciscan in her ability to work hard and long at whatever tasks she undertakes.

It was 1980 when Mother Alfredine came to stay with the Sisters. A tiny woman, well into her seventies at the time; she was retired from her years of teaching all over the United States, including Alaska. She was in the early stages of Parkinson's disease. This didn't stop her helping out at the school and the house but eventually her health deteriorated and slowly her physical strength began to ebb. She loved people and loved parties. She always appeared at the yearly Benefit Ball until she could no longer sit up.

Until she died in June 1990, she was tenderly nursed by the Sisters. For many years, they took turns caring for her during the night. But when she required more care and all the Sisters had daytime jobs, they hired a night nurse.

Mother Michael and Mother Margaret were carefully feeding her lunch one day when suddenly she began to choke. With presence of mind Mother Michael ran to the upstairs phone and called Ed Grenfell, Connie's husband, and a fireman trained in first aid. Ed was on a day off and just leaving the house when the phone rang. He was across the road and racing upstairs in minutes.

"I'm not a religious man but when I saved Mother Alfredine's life when she was choking, I felt as though God was in that room with me. It was the strangest feeling. I had never experienced God before."

For the Sisters, the presence of God in their lives is a given and God's presence is manifest in people like Ed Grenfell, their Saturday Work Party friends, all the wonders of the natural world and the joy that permeates everything they do.

As with any group of people living in close community, there are stresses and strains that have to be clarified and worked through. Sister Kathleen Ann was speaking with a friend one day whose marriage was breaking up with much rancor and bitterness.

"I just wish I could live in a convent like you do where everything is nice and peaceful."

Sister hooted with laughter. "You should try living with nine other women, especially when we're trying to make a decision about something and we all have strong opinions about how to deal with it."

Challenges and Responses

The area around the gatehouse needed a good cleanup and Sister Patricia decided to rake up all the leaves and broken branches and twigs from the trees. She set to work and soon had a huge pile ready to burn. There was no danger of the fire spreading, she'd taken care to keep the pile well away from the trees. What she didn't know was, a permit to burn trash is required by the Forest Service. She lit the pile and had it burning nicely when she heard sirens blaring.

"There must be an accident on the highway," was her first thought, "I hope it's not serious."

With the sirens coming closer, she realized the emergency vehicle was on their stretch of road and ran to the gate to have a look. A fire truck turned into the driveway. A ranger from the fire service jumped out.

"What do you think you're doing, don't you know you need..." and he stopped in mid-sentence. He was face to face with an innocent looking nun and for a moment was speechless.

Better he tell the story. This is Tim. "I met the Sisters when there was a report of a fire at Bridal Veil, my territory. We roared out with the fire truck and found a nun burning trash illegally in the front yard of the property. What am I to do? I can't give a ticket to a nun!

So I said to her. 'Well Sister, you need a burning permit,' then we helped her put out the fire."

"The Sisters were really nice and invited me to come back for dinner in a couple of weeks. It was marvelous. A whole baked salmon laid out very nicely, entertaining conversation and great hospitality. I brought one of my crew with me. I've been friends with the Sisters ever since."

Tim has become a regular at the Saturday Work Parties. He takes on special projects for them. "There are a couple of things I really enjoy and it gives me enormous pleasure to do them."

Tim and another ranger were hiking up Larch Mountain on a snowy winter day. "We had crampons, carried ice axes, ropes, full outfits. The snow began to blow and then up ahead on the trail I saw of couple of the Sisters in their brown habits. I thought, what are the Sisters doing up here on a day like this. I was concerned about their safety so we began to hurry after them. Somehow we lost them! They were moving so fast we couldn't catch up. Later when I asked them about being up there, they said they were just hiking and enjoying being outside. I couldn't believe it. This was before the young Sisters came. These were women in their late forties or early fifties."

Another Franciscan Sister arrived in late 1984 to teach at the school. Sister Anne Clare is Montessori trained. An American, she received some of her education in Europe and is fluent in several languages. She, Sisters Janet and Kathleen Ann are younger that the others in the community and are especially welcome. Dedicated young Sisters coming to Bridal Veil are essential for the community to grow and thrive.

A project the Sisters began to mull over at their weekly meetings was the need for a cemetery on the site. They brought George Erdenberger into their discussions and asked his opinion as to the best location. Ever sensitive to their needs, he gave each of them an outline sketch of the property and asked them to take some time and fill in where they thought the cemetery should be. Also, to draw other additions to the site. They'd been talking about a barn and garden plots, and to add those.

He also wanted them to think about putting in a separate road so they could drive their cars to a parking space at the back entrance of the house. They had limited access to that area by way of a makeshift gravel pathway branching off the main driveway near the fenced-in, disused swimming pool.

When they shared their sketches with the one George had done, there was almost complete agreement on where and how to make the desired changes. The cemetery plan was put on hold while they pondered the building of the barn mentioned earlier. The goats needed proper housing and Rosa, one of the original three, was pregnant. She'd been bred with an animal from another flock. Not only did the animals need shelter, the Sisters were in desperate need of storage space for their tools, hay and straw. Water lines had to be brought to the barn area.

In the field south of the gatehouse was a pile of stones, the remains of the foundation and fireplace of the small house built for Kathryn Reynolds by her brothers.

Sometime in the checkered past of the property, the house had been destroyed. Much of the stone was covered in weeds and vines. This pile of rubble was known, for some obscure reason, as Pig Hill. Not to waste this good stone, the builders of the goat barn used it to shore up the foundation. The land is on a down slope and the Pig Hill stones found their final resting place anchoring the barn to the lower edge of the slope.

The barn was built south of the gatehouse and it was here that Mother Francine's first goat gave birth to twins. And it was down to this barn at six o'clock every morning that Mother, cup of coffee in hand, made her way to milk Rosa. To a woman not enamoured of those early hours, this was a true labor of love. Besides there was no one else to do it. After all, Rosa was her goat.

An Unexpected Visitor

"Did you hear a knock at the door?" Mother Michael turned to Mother Margaret.

"I'm not sure. Maybe it was one of the dogs."

"I'd better check in case someone is there." She went to the front door first and finding no one there, hurried to the back. Standing there was a tall, good looking young man.

"Can I help you?" she asked, stepping outside.

"Excuse me, M'am. I was wondering if I could go up and see the falls?"

"Sure, go ahead." The Sisters were becoming more than a little annoyed at the numbers of total strangers driving up to their home, stopping to stare and then leaving, as though their driveway was a public road. Some even got out of their cars and walked around without the courtesy of asking permission.

Mother Michael liked the look of the young man and his polite manner. She returned to the kitchen. Fifteen minutes later another knock at the door.

Back she went and there he was again. This time with an apology.

"I owe you an apology Sister. I didn't tell you why I wanted to see the falls." Mother walked outside with him. "You see I used to live here when my grandmother owned the place."

"You did!" Her pleasure at meeting someone who could fill in some of the history of the house was plain to see. "Who was your grandmother?"

"Kathryn Reynolds."

"Well, for heavens sake, come on in and have some coffee. Mother Margaret will want to meet you. By the way, I'm Mother Mary Michael," and she went ahead of him to the kitchen.

Their visitor was Michael Collier, sergeant in the United States Marines, home on leave from Okinawa. He told them about his grandmother, what a wonderful person she was and the kind of healing work she did. The Sisters had heard many wild rumors about Mrs. Reynolds, all without substance and totally unfounded.

Michael walked through the main floor with the Sisters and was shocked to see what had happened to the beautiful ballroom ceiling and balconies.

It wasn't his last visit to the house. Whenever he was home on leave, he visited Bridal Veil. He loved the place. Being there brought back wonderful memories of his beloved grandmother.

The Return Of The Madonna

The beautiful painting, *The Madonna of the Chair* that Louise Lawrence purchased in Italy in 1926 was soon to return to its original place on the west wall of the ballroom-living room. Henry Day Ellis, a friend of the Lawrences, had acquired the painting when Louise Lawrence sold the Bridal Veil property in 1946. Mr. Ellis had presented it to Marylhurst College where it had been hanging ever since. When he learned that the Franciscan Sisters were establishing their foundation in the house he had known so well in the past, he asked the Sisters at the College if he might return the painting to its original setting. He planned to replace it with a tapestry woven by The World Tapestry Alliance, Inc. to reflect the life of Sister Miriam Theresa whom he wished to honor. An indepth study of the Sister's life was undertaken and a colorful tapestry depicting her many achievements was woven by a master weaver. It reflected the Aubusson tradition.

The return of the Madonna gave the Bridal Veil Sisters a piece of art which they could never have afforded. This beautiful painting is a source of joy to the Sisters and their friends. Part of the joy is having something back in the house that is part of its history.

A Diversion, the Ducks, Raccoons, a Rescue

With the barn built, the Sisters turned their attention to planning how and when to put in a separate driveway to the back of the house. The new road would have another use. For all the well-attended events held at the house, more parking spaces were needed. With their feel for the land and especially for the beautiful Douglas firs, they were going to have to make some tough decision. Perhaps some trees had to come down.

However, a minor disaster took them by surprise. Their septic system failed. Replacing it threw their various land-planning schemes into limbo. The Sisters are nothing if not flexible. They called in expert help. First on the list of things to do, dig out the old system. It was in the field behind the gatehouse. A man with a backhoe came to clear it. While he was there and handy, the Sisters asked him to scoop out a big area behind the new barn and close to the gorge wall. They wanted a duck pond.

Although the machine moved most of the earth, the Sisters and their friends did a lot of the digging by themselves. Into the muddy mess they went and when the area was prepared, they laid the septic system—with some expert guidance. Not content with that back-breaking labor, Sisters Mary Coleman, Janet and Kathleen Ann finished digging out what was going to be the duck pond.

"Boy, I'll never forget that!" Sister Janet winces at the thought. "And before we had recovered from that, we decided to put in a whole underground water system. You know what that means? We had to dig long, narrow trenches from the stream by the main house, and then, we had to lay the pipe! Of course, George was there helping and making sure we did it right."

"And," declared Sister Mary Coleman, "to give us water in different places around the grounds, we put in stand pipes." She was enthusiastic about this piping system they'd engineered. When she responded to a call from another Center in Michigan in 1988 to take over the duties of a teacher stricken with cancer, she wrote to say that she missed everyone and especially missed the water system.

The Ducks

No sooner was the duck pond filled with water when ducks arrived on the scene. Mostly white domestic ducks but with some exotic Chinese ducks, they paddled happily in their new home and nested in their own coop.

Within a year the ducks were laying eggs and attempting to hatch ducklings. Not content with the nests provided they flew through the open barn windows, making themselves right at home. Up in the loft one adventurous duck set up house, laid her eggs and sat on them.

This was not part of the duck plan the Sisters had in mind. So up climbed a Sister, removed the eggs, took them to the coop, hoping the duck would sit there. That didn't work. The windows were screened to keep them out.

Before long, marauding raccoons discovered a sitting duck. Going down early one morning to feed her chickens and ducks, Mother Margaret found a bloody mess. A raccoon had come in the night, killed the duck and eaten the eggs. The poor mother duck had put up a struggle and was torn to pieces.

This was not to be borne. The ducks must be protected. The Sisters had a conference. Ed Grenfell had a rifle. They asked to borrow it. Sisters Kathleen Ann and Mary Coleman said they'd sit up all night and shoot the raccoon if it returned.

Ed brought over his rifle. Neither Sister had ever handled a gun much less fired one. Ed taught them how.

He put a target on a tree and Sister Mary Coleman on her first try hit it dead center. Their target was a matchbook cover. Sister Kathleen Ann is left-handed but got off a good shot, hitting the edge of the target.

"Hey, you're pretty good." Ed laughed at the picture of Sisters firing his rifle. "That raccoon better not fool around with you guys."

The night was cold and the Sisters sat in the old rabbit hutch, now empty of rabbits. They were freezing. Close to midnight they heard a noise, saw the raccoon go into the barn. They waited and waited for it to emerge but it must have found another way out. They missed it and decided to go to bed. They were shivering from the chill night air.

The ducks were left in peace until July 1987 when another mother duck was torn to bloody bits and her eggs eaten. The rifle was borrowed again. Sister Mary Coleman said she'd tackle the animal on her own. Sister Kathleen Ann had a meeting next morning and needed a night's sleep.

July is the month for the F.S.E. annual retreat and this year it was the turn of the Bridal Veil community to host the event. Visiting Sisters were accommodated in the roomy, three bedroom, upper gatehouse apartment. The apartment below was given over to a priest, the retreat master.

Mother Francine decided to stay on guard with Sister Mary Coleman and lie in wait for the raccoon. By midnight with no sign of the animal, she decided to go to bed. The retreat master came out and offered to keep a lookout with the rifle toting nun. At 2 a.m. they heard a noise in the tree nearest the barn. The priest shone a flashlight showing up a raccoon on a high branch

"Here you hold the flashlight Sister and give me the gun. I can shoot." By this time two of the Sisters staying in the gatehouse had come out to see what was happening. Mother Shaun and Mother Rosemae thought Mother Francine should be in on this so Mother Rosemae hurried back upstairs to phone the main house.

She dialed and a sleepy voice answered. "Hello." Mother Rosemae in a dignified voice, thinking her colleague was half asleep, "Are you ready to catch the coon?"

There was a stunned silence. Mother Rosemae thinking Mother Francine was only half awake declared, "This is Mother Rosemae. Come on wake up!"

With that an aggrieved voice at the other end announced, "I THINK YOU HAVE THE WRONG NUMBER!" and hung up.

Nothing daunted, she tried again and this time roused Mother Francine and down she came. "I could see the raccoon's eyes shining in the light."

The retreat master holding the rifle and pointing it up the tree called, "Tell me where it is." He'd forgotten to put on his glasses when he came out and couldn't see.

Sister Mary Coleman took the rifle and got a shot away. The raccoon dropped to a lower limb. Now hidden behind some leafy branches it was out of her sight. Sister held her fire. Part of her wanted to finish off the animal and another part just wanted to teach it a lesson. To put the fear of God or the Sisters into it if possible.

In the general turmoil after the firing of the rifle a frightened chicken escaped from the coop and flew way up to the top of the peacock enclosure. It clung to the wire mesh seeming unable to move.

One of the younger Sisters staying in the gatehouse bent on rescuing the stranded chicken from its perilous perch began climbing the side of the enclosure. The wire swayed as she inched her way up. Reaching the top, she lay on her stomach and slowly slid across the sagging wire. The chicken clucked frantically as she caught it.

Getting up was one thing; bringing a struggling chicken back was another. This was not a tiny, compact woman. She was tall and slim. Backing up the way she came, she eased herself across the wire and handed the bird to another Sister who had climbed up to help.

"Whew, that's enough excitement for one night. Let's go to bed." Mother Francine figured that early morning prayers would arrive all too soon for the intrepid hunters and rescuers.

Awakening early, one of the Sisters in the gatehouse who had slept through the hunt and rescue operation picked up her habit where she'd hung it the night before. She looked at it with amazement. It was dirty. Threads were pulled. It was a mess.

"Who's been wearing my habit?" She sounded like one of the three bears in Goldilocks. It was her newest. The chicken-rescuing Sister wakened with a start. She looked at her friend's soiled brown habit.

"Oh, oh! You're not going to believe this but I crept out of here in the dark last night and grabbed my habit from the closet, and after Sister shot the raccoon, I climbed up on the peacock enclosure to rescue a chicken," she paused to catch her breath. "I guess I grabbed your habit by mistake."

"Run that one by me again. You were doing what last night?" In her wildest imaginings, she couldn't get her mind around what her friend was doing on top of the peacock pen, in the middle of the night, catching a chicken.

"Well, it was like this." And she told her about the rifle, the raccoon, the shot and the chicken. "I'm really sorry about your habit. Let me have it and I'll wash it and fix it up." They laughed as they examined the forlorn garment.

"It's more dirty than anything else so I guess you're forgiven. Only the next time you decide to do something crazy in the middle of the night, make sure you're wearing your own clothes." She was still smiling as she walked up to the main house for prayers.

The raccoon disappeared without a trace and for three years none came by to rampage through the ducks. "I think," said Mother Francine, "word must have gone out in raccoon land, 'don't mess with those Sisters. Stay away from those nuns or they'll get a gun and they'll get you!'"

Two Major Projects

With the septic system in place, the Sisters turned their attention to planning the cemetery. They decided to locate it where Louise Lawrence had her cutting garden. However the community could not put a cemetery on the property without permission from the county authorities. They required a lawyer to lead them through the process. Fortunately, one of the Earth School board members was a young lawyer and he agreed to handle the legal work.

The Sisters who could be spared from their tasks were on hand with their lawyer for the hearing. The proceedings went along without a hitch until one item made them blink.

"You realize," said a county official, "that the cemetery must be in use within two years or you'll have to renew your application."

Their lawyer turned to look at the assembled nuns sitting behind him, "Who volunteers to go first?" Even the officials laughed. The Sisters had their cemetery plans approved.

They laid it out in a square with intersecting gravel paths to form a cross. Grass was seeded by one of the Saturday Work Party women. Margaret Patricia seemed to have a special knack for growing grass from seed. She had reseeded the lawns at the front of the house and thought her help might be needed to reseed the "bowling green" lawn. It was being dug up to put in a sprinkler system.

Margaret Patricia is an old, albeit young, friend of the Sisters, "I've known them for twelve years. My two daughters went to the Earth School. I love coming to the Work Parties. It's like a ritual. Everybody gathers on the third Saturday and I enjoy working with all the people here. In a sense, it's like being part of something bigger than me. As though we're all together for a united reason. These Sisters represent the real Catholic Church and being in tune with them is like being in tune with the church all over the world."

While she's speaking, she's also catching her breath. A big digging project is going on. The bowling green lawn is a muddy mess as the Work Party digs trenches to install the sprinkler system. Margaret Patricia is muddy up to her knees as are all the others.

She looks down at her dirty clothes, "Look at me. I'm filthy from being in the dirt yet I enjoy it all. There's something special about working on this land. We come together and work on these grounds and it's not just for the Sisters, it's for all of us who come here and will be coming here. For me belonging to the church is working, playing and praying together.

"Somehow planting grass and flowers and digging in the dirt makes me more human and knowing the Sisters has given me an opportunity to know more about who I am."

Margaret Patricia is a nutritionist. She works in a hospital. She is involved with cardiac patients educating them about proper diet and exercise. "In our society we have diseases of over consumption and isn't it ironic we also have poor nutrition. I don't like to keep telling my patients not to eat this or that. I look at the problem in a deeper way, a more cosmic way."

"It's as though by over consuming, we take more of the world's natural resources than our bodies need, then they react with different disease states."

"There's a need for balance between work, play, and prayer and these are related nutritional concerns. I look at a human body and see what it requires for fuel, then I discuss that with the patient."

She began shovelling dirt as she continued, "my work in the hospital with patients is related in a way to what we're doing here on the land. There's a health about this place that has come through a lot of effort. No habitat is being taken away. The Sisters are not stripping the land to make way for something that doesn't belong. Everything is in the natural order of things."

"Even though we do a lot of work restoring the gardens to their original formal design, there is a wild, informal boundary to the property. We're human beings creating something for other people to enjoy and this gives me a sense of being part of something bigger than myself."

Her feelings were echoed by other members of the Work Party. M.J., as Mary Jane is always called, was busy with the leaf-raking crew. She's known the Sisters for twelve years.

"This is such a beautiful spot and there's a sense of belonging. The work is fun, even raking leaves! Everything is well organized and we accomplish things as we're working and being really appreciated. The Sisters are very generous with what they have and they let us claim ownership of what we're doing."

"They trust us. We're given responsibilities and we accomplish something important. I feel as though I own a little piece of the land I'm standing on." Then M.J. smiled, "And the social events are great and the people who work here are really nice."

Road Building

No project seems too difficult for the Work Party volunteers to handle. Stoop labor at the trout pond, digging out the field for the septic system, laying the water lines, all are done with great community spirit and much laughter as the Sisters and their friends toil together.

After lunch on one of the work Saturdays, George presented a new challenge.

"We need more parking spaces on the site as you know." His listeners nodded in agreement, "Also the Sisters think that some day the swimming pool should be renewed, not for swimming so don't get your hopes up." Groans all around.

"We've got a kind of long-term plan to put a greenhouse over it and keep water in the pool for extra fire protection. But that's not for awhile yet."

"That bit of gravel road that cuts in front of the pool to the Sisters' parking space at the back of the house will go. I've drawn up a plan that puts a new road cutting away from the main driveway. It'll loop around the back of the pool and come up close to the gorge wall, then to the house."

He unrolled his sketch for the group to study.

"Okay, George, what do we have to do?" This was Buzz Gilbert, retired in his early fifties, a man who radiates physical energy and works without tiring from morning to night.

"Well, we have a problem."

"George, if it means digging up another field forget it!" Sister Kathleen Ann turned to the others, "Don't you agree?"

"No, it's not a field," and George grinned at them, "we have to dig the roadbed. By hand."

"Come on, you've got to be kidding," Sister Janet wondered how everyone else was feeling. "Do you think he's serious?"

"Now just wait a minute while I tell you the problem. You haven't heard that yet."

"Okay, let's hear it," Sister sat back with a smile.

George continued. "Along the back of the property is a pipeline. It runs right alongside where we want to build the road. Inside the pipe is a cable, a transcontinental cable, and if we damage it in any way, repairs start at $10,000. If we bring in a backhoe or some other heavy equipment, it will hit the cable for sure. And, not to worry, you won't have to dig the whole roadbed, only the part beside the gorge wall."

Angie, an old Work Party hand, asked the important question. "How long is that part?"

"Oh, about a hundred yards, give or take a yard or two."

"And we have to dig this out?" Dave looked at George's sketch. "When do you want us to start?"

"Any time. Who wants to volunteer?" George thought he'd better give them a chance to cop out. With much dramatic moaning about sore backs and blistered hands, they all said they'd do it, all except Bethany Franceschi. She was excused; she was expecting her fourth child.

"Great. We'll get started next Work Day. I think we've got enough shovels but if you have one, bring it along."

George gazed at his motley crew on the appointed day. The younger Sisters in their long jean skirts and shirts, men and women of various ages and sizes, and a group of their children ready to carry away stones.

"I've put marker posts and run string along where the road edges will be. I've kept them well away from the cable so we shouldn't have any problem."

Sister Janet picked up her shovel, slung it over her shoulder and announced to the group, "You know what we look like. A chain gang." Then grinning at George, "I hope you don't have a whip to crack over our heads if we slack off."

With his own shovel in hand ready for work, George gave her suggestion a little thought, "Say I didn't think of that but maybe Mother Michael wouldn't go for it."

The workers were now in high good humor and in lock step, marched off to dig the road.

George is amazed at what they accomplished. "In half a day, we had the road roughed in. On the next Work Day, we ordered in fill and gravel. That all had to be put down and levelled off and we did all that. What pleased the Sisters though was that only two trees were taken down to bring in this new road and to create more parking spaces."

Walking the land with George Erdenberger is to have a lesson in spiritual ecology. "The sense of place here is a very deep feeling. There's a need to preserve special places like this house and this land. It has a soul as the Indians believe."

"The Sisters have set aside a piece of the natural world. It is sacred in a way. It is here to enjoy, not to use in the sense of taking and not giving anything back. They

Building the road

have given it back love and care. A sacred using of the land."

George and his wife, Georgia have close ties with the Bridal Veil community though neither is Catholic. "Think of the lives this place has touched, a touching of people's souls and that's a basic human need. And there's an unconditional acceptance by the Sisters. You are accepted here knowing there is an unspoken framework. We don't intrude on the Sisters' private lives and they don't intrude on ours unless asked to do so."

"And there's something else. We've isolated ourselves in our jobs, our cars, our homes but at Bridal Veil there is a sense of accomplishment, of being a real part of something, something that we are creating that will be here long after we're long gone.

"Remember the Sisters are Franciscans. St. Francis' life was about rebuilding the church, returning it to its origins. It was no accident the way the Sisters responded when they first saw the sadly neglected house and the land left desolate and alone. They knew instinctively that the house was well crafted, that underlying the pall of neglect was something worth saving and preserving for the future."

The Franciscan Montessori Earth School in Danger

Early in 1988 the Sisters were hit with a bombshell that gave them months of unease. Something they could do nothing about except pray. Their precious school in which they had toiled and brought up to enviable academic standards was in danger. The school buildings and its ground were leased. In 1988 with two more years to run on the lease, a religious organization began to make inquiries about purchasing the facility for their own school.

Representatives came to look around and liked what they saw. Little wonder, since the Franciscans had made their classrooms, offices, cafeteria and kitchen as near to perfection as possible. Students and teachers alike reflected the quality of their environment.

For Mother Francine whose life work as an innovative educator is bound up in the school she created from scratch, the days weeks and months of uncertainty were never ending.

"You just can't imagine how awful it was. We had no money to buy the school. With all the upgrading we'd done, the place was worth over a million dollars. We knew the group wanting to buy it had the money and we had nothing."

As the months crept by with the community and all their friends praying that the school would remain in their hands, the tension began to ease. The Sisters were finally put out of their misery when the interested buyers decided against the purchase.

With this crisis behind them, they realized that for the school to remain in its present location meant having to think about finding money to buy it.

They'd have to get into the big league of money raising. For women who had always relied on themselves to raise needed cash, the prospect was frightening. Cleaning offices, working in factories, benefit balls, Villas, Valentine luncheons were small potatoes in terms of money earned.

They turned to their Mother House in Connecticut for help in solving this dilemma. It was obvious that professional assistance was needed to sort out their financial requirements and the big question, how to go about raising the necessary funds.

It fell to Mother Francine as head of the Earth School to become educated in how to raise large sums of money. The amount required to purchase the school building and surrounding thirteen acres to meet the goals of the school and beyond was set at $1,500,000. A staggering sum of money for Sisters used to dealing in more human-sized dollars and cents.

To put such a project into a well-designed form took two years. The Sisters were now committed to a capital campaign. The goal of the first phase was to raise $500,000 needed to secure the present site and to set the stage for the next $1,000,000 required to complete the purchase and ensure future program development. The autumn of 1990 was the date set for the start of their fund raising. The Sisters hopes were high. Never lacking in courage, they were going into this important venture with the same dedication they bring to all their activities.

"The philosophy of the Franciscan Montessori Earth School includes the belief that all children are born with a drive to develop themselves. Children learn best from their own physical activity and senses if given freedom to explore and create in an enriched environment with supportive guidance based on observation of the child's interests and needs. As a result, educational experiences must vary in kind and degree in order that each student's unique potential may be challenged." Mother Francine is eloquent when she speaks about the school.

Notwithstanding their anxieties about losing their school building and then having to become involved in the tremendous effort to raise money to buy it, work continues apace at Bridal Veil. The animal barn didn't have enough storage space for the various pieces of equipment now required for the work being done on the site.

One important piece of machinery is a snowplow. Clearing the long driveway after an east wind has dumped mountains of snow is virtually impossible to attack by hand. It was done by hand during the first winter, after that the Sisters knew they couldn't cope and bought a snowplow.

As the various projects fell into place shovels, rakes, hoes, forks, wheelbarrows had to be housed. A tool shed was built.

To hear the Work Party volunteers tell it, this was a real "fun" time. "I remember shovelling gravel and shovelling gravel," groaned Joe. "It was like the magic rice bowl in the old fairy tale. I didn't think we were ever going to get to the end of it."

"And what about all that concrete we mixed and moved around?" Helen had been coming to the Work Parties from day one. She thrived on the work and seeing their efforts bear fruit. "I'm just glad I didn't have to build the thing."

The actual carpentry was left to the men with the necessary skills. It took from March to the following November to finally complete the barn. Somehow in the reworking of their plans, it had grown from a tool shed to a fair sized barn and was named after Mother Michael's father who was a railway man. Known as the Bartley Shed, his old railway insignia circles his name right above the door..

The Bartley Shed is a dual purpose building. The Earth School has a two-week summer program as well as other farm experience outings for the students. To accommodate their needs, a child size washbasin and washroom were added. All these changes on the land have to be approved by a specially appointed state committee to ensure developments in the Gorge area do not harm its natural beauty.

The Sisters also created a classroom in part of the lower gatehouse where the Jacobsons once kept their three cars. Bridal Veil is a wonderfully child centered place. Two neighbor boys, Taylor Grenfell and Benjamin Franceschi are allowed to hurtle down the driveway on bikes or skateboards. Babes in arms, toddlers, older children and teenagers arrive on Work Party Saturdays with their parents. There's always someone around to look after a baby or a two-year-old while their parents work. The Sisters have collected playpens and highchairs from here and there so the children can be cared for safely.

Once a year, the third Saturday in November, the Sisters prepare a magnificent Thanksgiving dinner for all their friends who've helped restore the land, dig roads, septic systems, build barns, clean ponds, plant the rose garden and rake leaves, etc.

George Erdenberger having been given the responsibility of organizing the various developments on the site, gives the assembled, turkey dinner-filled group a description of what they've accomplished the past year, using a flip chart to give visual impact to his words.

It's a very special occasion when memories are shared. The Sisters and their friends have created an unusual community where good feelings abound. This is something they have done together. The work has sometimes been easy, sometimes hard, usually dirty, wet on rainy days, and month after month, year after year, the people arrive ready to do whatever is asked of them. Some come a few times, the odd one or two turn up for one day and never return but most, like the Sisters, are there for the long haul. How does it happen?

The question was posed by my husband on one of our visits to Bridal Veil. We were sitting around after dinner talking about what had been done since 1980 (when the Work Parties started) and how it had been done.

"Do the other F.S.E. communities have the same facility in recruiting volunteers as you do?" He was teasing which brought loud laughs from the Sisters and almost as a chorus they called out. "Yes they do!"

Bill pressed on, "Is this something they teach in school, the kind of non-directive direction you are expert in?" He still remembers cleaning eavestroughs, trying to start an ancient and balky lawnmower that had seen better days and being sent off, he swears, halfway to the coast, to pick up their photocopier, in for repairs.

When Mother Francine stopped laughing, she said, "Yes that's part of who we are." Since that didn't satisfy, Mother Michael chimed in.

"It's the Franciscan way of begging. Francis was a beggar so when you're needy you go and ask for things and that's what we ask for and that's what we get."

This prompted Mother Francine to say more. "In India beggars have a begging bell. That makes a sound to say they are in need. While we don't actually say it, the need is there. And there's a reciprocal need and that's what draws people."

For Sister Kathleen Ann, "It's a person to person contact. One is attracted and meets another and that's the way people are drawn together. It's hard to explain but there's nourishment for body and soul while we're out there working. There's a sharing and our friends go back feeling ten times better and we've also been nourished by their presence and gained something from it. So people keep coming back."

The community added two new members in 1988. Sister Karen Marie, a soil scientist found a job in a Portland laboratory. Sister Karol Marie is a teacher with special qualifications to work at the Earth School. Both are young and full of energy. They arrived at Bridal Veil just in time to hear George announce the next grand project.

"We're going to put in the rose garden!"

With years of experience behind them, none of the volunteers was under any illusion that this would be an easy task. They all knew the original site of the garden. It was now a miserable looking weed strewn disaster. The Sisters had some small success planting flowers there but since it was to be resurrected as the rose garden, they let the flowers go.

The rose garden as planned by the Jacobsons is below the level of the bowling green as the ground slopes towards the river. Centered by the pineapple fountain, steps lead down either side to the garden. The fountain facing the rose garden has the face of Poseidon, Greek god of the sea, set into the wall.

"What we have to do first is clear the area of weeds," George has his crew in tow, "then dig it all up turn over the soil, add peat moss and prepare it for the roses." Not wanting to delude them about the extent of the work, he added. "And we also have to dig out and lay down a gravel pathway around the garden and crisscrossing it."

The workers had been refreshed with coffee and sweet rolls on their arrival and would have a delicious hot lunch from Mother Margaret's kitchen at the end of their morning's labor. In the warm weather, she brings out

Work Party

ice-cold lemonade and everyone has a chance to take a break, lean on a shovel or sit in the dirt.

With their usual communal spirit, the laborers bent to their task. Many Saturdays passed before the garden was ready for planting. Gravel was wheelbarrowed up from where it had been dumped at the side of the driveway and raked smoothly on the paths. Hours of toil went into giving the roses a home.

Unique rose bushes were given by friends to com-memorate special events or as a memorial to someone who had died. The sprinkler system was put in place before the paths were laid. The last item added to the center of the garden was the original marble birdbath that once graced the middle of the bowling green lawn. Somehow it had survived from its Jacobson's origins down through the years, a piece of garden history in the midst of the beautiful roses.

For the Sisters and their friends, bringing this garden back to life was a joy. It was a thing of beauty to be savored. So much of the work over the years were practical projects. The rose garden was an absolute visual delight.

Goats

Rosa, Mother Francine's first goat had a difficult time giving birth to twin kids. She was never completely well after the delivery. Needing special care, she was not bred again.

As for the twins, they bounced around the field doing their best to keep away from Israel. He butted the frisky kids at every opportunity sending them tumbling. The Sisters decided that four goats were enough. A home had to be found for the two little billygoats.

What to do with them? The dilemma solved itself. A young couple bought a house a couple of miles from Bridal Veil, on the Crown Point Highway. It wasn't long before Pat and Ellen Brothers became friends of the Sisters. They liked goats and had a large property.

"We'll take them." Pat thought that having two goats for pets was a great idea. The Brothers treated the goats like pet dogs. They did, however, draw the line about having them in the house. There were cozy stalls in their small barn. The twins now wore collars with their names inscribed. Casey and Francis liked nothing better than to go walking with Pat and Ellen, each on a leash.

Seeing goats walking on the leash brought some rude remarks from passing motorists. "Hey, why don't you get a dog?" shouted one. Others slowed down to have a better look at this phenomenon. As for Casey and Francis, they were in goat heaven. When Pat and Ellen sat on their patio in the summer time, they'd snuggle up to them hoping for tidbits or some nice strokes.

The Brothers both worked and Ellen was now in line for a major promotion. This meant being away from home for three to four months. Pat's job was also taking him out of town during that time. What to do about their pets?

What else? The Sisters said they'd take them back and look after them. As it happened, my husband and I were visiting when it came time to collect Casey and Francis.

Sister Kathleen Ann, Mother Francine, Bill and I went in their station wagon to pick up the goats. Bleats and sad goat cries greeted us as we opened the barn door.

"Well, well, are you lonely then?" Sister Kathleen Ann's soothing words calmed them and we all petted them and talked baby goat talk as they were led to the car.

Mother Francine crawled into the back of the station wagon and the two half-grown goats were handed in to her. She held her arms around them as best she could and they, knowing a goat lover when they saw one, cuddled up, pressing against her and one ended up lying across her lap.

Sister Kathleen Ann began the drive back to the house while Mother Francine kept the goats company. She stroked and talked to them. I was leaning over the backseat entranced by this bizarre scene when she began a little prayer.

"Please God don't let them do anything. Please God keep everything inside them."

I burst out laughing, "Oh, my gosh, if they pee on you you are going to be in a mess!" Her prayer was answered. They didn't.

Put in the field with the other goats didn't please Israel. He butted and pushed them around. Even Rosa no longer recognized them. The little animals were on their own with no protection. Plainly this would not do. Israel might injure one or both.

A small fenced enclosure next to the peacock pen was fixed up for them. Bales of straw stacked on three sides with some boards for a roof made a shelter. They were provided with plenty of food and water. But these little creatures were miserable. They wanted out. They wanted to be petted. They wanted tasty tidbits. So they cried. When anyone came near the pen, they bleated so pitifully that whoever it was had to stop, pet them, scratch their ears, speak loving words and feed them little treats. To walk away was to hear their pitiful cries.

Slowly the goats became used to their temporary quarters and soon were tough enough to face Israel in the big field. He tired of the butting game and left them alone.

When the Brothers returned home, the twins left and another animal joined the brood. Not a goat this time, a Shetland pony.

"Oh, no, not a pony! We don't need a pony!" Mother Michael was doing her best to keep their animal kingdom under control. The Sisters were at their weekly meeting when the possibility of owning the pony came up. The fourteen-year-old animal was offered to them by a friend. He would come complete with harness, pony cart, everything a pony owner might desire.

"Who'll be responsible for it? Ponies need exercise. They have to be groomed, fed and watered. I think we've got all we can handle right now." Mother Michael looked around her community for support.

Before anyone had a chance to answer, Sister Karen Marie spoke up, "I'll take care of him." Then to add more punch to her statement. "When we have children visiting, I'll take them for rides in the pony cart."

"Now Sister, when will you have time. It takes an hour each way for you to drive to work. You leave early in the morning and get home late at night." Mother Michael's concern for this slightly built young Sister was obvious but she felt in her heart of hearts that she was going to lose this round. Sister Karen Marie is up at the crack of dawn every morning to go for a run, not a jog, a run for miles down the road. She had enough energy to cope with a fourteen-year-old pony after her day's work.

"But don't you think it will be fun for the children who come out on weekends to have pony rides and learn how to care for him."

Sister was touching a vulnerable nerve in her assembled colleagues. Where children were concerned, they liked nothing better than to give them opportunities to be with and handle animals.

"What do the rest of you think? Do we need a pony?" As she looked around she knew she had been outflanked by Sister Karen Marie. The assembled Sisters thought the gift of a pony with his accoutrements was just fine. Ever graceful in defeat, Mother, joined in welcoming the newcomer.

The pony, cart and harness came to the community in August 1989 just in time for our grandchildren, Fraser and Taylor, to ride off with Sister Karen Marie in the cart.

Juniper has a new name in keeping with his new home. He is called Juniper, after one of St. Francis' favorite disciples. Put to graze in the field with the goats, he crossed Israel's line of vision. Something new to intimidate. He came at Juniper with his classic butt attack. But Juniper was bigger than Israel and kicked at him. The stand-off lasted a few seconds and Israel tried again. The pony turned his back on the goat and kicked him hard with his hind hooves. That ended Israel's attacks on Juniper. Peace was declared after this skirmish. Intimidation only works on smaller and weaker subjects.

When the Earth School children arrived for their two weeks of summer school one of the Sisters' loyal friends,

Curt Von Ahn, came over to take the children for rides in the pony cart. Now retired from forty years with the United States Forest Service, Curt and his wife, Gerry, have spent hours at Bridal Veil with the Work Parties and helping at various social functions. Curt well remembers the making of the rose garden.

"We finished it in the rain." But for him after forty years in the Columbia Gorge area, a little rain didn't dampen his enthusiasm.

Juniper had plenty of exercise during summer school. Sister Karen Marie looked after his grooming and feeding at night. She was still running for miles down the road in the early, barely light, morning hours and this became a concern for Mother Michael and Mother Margaret. Visiting friends out for their morning exercise noticed young men alone, some acting strangely, one waving his arms and talking to himself. The road is a lonely place in the dark of the morning and evening. At a community meeting, the Sisters thought it best for her to find another way to exercise.

She solved the problem quickly and killed two birds with one stone. Both she and Juniper need exercise. With Juniper in tow, this young Sister races up and down the driveway, up the path to the falls her veil flying behind her and her brown habit slowing her not a whit.

All this running has energized Juniper and instead of standing around the field, head drooping as though asleep, he takes quick gallops, kicks up his heels, nudges Israel to get something going but Israel won't play. This frisky pony is too much for him.

The Way Ahead

Sister Patricia finished her training as a mortician and left to join their Mother House in Connecticut. Sister Mary Colemn, so far away in Michigan, seemed destined not to return to her beloved Bridal Veil. Her expertise as a teacher and adult educator filled a growing need in the Center she had joined. Everyone missed her and nourished the hope that one day she'd return to her home Center.

Sister Anne Clare's gifts were much in demand as a teacher of German and she responded to an invitation to lecture on the German language at a college in Montreal, Quebec. Scarcely was she back in Bridal Veil when she was asked to travel to Rome and become part of a Vatican-sponsored study into how the church might become more sensitive to various cultures around the world.

"She's a real academic and loves research. We're sorry to lose her but she'll be returning to us." Mother Michael hopes this is not wishful thinking. Her small community can ill afford to lose someone of Sister Anne Clare's caliber.

The "what will we do next" question is one that George addressed at the 1989 Thanksgiving dinner for the Work Party.

"We've been talking for years about redoing the patio behind the chapel. Those flagstones are uneven and a real hazard for anyone walking or sitting out there.

"Then there's the rock garden back there. It's still a bit of a jungle so I think we'd better tackle that next year.

"But what will happen if we run out of projects and there's nothing for the Work Parties to do?" For Mother Michael and the other Sisters, these Saturdays have become a very precious part of their lives. "We won't have anyone come out to see us!"

This brought loud laughter from the assembled group of well fed friends gathered in the ballroom. "Just try to keep us away!" This came from Michelle, a university student. A relatively new worker, her brother and sister attend the Earth School and she appreciates the education they're receiving. She is also candid about why she comes to the Work parties.

"I like the food. I get away from school food and it's really nice to help out. The atmosphere here is great. The Sisters do a lot for us and I guess I just like the way they are."

"Don't worry Mother, there'll always be lots of maintenance to keep us busy." George was laughing along with the others.

"And don't forget," Sister Kathleen Ann raised her voice to make everyone hear, "there's always the reservoir under the falls to be cleaned out every spring."

It was to her that two visiting children came running on a Work Party Saturday. "Sister guess what. There's a deer under the falls and it's dead!"

With the children running on ahead, she hurried after them up the path to the falls. And there was a deer, its head hanging over the reservoir wall, quite dead.

"Well, the poor thing. I guess it got too close to the edge up there and fell over."

"It must've been awful to do that. The falls are so high." The ten-year-old girl stared with horror at the water pouring over the top and pictured the animal tumbling down. She shivered. "What are we going to do Sister?"

"We've got to get it out of there, that's for sure. Come on, let's find Sister Janet and some of the men to help."

Dislodging the deer from its watery grave wasn't easy. It was a half-grown animal and most of its body was in the reservoir. Someone had to climb into the freezing cold water and push it out while the others pulled from the front. One of the men volunteered to be pusher and hoisted himself over the wall.

"Let's be quick or I'm going to freeze!" Up to his waist in the water, he was also being drenched with spray from the falls.

The children watched fascinated as the two Sisters and the other man standing in the stream tugged and pulled and finally dragged the deer out and flopped it on the ground.

"Boy that was hard." Sister Janet shook water from her skirt and listened to the water squelching in her sneakers. "Now what are we going to do with it?" They stood and looked at the once beautiful creature.

"That's going to need a big hole." Sister Kathleen Ann came up with an idea. "We've got those deep trenches we've dug for the water lines, let's dig one of them deeper and bury it there."

They weren't sure how the others would like this idea so they managed, with some stealth, to drag the carcass behind the house and while the workers were busy digging trenches down near the swimming pool, prepared a grave for the deer. It is buried somewhere. Its final resting place unmarked and mostly unknown.

Sister Kathleen Ann, once a city girl unused to hard physical labor, will climb into the reservoir herself to clear out the big rocks that fall from the top.

"It's great fun once you get used to the cold."

Is there nothing, I wonder, that these women will not do to preserve this land, this house and this waterfall with its tumbling stream rushing down to join up with the mighty Columbia River.

When they arrived in 1975, their only plan was to survive. And survive they have. The way they've survived is nothing short of a miracle. In their wildest dreams they never imagined the future that lay ahead. All they knew for sure is this. They are Franciscans. They know the meaning of hard, dedicated work. They have their firm and absolute faith in God. They are also blessed individually and collectively with the gift of humor. It has seen them through many a dark moment.

Looking back on those years, Mother Francine smiles, "We've never had anyone within the church hierarchy say we can't do this or that. 'By their fruits ye shall know them' and by our lifestyle, we've shown we belong heart and soul to the church and, in fact, are in the heart of the church."

She went on, "It's hard to put together in the minds of some Catholics that our wearing of a simple habit makes sense. It makes it hard for them to deal with us. We've created a kind of conundrum for one or two!"

"Some other women religious find it hard to deal with us because we wear a brown habit. They think we're a throwback. Well we tried civvies then a simple short brown dress and now we're in this long one."

"But doesn't wearing a distinctive habit set you apart and maybe people wonder why you're doing it? Couldn't it be seen as setting yourself up as something special. What does setting apart do for you?" I'm acting as a kind of devil's advocate yet am truly interested in their motivation.

Mother Michael picked this up, "It's just a way of being a witness. I think people need a witness to something. Take the time a couple of weeks ago when we were at the airport to meet another Sister and we passed a group of extremely well dressed people. One of the men turned to another and said, 'Isn't it good to see Sisters again.' I think people need to know we're still around."

"You symbolize something then?"

"Well, those people at the airport looked as though they had everything they could possibly want in this world. Why would they need to see Sisters and feel good about seeing them?"

"The witness part is really important," added Mother Francine, "as consecrated religious women who vow chastity being a witness is part of that vow. And we vow poverty as well. It's expensive to have a large wardrobe. What we have is a simple wardrobe. We've given ourselves to the Church and our energy goes into the work of the Church.

"This habit is a way of saying who I am but it doesn't define me as a person. The challenge to us in expressing who we are is much broader and goes beyond the fabric we wear." She also wanted to clarify something else.

"I don't want to imply that Sisters who wear secular clothes are any less devoted or committed to the Church. There are hundreds of dedicated religious women who have opted not to wear a habit. We are readily identifiable as Franciscans and we're seen all over the world. It's interesting to visit Italy, Jerusalem, Meriden and other places, and there we are."

"I was in a store the other day," Sister Kathleen Ann joined the conversation, "and a woman came up and said,'don't you work at the Corinthian Funeral Home?'

"No, I didn't, but Sister Patricia did. Then she went on, 'I recognized your habit. I heard Sister Patricia speak at one of the parishes and I've often thought how wonderful her talk was', so again, we're reminded about the witness of wearing the habit. And Sister Patricia's talk, the woman remembered was on death and dying.

"I think some Vatican II changes have been misunderstood to some degree. For some, it meant leaving off the habit they'd been wearing. It really meant to renew from within."

The Sisters find it easy to talk about themselves, their devotion to the Church, their witness to the faith, their professional work and the deep and abiding love they have for their friends. When asked how people become more at peace within themselves and more balanced by coming out and working on the land, Mother Michael has a simple reply:

"God uses people and works through them. There's something that comes from living in a community. There's synergy. It's the energy that does it.

"A group living together, pooling everything. There's a unity about a lively community, a wholeness as a circle is a whole. I think that's what makes the difference.

"You have to always remember that we are Franciscan Sisters of the Eucharist and that means giving totally of ourselves. When there's a crisis, we're there for each other. A real awareness of one another. And the intensity of our prayer life is the same as our everyday lives. We try to balance our lives so that everything we do brings us stronger into the community."

"And we can get excited and concerned when Mother Alfredine is really low and can get just as excited when Juniper hops a little faster the next day!" Sister Janet then adds, "There's a blending of all our experiences, constantly creating a sense of the community as a whole."

"But what happens when a new Sister arrives and has to blend into this community? How was it for you, Sister Karol Marie?" I turned to this young Sister, the newest arrival.

"It is hard. I came from the novitiate. That was a good year. Although I was working it was different from working here. In a way, it's like coming into a different culture, yet there is a sameness. This Center is part of a larger body," and looking at the other Sisters added, "and hard work is nothing new. If you're a Franciscan, you work hard."

"My work at the Earth School is fascinating. I'm taking courses in how to integrate autistic children into a classroom of normal students." Here she becomes eloquent. "I'm working with the mother of an autistic boy to see how we can give him the best chance to succeed in what will be, for him a stressful environment. And we don't want the other children to have too much difficulty either in coping. We see it as a great learning opportunity for them. They'll be able to help as well."

What is it the Franciscan Sisters are modeling both at their school and with their Work Party friends? Not a conscious, "be like us" model, nor a "this is the way to do it" model. Nor would they like to be seen as models of anything except their own living, breathing selves.

Dave put his thoughts about the Sisters this way. "They respect individual differences. My two daughters attend the school and I'm pleased with their growth. One of them comes out with me now to the Work Parties. There is a kind of church feeling. People are willing to invest their physical labor and when you're willing to invest your sweat and your muscles, you are really putting your soul into it.

"I've invested myself into that rock wall, the grass, the roses, even the buried water line. People have invested themselves deeply in the earth and the plants that are here. It's part of ourselves and we know it's going to remain long after we're gone."

"And that's what the Franciscans are doing with the children. They're investing themselves and they leave in those human lives, their heritage. Their religious world is so easy to be part of. It never seems stale, never seems dogmatic or rule ridden."

It was the third Saturday in November 1989 when I caught up with Kathleen, a fairly new recruit to the Work Parties. "What brings you out here with your son?"

"This is my third time out. I look forward to this every month. It's the kind of community atmosphere I like and I plan to come to every Work Party.

"I met the Sisters through the Earth School, my son is there. We moved here from North Florida in August. In September, Sister Kathleen Ann said, 'We're having a little get-together on Saturday. There's a few people who come out and we work in the garden and we have a nice lunch. It's from 9 to 4 and there's some snacks, and it'll just be lots of fun.' I figured it'd be a chance for us to meet people since we didn't know many in town.

"Well, on my first Saturday when I drove in, I thought, this is like a parade or something with people coming in and playpens being set up for the babies. I couldn't believe my eyes.

"Mother Francine was going around with a list of who will be doing what, where they'll be doing it and with whom. She said, 'Kathy, you'll be working with that person over there.' So we went and worked on the path and later I realized they plan their jobs very well and they orchestrate the whole thing. They make it more than a work day. It's like planning a dinner party where you seat your guests according to their interests and personalities.

"I met people and it was good for me and the food was great too!" She broke into a big smile. "I was so elated at the end of that day. It was good to work, to get outside and it's a way of having a social event without just sitting around. You actually feel better and you actually put something in. I said I'd come every Saturday I could.

"At lunch I asked different people how often they came out. Some said three months, another woman said eleven years. The second Saturday we were supposed to come out, it was pouring rain and I wondered whether we should just stay home but I figured the Sisters would have something arranged.

"So we gathered in the kitchen and had sweet rolls and coffee and everyone was in a happy mood and laughing, having a good time. Then the Sisters said, 'We work in the rain. We have rain gear, boots and gloves, and guess what? We work in the rain until we can't see.'

"I was given a job over in the corner of the garden with George and it got dark early and was cold so we stopped a bit earlier than usual.

"It's a bit like a family reunion only better. It's good for me because I'm under a lot of stress studying at the Chiropractic College.

"When I looked at their school and saw it as a community that tries to involve the whole family, thus making the child a whole person because the child is part of the family, I knew it was right for my son and me. They plan their events to have the families involved. I already know a lot of my son's friends' parents. I go to different events and say 'Hi'. Although we've only been in Portland since August, through the school and the Sisters and coming here, I feel as though I've been here longer. It's like a blessing to me, being a single Mom and a long way from home.

"Being here is just like a vacation. Look at my son over there working with Buzz. Owen's Dad died five years ago and he misses his father. Owen is so happy. The Sisters are aware of his needs. Here he's with people in a social way, having a good time."

Into the 1990s and Beyond

Sixteen years later and the Franciscan Sisters of the Eucharist at Bridal Veil are as enthusiastic about their community as they were at the beginning. The original group have aged! Mother Michael feels inside as she did back in those early days but "my body knows otherwise! I look back on what we've done over the years and wonder how we did what we did, especially those first few years when we seemed to be working all day and most of the night."

Even though the years have brought grey hairs and more than a few aches and pains, the flame of their commitment to their community, their school and their friends burns brightly. The younger Sisters who have joined the community over the years, bring their own unique personalities. As with the original group, they seem blessed with more physical energy than the average human being in this world.

To do yard work with any of the Sisters is wearying. They just keep on and on. Mother Michael no longer does yard work. That doesn't mean she is idle. She helps with the animals, weeds the garden and looks after the chickens along with Mother Margaret. These tasks don't count as yard work.

Early in their time at the house, Mother Michael took to wearing a bright red apron, the kind with a bib top. It has become as much a part of her during working hours as her Franciscan habit. During Work Parties, she likes to be out on the grounds chatting people up, finding how things are going and with her ever present sense of humor, lighting up the day.

Both Mother Michael and Mother Margaret are well into their seventies. Their distinctive personalities are an

Mother Michael, George Erdenberger and Sandy Olsen.

interesting contrast. Mother Michael, exuberant, gregarious, very intelligent, given to great bursts of laughter, often at her own expense.

Mother Margaret at first glance appears very quiet and self-effacing. A second or third glance finds a super-efficient, supercompetent woman, her sense of humor laced with a gentle wit. Never pushing herself forward, people are drawn to her. Working with her in the kitchen preparing for one of the big events is to see her at her working best.

She's given me tasks for which I have little skill, making radish roses, or preparing vegetables or filling tart shells. She'll demonstrate then leave. Walking by, she may notice that something isn't quite right. Mother Margaret never uses the word, "don't." This is how she instructs.

"Honey, I think you'll find it easier to do it like this." And she'll show me again all the while saying nice encouraging words.

"You're doing fine. The slices just have to be a little thinner." I glow inside, smile happily and feel good. And I make the slices thinner and even the radishes turn into roses.

All the Sisters are delighted to have children around. My grandchildren love being at Bridal Veil. For them, Mother Margaret is like the Pied Piper of Hamelin Town.

They'll follow her everywhere, eager to help. She taught them to enter the chicken enclosure slowly, to speak quietly so as not to agitate the birds. They've gathered eggs under her guidance without breaking one.

One of the high points of that particular visit was moving tiny baby ducklings from one place to another. Mother duck and her twelve ducklings are in a small shelter in the field behind the gatehouse. The pen has chicken-wire sides, a wood roof and sits right on the grass. Fresh water runs into a large bowl. Food dishes are off to one side.

The mother and babies are being protected from raccoons, hawks and roving minks. The minks are in the area thanks to a past neighbor, thinking to strike it rich with a mink farm, fell on hard times, and rather than destroy the animals, let them go.

The shelter is now in a fresh location. Mother Margaret picks up the mother duck and pops her into the pen. The children are shown how to pick up tiny ducklings. Taylor, then four years old and Fraser, eight, are given a lesson in handling fragile baby birds. Fraser did just fine cradling the ball of fluff in his hands. Taylor picked one up by its neck.

Nothing rattles Mother Margaret when she's dealing with a child. "Taylor, honey, it's better to hold the baby this way, otherwise it might choke." And she takes the duckling, shows the child how best to carry it and gives it back. This is as good an illustration as any of how the Sisters approach both children and adults. They give them their trust.

Buzz Gilbert and his wife, Annette, are regular helpers and visitors at Bridal Veil. Annette, whose sister, Madge Nepper, once ran the Columbia Gorge Nursing Home on the property, loves being with the Sisters and they love having her.

"It's really nice for me to come back to this place that I remember from when I was fifteen."

Buzz thrives on hard work. He built the addition to the goat barn to house Juniper and will undertake any task handed to him. His eyes light up when he talks about the Sisters and what they mean to him.

"They really, truly appreciate what you're doing for them. Even if you don't get a specific 'thank you', you still get that wholesome feeling.

"They never judge. They accept who you are. They let you work to your own ability. I guess it's like the Montessori Earth School, teaching a child in a spontaneous way. This is spontaneous teaching of adults! If you want to excel, go ahead, they won't stop you. Go at your own pace and if you've got some skills, they let you go ahead with some guidance rather than correction."

Buzz went on to express many of the same feelings other friends had voiced. "I really enjoy coming here and working with the Sisters. But, you know, it's really for me, not for them. It kind of makes a whole person out of me. I feel good when I leave. I have a kind of bond with the Sisters. That's what keeps me coming back."

Mother Francine, one of the original founders of the Bridal Veil community, is now in her early fifties. Still full of *joie de vivre*, her many intellectual gifts find fulfillment in the school she and the community established. To know her is to love her. She is a delightful companion, fun to be around yet with a deeply serious and deeply rooted love of her Church.

With her abiding fondness for goats, it was inevitable that she'd find a way to add more to their flock. The latest additions are two pygmy goats. These small creatures are perfect for children to pet. Alice May was bred to a white angora goat and has produced a beautiful white kid.

There were two sad events during 1990. Mother Alfredine died peacefully on a June afternoon with two loving Sisters holding her at the end. Her death was not unexpected and with Mother Michael and Mother Margaret beside her, she left the world gently. She died just a few days before the Benefit Ball and the Sisters wondered if the Ball should be cancelled.

"She loved a party. When she was bedridden, she liked to hear the music at the Ball and was always interested in who came and how it all went." Mother Michael smiled as she recalled her old friend, "I'm sure she'd want us to go ahead."

So it was decided. Sister Patricia, now a licensed mortician, came from the Mother House at Meriden. Mother's body was taken to the funeral home where Sister had a colleague who trained with her. There she prepared Mother Alfredine for burial in the Bridal Veil cemetery, the burial to take place after the Ball.

The altar in the chapel became the focal point for those of us who knew Mother Alfredine. Some of her personal belongings were there, a basket of the powders, soaps and lotions used to make her last months comfortable. And a notebook that contained the name of every student she had taught over the years. Her life is celebrated. It was a life dedicated to children. She will not be forgotten.

1990 was also the year that Mother Francine's dear, old dog, Jessica, had to be put down. Unable to walk and in a lot of pain, letting her suffer any longer would be cruel.

Sister Kathleen Ann went along with Mother Michael and Mother Francine to the vet. Jessica had been with them since their days in British Columbia and is a special part of their history. They held her in their arms while the vet gave her the injection that freed her forever from pain.

"Of course, we all cried because she was so special," Mother Francine went on, "we brought her back here and this is where she is buried."

Before long, another dog was acquired. This Sheltie, a young male, has decided to be a guard dog, giving vent to loud barks and growls when anyone other than the Sisters approaches.

Margot Waltuch, their Montessori consultant, was visiting shortly after the Sheltie arrived. Looking at him with her expert eye, she decided he had to go to obedience training. "With so many children coming here, he has to know not to snap at them or anyone else."

No one seemed to be listening to Margot's words of wisdom, so she picked up the Portland telephone book, located a dog trainer and catching Mother Francine's attention by standing over her with the book declared, "Now I've found someone for you so I think you'd better phone."

It has fallen to Mother Francine to be trained along with the dog. With fear of failure as a dog educator hanging over her head, she went off to obedience classes. Both she and the dog passed.

The Bridal Veil Sisters look around their home and the surrounding land and feel blessed. "The real story here is not about us," Mother Michael is adamant on this point. "The real story here is about all the friends who've come over the years to work on the land, to support the

Mother Francine and Mother Michael planning the yard work.

events we put on, who have given us their love and their trust. Without them, we couldn't have done any of it."

The Sisters have become more closely tied to some of their friends, giving them spiritual direction. "We pray with them and challenge them to live their Catholic lives to the fullest." Mother Francine sees this as an important part of their Franciscan heritage.

"Then there are some of the Work Party volunteers who express a desire to be in a closer relationship with us in prayer.

"There are a several levels here, the Franciscan apprentices, sort of like the Third Order of Franciscans. These are the people who have been around here with us a long time. We meet a couple of times a month and we pray together. We're involved in family rituals and celebrations with them, baptisms, birthdays, anniversaries. We're a kind of spiritual base for them.

"Then there are the people in similar professions, such as Montessori teachers who have formed a community that clusters around us. We meet with them regularly and work through a process of commitment to their work within the Church.

"And we work with a group of lawyers who hold in trust our land and we see all these connections with small groups of people as our call as Franciscans. That is, to develop within their communities, quality of life as families and in their relationship to the Church.

"Community is many layered. There's our house community here, our broader F.S.E. community, other religious communities and the lay community. We do what we can to lend encouragement and to support them.

"All the time we were forming this community at Bridal Veil, then starting the school, we always had a sense there was support out there."

Now and again when asked Mother Michael and Mother Margaret will share their visions of the future.

"We'd love to be able to have more land out here and build a cluster of small houses where elderly people could live out their lives in dignity."

"Good nutrition is so important for everyone and sometimes it's hard for an old person, perhaps with physical problems, to put together good meals." For Mother Margaret, simple food, well prepared is something everyone should have to thrive.

"Or we thought about having the same kind of set-up for people suffering from some mental disability. Why there's Bethany right next door to us, upgrading her nursing skills to qualify as a psychiatric nurse." Once launched on her future vision, Mother Michael is hard to stop.

The Franciscan Sisters of the Eucharist at Bridal Veil are a continuing story of love and devotion to their

Church, their friends, their school and their various animals.

"I hope," says Mother Michael leaning across the kitchen table and catching my attention, "you are writing about Jessica. Afterall she was with us right from the beginning."

So to finish, here is Jessica's story.

Jessica and the Therapist

Jessica is Mother Francine's dog. Having had a somewhat checkered career, it's little wonder her temperament is not as reliable as it might be. She was a five-week-old foundling offered to the Sisters by a little East Indian boy. This all happened when they were living and working in British Columbia.

The child approached them on the street holding in his arms a greyish, whitish, blackish bundle of fur with two bright, watchful eyes peeking out.

"Excuse me but would you like to have this dog?" The child's big brown eyes looked up at the Sisters and down at the puppy he carried so gently. "My mother says I can't keep it." His voice trembled. He was on the verge of tears.

Mother Francine knelt down. "Are you sure? We wouldn't want to take your puppy."

Tears trickled down his face, "She says I have to get rid of it and I don't know what to do." He was about nine years old and the Sisters couldn't bear to think of him being so sad.

They looked at each other. Mother Michael put her arm around his shoulders. "Now don't you worry about a thing. We'll take your puppy and we'll look after it real well."

The boy put his dog in her arms. "Now before you go, how about giving it a nice hug and telling it good-bye.

Why you might meet us again and you'll be able to see how big it's grown." She was doing her best to cheer him up. He gave it a big hug, them a big smile, and ran off.

"Well, I guess we have a dog, Mother. I wonder what it is." She turned the puppy upside down to have a look. "It's a girl."

What to name her? Using the Bible as their source, they flipped the pages and let it fall open. They picked whatever name appeared on the page. There were two, one was Mount A., just that and the other was Jesse. "Well we can't call her Jesse, so we'll call her Jessica."

Jessica was a funny looking animal of unknown and very mixed parentage. However, she had a certain allure because shortly after she took up residence with them, she was dognapped.

At the time, the Sisters were living right next to the beach near Tsawwassen and Jessica ran around freely. One day she disappeared. Mother Michael, by now quite smitten with the puppy, went up and down the beach calling her.

"I couldn't believe she'd wandered off. I was really upset and kept looking everywhere for her."

Mother Francine and Sister Dorothy were on their way home from school and Sister saw a dog that looked like Jessica.

"Isn't that Jessica?"

Mother Francine ran over. "Yes it is but she's not wearing her collar." She picked the dog up and asked, hoping but not expecting a reply, "Hey, what are you doing here?" Jessica knew but wasn't telling. They found her on a road away from the beach.

The intrepid nuns set out to solve the mystery after taking Jessica home. They returned to the scene and found two small boys who appeared to be looking for something.

These were the dognappers. They'd been down on the beach and seeing roly-poly Jessica decided to take her home. Small they may have been but smart they were and removing Jessica's collar, buried it. Home they went and told their mother they'd found a lost puppy and "Please, can we keep it?"

The Sisters walked with the children to their home and their mother persuaded them to tell what they had done with Jessica's collar. It was buried in the sand and like pirates digging up lost treasure, the boys uncovered the loot.

The Sisters told the boys they could come down any time and play with Jessica but had to promise not to take her away again.

This, then, is Jessica. Boss of the ranch, you might say. When Sister Paula Jean brought in her own dog, Jessica became very protective of her turf and as the years went by and arthritis began to pain her, strangers were warned not to pat her or make sudden moves. Work Party friends knew when to leave well enough alone. Even when she was young and ambling around the grounds, she was approached with caution. She might snap, then again she might enjoy having her ears scratched.

It was summer, 1987, when relatives of one of the Sisters dropped by for a visit. Into the kitchen they came for coffee and cookies. Jessica was sleeping under the table.

"Be careful of the dog. She's right by your feet." Mother Michael warned them, "She might snap but don't worry she'll be okay if you leave her alone."

"Oh, I know dogs, she won't hurt me," and with that the man leaned down to pat her. She bit his finger. Hard. Blood poured from a nasty gash.

The Sisters were frantic. To have a visitor hurt like this was a shock. "Let me clean your finger," Mother

Margaret brought out the first aid kit. "I think you're going to need stitches. One of the Sisters will drive you to the emergency."

"No, no. It's all my fault. You told me not to touch her. Just tell us where the nearest hospital is and we'll go there. My wife will drive."

He needed fourteen stitches. Mother Michael and Mother Francine worried themselves into thinking that something was seriously wrong with Jessica. She had bitten others but never as badly. "I think," said Mother Francine, "that we'd better take her to a dog therapist."

"A what?"

"Someone who can tell us what to do about her behavior. Maybe she needs some kind of special training or something."

In the yellow pages of the Portland phone book, they found the name of a woman, Ann Childers, who was listed as handling behavior problems in dogs. The two Sisters took Jessica to see her.

"So there we were, describing Jessica's snappiness and her other sterling qualities when it became apparent that we were the problem not Jessica!"

"And you," declared Mother Francine pointing an accusing finger at Mother Michael who looked the picture of innocence, "every time the questions got too close to home you said that Jessica had to go for a little walk and disappeared for minutes at a time."

"The difficulty as I see it," Ann Childers next words came as no surprise to the two Sisters, "Jessica rules you two and you two (this with emphasis) should be ruling Jessica."

"What could I say?" laughed Mother Michael. "Of course she ruled the roost but at age thirteen and with her arthritis paining her, I didn't think her disposition was about to change.

"And you should have seen Mother Francine's face as we were being chastised for letting Jessica be the boss. She looked so crestfallen. As an expert educator of human beings, she felt guilty about not educating a dog properly.

"Well, we were told to start massaging Jessica, gradually working from tail to head. This was to get her used to being stroked from back to front. The theory being that hands coming at her from behind might alarm her unless she was used to it.

"I decided to take Jessica out and put her in the back seat of the car and wait for Mother Francine outside. I didn't want to hear anymore! Then I remembered I had the check book and went back to pay Ann.

"When we returned to the car, Jessica, old, fat and arthritic, had clambered from the back into the front seat and was sitting happily behind the wheel.

"Well, we leaned against the car and laughed and laughed. I tell you, she was making it quite clear that she didn't want anyone messing around with her rules and if we weren't careful, she might drive off and leave us.

"The funny thing is, she'd never done such a thing before. How she did it, we'll never know."

Epilogue

The Franciscan Center at Bridal Veil, Oregon, is one of the Life Centers spread from the East Coast to the West Coast. The Mother House at Meriden, Connecticut, centers the entire community. Bridal Veil is called the Life Education Center. Because of its focus on formal education, it embodies the mission of the Church to "to teach all nations, baptizing in the name of the Father, the Son and the Holy Spirit." This is the outreach to everyone.

Moreover, in the spiritual tradition of St. Francis who was called to "rebuild the church" in his time, the Sisters are dedicated to rebuild within individuals a respect for the deep truths of their inner being. This brings each person to a reverence for the sacredness of all life and fosters a fidelity to the transcendent values of human life.

The Franciscan Montessori Earth School in Portland, Oregon, is the formal embodiment of the Life Education work. But education takes place on all levels of human life from birth to death. And so, everyone who comes to Bridal Veil is in some way included in the education process.

Eight Sisters are living at the convent at the present writing. Five work at the school. Two are at the Bridal Veil site to care for the Center, and one Sister works at a laboratory, testing soil, water and feeds to build a healthier environment. Whether they are at home, at school or in the larger community, there is a sense in which all have entered into the process of education and are thus fulfilling their call to build the Church.

> Mother Mary Michael Costello, F.S.E.,
> Franciscan Sisters of the Eucharist,
> Bridal Veil, Oregon.
> U.S.A.

Sources

"Bridge of the Gods Legend, its origin, history and dating." *Mazama*, Vol. 40, pages 33-41. (1958) Donald B. and Elizabeth G. Lawrence.

Columbia Gorge History, Volumes One and Two, Tahkie Books, Box 355 Skamania Rt., Stevenson, WA, 98648
Copyright Jim Attwell, 1974, 1975.

Encyclopedeia of Northwest Biographies, 1943.

Frozen Music: A History of Portland Architecture, Gideon Bosker and Lena Lencek, Western Imprints, Oregon Historical Society, Portland, OR.

Historical Notes of Bridal Veil and Palmer, Oregon, Sara A. (Gussie Moore) Judd and Alva Horton.

Presentation given by Dr. Donald B. Lawrence, prepared for oral presentation by Friends of the Columbia Gorge at hearings on the Columbia Gorge National Scenic Area Act held September 10, 1982, Hood River.

Wildlife of the Columbia River Gorge, Oregon Historical Society Press, Jack Murdock Publication Series. Oregon Historical Society, Portland, OR..

Index

A

Alfredine, Mother, 218–19,
    256, 264
Angie, 235
Anne Clare, Sister, 222, 251
Astor, John Jacob, 20

B

Barrett, Mary, 12
Bassett, Robert, 77, 81–82, 93,
    95
Bassett, May, 82, 93
Benson, Simon, 31
Bernice, Sister, 184–85
Birt, Bill, 183–184, 242, 246
Boly, Craig, S.J., 168–70
Borkowski, Fr. Edward, 6–10,
    67, 143–146
Bradley, J. S., 22
Bradley, Mrs., 22
Brothers, Ellen, 245, 247
Brothers, Pat, 245, 247

C

Carlin, Br. Nick, 6

Carruthers, Roy, 45, 47
Childers, Ann, 271–72
Clark, Phyllis, (see Duncan)
    128
Cole Mr., 47
Cole, Dorothy, 47, 75, 80
Collier, Michael, 108–111, 115,
    120, 225
Costello, Frank, S.J., 168, 176,
    184
Cusack, June, 120

D

Dave, 235, 257
Deragisch, Martin, 143
Dorothy, Sister, 269
Duncan, Phyllis, (see Clark)
    128

E

Ellis, Fred, 98
Ellis, Henry Day, 97, 225
Erdenberger, George, 194–97,
    212–13, 222–23, 227, 234–37,
    241, 243, 252
Erdenberger, Georgia, 195, 237

F

Fabian, Frank, Sr., 106, 113, 119, 125
Fabian, Frank, Jr., 106–7, 113, 115–17, 120, 147–49
Fabian, Gordon, 106–7, 113, 116-18, 120
Fabian, Janis, 105–7, 113–14, 116–17, 120
Fabian, Lois, 105–6, 113–14, 116, 118–19, 125
Falls, Terry, 58, 173, 174
Fitzgerald, Father, C.S.S.R., 135–41
Franceschi, Benjamin, 241
Franceschi, Bernard, 198–99, 211–12,
Franceschi, Bethany, 198–200, 211, 236
Francine, Mother, 1–2, 5, 8, 12–14, 17, 49–51, 53–54, 57, 59, 62–64, 68, 70–71, 73–74, 151, 153, 155–58, 160, 162, 164–65, 168, 170–72, 175, 177–81, 183–84, 186, 190–93, 196, 215, 224, 229–31, 238–40, 242, 246, 249, 254–55, 258, 263, 265–66, 268–69, 271–72
Francis of Assisi, Saint, 4, 15, 60, 69–70, 152, 164, 172, 237, 248, 273
Franklin, Minnie, 27
Fraser (Birt), 248, 262

G

Gibbon, Don, 53, 157, 160–62, 167, 193
Gibbon, Kay, 157, 160–62, 193

Gilbert, Annette, 126–27, 263
Gilbert, Buzz, 235, 259, 263
Gilbert, Ramona, 185
Gray, Captain, 18
Grenfell, Connie, 187, 208, 219
Grenfell, Ed, 219, 228
Grenfell, Taylor, 241

H

Hagen, Mr., 83
Hanks, Grace, 127–29
Harnan, Mrs., 88–89
Harwood, Nellie, 111–12
Hefty, Mr., 40
Helen, 240
Holloway, Olive, 111
Horton, Alva, 22
Howard, Most Reverend Edward D., 143
Hubert, Brother, C.S.S.R., 136
Humel, Very Reverend Frances, S.V.D., 143

J

Jacobson, Clarence, 27–28, 31–32, 34, 38–40, 44–45
Jacobson, Dorothy, 27–34, 37, 39–42, 45, 47–48, 66, 75, 77, 80, 119, 125, 154, 213, 241, 243–44
Janet, Sister, 184, 194, 210, 222, 227, 235–36, 253, 256
Jenny, Chris, 45, 48, 77–78, 82
Jenny, Irene, 43, 48
Jenny, Mrs., 91
Jenny, Verna, 91
Jerome, Brother, O.M.I., 52, 55, 57–58, 62, 67, 70, 152, 189

Joe, 240
Joesph, Frank, 1, 4–5, 10–11
June (see Cusack), 108, 112,
    117–18

K

Karen Marie, Sister, 243,
    247–49
Karol Marie, Sister, 243, 257
Kathleen Ann, Sister, 185,
    215–19, 222, 227–28, 235,
    242, 246, 252–55, 258, 265
Kathleen, 258
Keith (Reynolds) 101–3, 105,
    108, 117

L

Leitzel, Caroline, 45
Leitzel, Clarence, 43, 45
Leitzel, Elizabeth, 42–43, 45,
    77
Leitzel, John, 32, 34, 38–39,
    45, 48
Lawrence, Donald, 19, 25–26,
    76–77, 81–87, 95, 97–98,
    213
Lawrence, Elizabeth, 84–87,
    95, 97–98
Lawrence, Jean, 84, 88–91,
    93, 95–99
Lawrence, Louise, 25, 47,
    75–82, 84–93, 96–99,
    101, 125, 213, 225, 231
Lawrence, Mabel, 81
Lawrence, Sophie, 81
Lawrence, Virginia, 76–77,
    87–88, 95, 97–98

Lawrence, William C. I (Will),
    25, 75, 79–80, 82–84, 92,
    97–98
Lawrence, William C. II (Bill),
    76–77, 81–84, 87, 91, 95,
    97–98
Lawrence, William C. III
    (Lawrie), 84, 88–93, 95–99
Liguori, St. Alphonsus, 136
Luscher, Fred, 81, 87, 90

M

Macdonald, Angus, 12, 72
Margaret, Sister, 49–56, 58,
    64, 67, 69, 72, 74, 152,
    155, 157, 159, 161–62, 167,
    174–75, 179, 181, 188, 191,
    194, 199
Margaret, Mother, 200–202,
    204–9, 219, 224–25, 228, 243,
    260–62, 264, 267, 271
Margaret Patricia, 232–33
Marie, Sister, 204–5
Mary Coleman, Sister, 165–66,
    177–79, 186, 194, 199, 211,
    216, 227–29, 251
Mary Gregory, Sister, 154–55,
    158–59, 162–63, 173, 189
Mary Jane, 233
Meier and Frank, 24
Meyer, Adolph, 78
Michael, Mother, 1–5, 8–11,
    13, 17–18, 49–50, 52, 55,
    59–61, 64, 68–71, 74, 151–52,
    155–56, 158–61, 164–66,
    169–71, 175–76, 178–79, 183,
    186, 191–92, 195, 199–200,
    202, 205–7, 211–12, 215, 219,

Michael, Mother, (cont.)
    224–25, 242, 247–49, 251–52,
    255–56, 260–61, 264–72, 274
Michelle, 252
Missen, Fr. Nicholas, C.S.S.R.,
    136
Moffatt, Mr., 63–66
Mother Guardian, 69, 179
Moss, Linda, 113–14

N

Nancy, 214
Nepper, Bud, 132–33
Nepper, Jack, 126–33
Nepper, Madge, 126–33
Nuttman, Fr. Joseph, C.S.S.R.,
    136

O

Oliver, Brother, C.S.S.R.,
    135–41

P

Patricia, Sister, 153, 175, 216,
    221, 251, 256, 264
Paula Jean, Sister, 1–2, 6, 8,
    18, 53–57, 60, 64, 66–67,
    71, 73, 152, 154, 156, 158–59,
    169, 175, 206, 270
Pope Paul VI, 15
Poppy (see William C.
    Lawrence I) 88, 90, 92, 97

R

Reynolds, Kathryn, 98, 101–3,
    105–15, 117–21, 125–27
Roosevelt, 119
Rosemae, Mother, 11, 62, 229

Ross, Harry, 105,
Rudfelt, Dick, 2–4, 58
Rudfelt, Katie, 3, 4, 58

S

Schmidt, Caroline (see Leitzel)
    44
Shaun, Mother, 62, 229
Shigo, Father, S.V.D., 65
Shiomi, Dr., 115
Smith, Virginia (see Lawrence)
    84
Stahl, Dr. Gerald, 102–3
Suzanne, Mother, 12, 215

T

Taylor (Birt), 248, 262
Thiele, Henri, 39–40
Tim, 221–22

V

Vanetta, Lester C., 125–26,
    128–30, 132–33
Von Ahn, Curt, 249
Von Ahn, Gerry, 249

W

Waltuch, Margot, 171–72,
    177, 190, 265
White, Father, 186,
Whitehouse, Morris H. 29–31,
    33–34, 36–37, 47–48, 61,
    128, 139, 197, 213

Z

Zifcak, George, 191
Zifcak, Isabelle, 191

The Author

Anita Birt, in a casual conversation with Mother Michael, remarked, "Someone should write the history of this place." To which Mother Michael replied, "Why don't you?"

During her research for *The House at Bridal Veil*, the author was intrigued by a series of coincidences that opened up lines of communication with many people involved in the past history of the house. From Montana, Minnesota, California, in and around the Portland area, they came, to remember their time at Bridal Veil.

Anita Birt is the daughter of a storyteller. Her mother, Elsie Bell Gardner, wrote *The Maxie Books for Girls* series during the 1930s.

Anita received her training as a Human Relations Counselor in Toronto, Ontario. She now lives in Victoria, British Columbia with her husband. They have two children and four grandchildren.

Backcover photo:
Sister Karen Marie, Fraser and Taylor Birt taking a ride in Juniper's pony cart, August 1989.